MeN aRe Pigs

Men are Pigs

STORIES WHICH PASSED THE TIME OF TESTS

JED SOMIT

atmosphere press

Published by Atmosphere Press

ISBN 979-8-89132-207-3

Cover design by Felipe Betim

Atmospherepress.com

Table of Contents

Foreword

Preface.
Quadrilateral.
Pinafore.
Typing Monkeys Working Overtime.

Aye, Aye, Sir!

Preface

Have fun. Enjoy. That's what these stories are about.

The stories' genesis was to entertain a young granddaughter during the "shelter at home" phase of the Covid pandemic. Meant to be read to her, there are musical and literary and science and pop culture references, puns and other word play material, for the adult reader as well.

Please read the stories aloud, even to yourself; that's the proper tempo. Make them interactive and funny. Emphasize the essential silliness of the stories. Encourage younger children to sing along, repeat silly names or even take over a role. Ad-lib, especially sound effects. Some stories expressly direct you to ad-lib, so create some fantastic passages. Insert some *bon mots* of your own. Let me know how it goes.

Interrupt to play the songs mentioned (or don't. No copyright holder allowed free use; most lyrics originally in the stories were removed or truncated). Take a tangent to read or explain the underlying fables, tales, or stories. Explain the references and the play with words. Use silliness about gender, religion, etc., as an opportunity for discussion.

Before reading to a child, please read the story in advance to learn where to edit. As the child matures, the story will change as you edit less or the child understands (or personally reads) more.

No sex scenes, no blood and gore, so nothing of that sort to skim through the book for. There are some puzzles and word games; I hope you'll discover something new with each re-reading. Did you get each owl or tree species?

The accusation that some stories were written simply to

reach one awful pun is a filthy libel that doesn't ring true. There's always more than one.

If you are offended by my ridicule of religion, politics, or other of your core beliefs: tough nuggies. I tried to be an equal opportunity satirizer. If not anywhere offended, I apologize that I overlooked something sacrosanct to you.

For insights on any reference, issue, passage, or to comment, contact me politely at jedsomit@jedsomit.com.

Jed Somit
Kauai, HI 2023

Birdies on the Golf Course

Twice upon a time, there was a dark, dangerous cloud over the land.

Twice? Yes, once then, a long time ago (older than Gramps), the time of our story, and once now. This book is about then. You'll have to make up, or live, your own stories about now.

Imagine, if you will, an already tense family holiday gathering, planned for a dinner and sleep-over, prolonged indefinitely, testing the outer limits of family harmony. Hear the town criers shouting, "Stay inside. Dark bodings. Death in the clouds!" while overhead, a dark, angry surf slowly blots out the sun, and at night, hides the moon and stars.

Because of that sickly overhang, not only visible in the sky like angry thunder clouds but scattering dead birds and animals in its wake, all the people in the land had to stay at their homes and couldn't visit one another, or even go to school, or to playgrounds, or even to the library or a skating rink. It was a lonely, frightening time, with just nothing going right.

Nobody, not even the magicians and wizards, the sage advisers, the parents and doctors, the talking unicorns and tea kettles, nobody at all, knew when it would end. But it would be a long time, people felt, shaking their heads sadly with a look that said, "Don't blame me."

Old and young were just stuck in their homes, with only their family as friends and playmates. Now, family is fine, and you should like to spend time with your brothers and sisters, aunts and uncles, nieces and nephews, and mom and dad, whatever you have, but after a while, perhaps a long while for you, and a short while for other families, it does get dull, and you would like someone new, almost anyone, even an annoying person, say, to talk to and play with!

Among the people trapped in the house, waiting for the Evil Cloud to lift, was a beautiful young girl (maybe 5 or 6 years old, depending on which fingers you use to count) and her younger brother, who was just a toddler. The gathering was at their home.

Beautiful? Yes, she was. Grandmothers always think their granddaughters are beautiful, but this young girl was beautiful even to strangers, even to other peoples' jealously critical grandmothers. She had blonde hair, like her mother, and a happy, smiling, shining face, which went well with her quick laugh and easy giggle. She would frequently offer to dance and sing her favorite songs and stories from the Dizzy Fables book (a prized birthday gift), not because she wanted to be a celebrity—there were no movies or TV then—just for the joy of it.

She often pretended she was a princess; she identified with the princess in each fairy tale she read or that Dad told her at bedtime. So, since she had one of those old-timey names, like "Cruella" or "Dweeble" or "Hortensia" or "Rottensocks," which, much for the better, are now out of favor, we'll call her "Princess."

Because of the family reunion, when the Evil Cloud came down, there were many people in her house besides her Mom and Dad and brother. We'll meet those people by-and-by, which means "sometime soon, but don't hold your breath." And there were also some animals, most notably (especially to himself) a cat. You may name the cat as you please, since his own name for himself was too long: "Graceful And Handsome Four Footed God Who Rules Over Humans And Mice." A cat by any name purrs just as soothingly. The family dog was missing, believed to be at Nana's, where he occasionally wandered because Gramps was an easy touch for a treat or a lengthy scratch behind the ears.

One day, a long time into the quarantine, so long that all the "take-home" packages of leftovers from the holiday meal had been eaten as snacks, so long that Princess had performed her favorite fables for each relative a few times, played with every cousin near her age all the games they knew, and was going out of her mind with tedium—maybe the third day—the people trapped with her in the house gathered together and gloomily glared at each other, bored. They asked, "What shall we do to pass the time?" (Mom and Dad didn't join in that discussion; with all the guests, they didn't even have time for all the chores falling upon the hosts of a host.) Some of the adults made suggestions that I simply won't repeat, as they are not fit for young ears, while some others' notions told us much about them but really weren't very helpful: no one else shared their enthusiasm.

"Eat," said one youngster. Then that one added, "Bake a chocolate cake, ice it and eat it."

Do you know the word "pudgy"? Have your mom or dad explain it to you. Those suggestions, and similar ones about Jell-O, and turkey and mashed potatoes, and peanut butter and jelly, and omelets and oatmeal, all came from that pudgy person.

And a lanky kid, who passed his time by jumping over chairs and couches and running up and down the halls and walls, and leaping from place to place, said, "Let's have races, with prizes for the winner!" The pudgy child, believing the prizes would be pieces of that chocolate cake (which hadn't even been baked yet), and knowing he or she wouldn't win any race, except maybe a pie-eating contest, said, "Naaaaaaah," and mouthed a five-note descending bass line.

You ask, "Why not watch television? Listen to music? Facetime with a schoolmate? Play some movies? Just ask Alexa for some more games or suggestions?" But this was long ago, before phones, television, dental floss, or a snooping Alexa. There weren't even ways to have music except for someone to sing or to play an instrument, although the pudgy kid was sometimes a good stand-in for an orchestra.

Princess (also in favor of baking the chocolate cake) said, "Let's tell stories to pass the time."

"Yes!" said her parents, speaking together as they often did. "That's a great idea."

Just as Princess was about to offer her favorite story—about a lovely teenaged mermaid princess who lived under the sea and fell in love with a handsome sailor, but as a sea creature she had fins and could only talk in bubbles, so to be able to be near and speak with her love the princess sold her lovely face to an old hag witchy lobster in exchange for feet and a voice, but then the sailor didn't recognize the princess (whose beautiful face and bubbly voice he had fallen in love with) with her now big clumsy feet (that mean lobster!) and an ugly face (the lobsters' horrid visage), and pining for her, the sailor almost fell under a spell from the lobster (who, using the sea-princess' face and voice, pretended to be her) and he was on the verge of becoming Mr. Claws, but luckily all was put right by the princess' guardian clam, so they lived happily ever after, although the sea-princess sometimes answered her sailor husband with bubble-talk until he said, "Whhhhaaat?"—well, just as she was to start that wonderful Dizzy story, with a song and dance for each scene, one of the older men, usually a sullen and ill-tempered fellow, so much so that behind his back everyone called him "The Grouch," said, "I've got a story." And not only does that sentence finally end, but so did Princess' chance to tell her mermaid tale.

Since The Grouch would only get grouchier if he didn't get his way, just like some people I know, he was allowed to tell the first story, while outside, the Evil Cloud swirled and howled and picked on unfortunate owls and mice.

Birdies on the Golf Course

I play golf. That game with small, hard balls. They are about the size of grouse eggs and look much the same. But when you hit grouse eggs, they don't go far; they just explode into your face. So, we play with golf balls.

On this day, I was playing golf with three other people. We had two golf chariots, each drawn by a pony. It was late in the day; the sun was behind a mountain, so it was almost twilight. Our group was basically alone on the golf course. We only had a few holes left to play.

I hit a great shot, of course, far down the fairway, maybe twice as long as anyone else's drive. [There were some sniggers at this from people who had played golf with The Grouch, folks who thought he was confusing a tall tale with a long shot.] After everyone else completed their first shot on the hole, their "drive," as it is called, I made my second shot, which landed right where I wanted [more sniggers, and a "harum-mph" or so, each getting a sharp look from The Grouch] near a lake, just an easy pitch to the green.

As I came to the lake and found my ball, several ducks waddled towards me. Then, several swans. A few nene came as well. Soon, there must have been 20 birds between me and my ball. ["The closest he ever came to a birdie," whispered one listener.] I started to swing my club to move them away, but the birds, and more birds still, came closer, even flapping their wings in my face, so I stopped.

The other players in my group came over and were soon also surrounded by birds. I tried to bend down and pick up my ball so I could leave, but a big turkey vulture came down from the sky and sat on my shoulder. ["The closest he ever came to an eagle," whispered that listener.] He shook his head at me and then started preening his feathers.

One of the bigger swans, the one with a long black neck, white head and black beak, spoke to me. At first, it sounded only like a lot of honks and quacks and snorts, but very soon I could make sense of it; by their nods, I could see that the others in my golf group understood as well.

"You stupid wingless two-leggers," said the swan while

wagging her head back and forth disapprovingly, "have no idea how to care for eggs. Men are pigs. Little chicks come from eggs. ["The closest he ever came to a chick," whispered a listener.] You don't hit them. You don't pick up sticks and smack them. Idiots!" The swan stopped shaking her head and looked me straight into my eyes. Then the pen (a female swan) sighed and continued, in a softer tone

"You surround eggs with tender grasses. You should sit on them and keep them warm. When you sit, you go down carefully, and wiggle your behind just like this," as she demonstrated, "so the eggs are covered and safe from wind and rain. You and your mate take turns, but you must never leave the eggs alone."

The swan paused for a minute, looking at the other birds, who were nodding their approval and occasionally honking at us. She brought her wing tip to her head, like a man would do with his index finger while thinking, and again looked straight at me.

"I bet you have more eggs in your bags and pockets. I've seen you before, taking them out. Now, put them all next to that egg there," she demanded.

I hesitated for but a second. The turkey vulture, still on my shoulder, nipped my ear, so I emptied my pocket of golf balls, and went to my golf bag and took out six more balls from there. The other people in my group, with the swan watching them closely and the other fowls honking and quacking, did so too, after the birds started pecking at their feet and ankles. After a bit, there were maybe 15 balls in a heap in the middle of the flock of birds.

Immediately, many birds brought over twigs and grass, and plucked and pulled them together like they were weaving a basket, so that a kind of nest was built under and around the golf balls.

"Now I'll show you how to sit on them so they hatch," said the talking swan. "I don't trust you to do it, since you're so big and clumsy and haven't a clue."

The pen waddled to the pile, wiggled her big behind about five times just as she had demonstrated before, twirled around twice and then sat down gingerly, so well placed that every one of the golf balls was covered.

"A little love and they'll come out just fine," she said in a soft voice, almost like cooing.

I don't know how long we were there. ["Probably until you sobered up," murmured that listener, getting another angry glance from The Grouch.] We couldn't leave, because when we turned away, the birds would fly up in our path and flap their wings into our faces and block us at every turn. The sun had almost fully set.

We were all very tired by the time the swan said, "It's happening. They are hatching!" She stood up so we could see.

I couldn't believe my eyes. I had never seen anything like it before. All of the golf balls were breaking open, with something alive inside trying to come out.

There was a ragged chorus of "Congratulations! Have a worm!" from the birds, many of whom flew into the air and in circles, swooping past the swan and the nest. I could hear some clucks and chirps, and other, louder sounds, coming from the hatching golf balls, and the entire nest had an eerie glow, like the wavering lights you see in the dark of a forest on a summer's night.

The chariot horses, who had been patiently chomping at the grass while we were surrounded by the birds, glanced at the nest and were thoroughly spooked. They took off running, with the golf chariots careening wildly from side to side behind them as they raced away.

My chariot-mate, a distinguished professor at the state university, a man who knew almost everything there was to know, and a great deal beyond that as well, said in an awed voice, "Will you look at that! Never in my life! I have studied birds and know the science of hatching, but this is by far the strangest and most marvelous event I have ever seen. I shall write a paper about it."

The players from the other cart were a doctor and her husband. The doctor said, "That is amazing. That is the most beautiful thing I have ever witnessed. Do you see them all? Are they real or just phantasms? What will they become? Oh, I wish I had a camera."

Her husband joined in. "This is unbelievable. I hope they are friendly. How big will they get? Are we in danger?" He took his wife's hand in his own and squeezed it gently.

That was the strangest day of my life.

The Grouch sat down. Everyone was stunned for a bit. "What were they? What did you see? What did they look like?" they all asked. The Grouch wouldn't say another word, except, "That's the end of the story."

"That pen," one listener commented, "was mightier than hisword."

Mom quieted the crowd by serving cheesecake-filled chocolate eggs, with espresso for the adults and strawberry milk for the youngsters.

Through mouthfuls of sweets, it was agreed to have a story or two every night.

The Cat Who Wouldn't Bow To A Hat

Dawn broke the next day with a sullen whimper. Scattered rays proved the sun was doing its job, but the Evil Cloud, looking like several layers of pudding scum 200 feet above (like Los Angeles today), allowed only a feeble pout to reach the house. A masked solitary traveler, on what had been a well-traveled road, dropped a leather band at the house's street door, knocked, but went on without waiting.

Later that morning, Dad opened the front door in his habit of getting the mail, forgetting the mail no longer came. Mom, across the house in the kitchen, heard his sharp intake of breath and, attuned to his moods, his soft whimper before he closed the door, leaving himself outside. She hurried across the huge entry room, opened and quickly closed the front door, and drew Dad into her arms. He was weeping as men do at sad stories: tears rolling down his cheeks but pretending nothing was amiss. In his hand was a dog collar; visible was the engraved name "Φdo."

"Don't tell the kids," they said to each other. "They'll think he's still at Nana's." Mom brought a small memorial candle, which Dad lit and left outside the door.

That night as the family straggled into the great hall, most of the gathering was still grousing (no, not talking of eggs this time, it means "complaining") about The Grouch's tale, saying, "What a cheat!" and similar whines, when the running boy, in a somewhat high-pitched, frightened voice, said, "Anyone have another tale?"

His voice was strange because, just a moment before, while running through the great hall, he had flopped the cat's ear with his toe. The cat had been fast asleep in a catnap, dreaming catnip dreams into which a few of the humans' words had penetrated, causing the dreams to be flavored by turkey, omelets, and the pursuit of hatching chicks. Remarkably fast, considering the feline's catatonic state, the cat's paws rushed up as fast as a Category-3 hurricane and scratched the running boy's ankles, making his words jump, just like he did, an octave or so.

Graceful And Handsome Four Footed God Who, oh heck, the cat, was still half-asleep. Without thinking, he answered the running boy, "I have a tail. I have the *finest* tail!"

Everyone was stunned. The cat could talk?

And, they thought, what could his story be? They waited, silent, curious as a cat. The cat fought off the heavy blanket of sleep fogging his brain. One of the uncles finally growled, "Where's the cat's tale, already?"

"Cattails are in the pond," the cat answered, still without understanding. He wet his paw with his rough tongue, and smoothed out his whiskers. Everyone was still looking at him.

"No, no," explained Dad. "We are telling stories. You said you had a tale to tell, so we're all waiting."

"Oh, that kind of tail," purred the cat to himself. He was unwilling to admit he had been confused, but was still too sleepy to think straight, so he sought a way to assert his superiority and stall for time. "I have a fine tale to tell," he said, arching his back and stretching, and raising his tail so it seemed to point right at the ceiling. "But first, I need a saucer of milk." Mom obligingly went to the kitchen.

Princess said, "While we are waiting, I have a fine story about a young girl in the middle of the ocean, who everyone ignores because she is a girl and small, but who fights the volcano god and saves her people. I have songs and dances for it." But the cat, ever proud and haughty, said, "No. My tale next. Wait."

After the cat leisurely lapped his milk, and then spent

about five minutes carefully cleaning his entire face, he stood up and began his story.

The Cat Who Wouldn't Bow To A Hat

This is a true story, every word. It takes place only a few generations ago, when cats still acted like humans and stood on two feet, and farmed, and gardened, and used tools, and lived in houses and villages. Since then, we've discovered it's so much more rewarding and comfortable simply to follow the sun around a human's house, sleeping here and there, playing when we like, and letting humans do all the work.

We cats can all talk, of course, if we want, but why bother when a simple "mieouwww" or rubbing against someone's leg gets us what we want without any effort, or the kind of expectations or responsibility that showing our skills would bring? [As if to make his point about how easy life was, the cat yawned, a big yawn starting at his whiskers, and continuing in waves through his entire body, until at last the tip of his tail flicked the yawn into the gathering, onto the pudgy one, who yawned him- or herself.]

This story was told to me by my grandfather, when he was very old and his sight was failing due to cataracts, and is exactly right. A cat never lies. ["I've seen that cat lie all around the house," said the Whisperer, but the cat ignored her.] It happened in the village my family comes from, called "The Catacombs," in a place in Spain known as "Catalonia." My family there owned a great store, called "Purrrena, with the very best food for felines." We also did catering [which he pronounced as "cat-ering"] for parties, and catalog sales.

My great-great-grandfather was the most active person in the town, well respected: a catalyst for whatever happened. He owned two boats; one with dual hulls – what's the word? – oh, yeah, a catamaran. The other was a catboat. [A catcall was heard, but which catty guest made it was unknown.] When the boats came in from the sea, there were always many fish, a fine catch [which he pronounced as "cat-ich"].

I remember the story well; my grandfather spoke in a husky voice, due to catarrh. It was right after Sunday School at the catholic cathedral, where grandfather taught catechism and helped the slower boys catch up [all pronounced to say "cat" clearly]. We were in his small office, at opposite sides, sort of kitty-corner to each other. There was a vase of cat-kins and cattails on his desk; gifts from the kittens he taught. I had just finished my lunch: catfish with catsup. Granddad gave me a present: a big blue cat's eye marble.

[Mom had been looking at the cat with obvious amuse-ment; she was almost snorting. She had a clear memory of bringing home a tiny orange kitten, only about a handful, from the Dog Pound, no less. This cat with his tale, she knew, was putting on airs. The cat looked at her, staring at her, dar-ing her to say anything, like a king glaring at an impudent courtier. He waited; she was silent. "Cat got your tongue?" he asked, but then went on with his story.]

"Not long ago," Grandfather said, "at a time of great catastrophe, this land was ruled by dogs. My grandfather, who was known as a fine singer—considered the best at cater-wauling in the country—was also an admirable archer. Kittens would throw stones in the air, and from 150 papaws away, he could hit the stone with his arrow.

"The dog ruler was a tyrant and a vain breed. He sent his wolf-dogs to collect taxes from all the cats, even the scaredy cats who scarcely could spare a flea. The dog [the cat virtu-ally spat out the word] demanded, on pain of thrashing with a cat-o-nine-tails, that all bow down to him when he passed.

"One day, that dog of a dog went even farther. He put a stick in the village square, hung his hat on it, and barked that all the cats, even the hepcats, had to bow-wow down to the dog tags!

"That was too much for your great-great-grandfather. He went to the catwalk on his castle [pronounced "cat-sil"] and shouted, 'We are not cattle, we are cats. I'll never bow to a dog again.' He went to the village square and tipped the dog's hat off the pole, into the dirt, and kicked it once or twice, finally throwing the hat into a muddy catchment.

"Soon after, of course, the wolf-dogs came for him. The mangy top dog had thought up a fiendish punishment.

"'I will take your oldest kitten – Catandra, I believe – and tie her to a stake in the village square. I will put an apple on her head. If you, who brags so much about your markscatship, hit the apple with your one chance, you can go free, and her as well. But if you miss ... .' Here the mongrel gleefully howled and howled.

"So, they tied Catandra to the caterpillar with catgut; she was paralyzed with fear: cataplexic. All the villagers were herded there; they even took the cat-burglar from the jail and forced the crowd from the cathouse to watch. The dogs hauled your great-great-grandfather out, none too gently, and let him get his bow and quiver, which held two arrows. They counted off twenty paces twice, then twenty more, and then twenty still further. None of the dogs could even hit a cow from that distance. 'Okay, furball, here's your chance to avoid death,' the cur said, drooling with cruelty.

"So, your great-great-grandfather lifted his bow (he would bow but not bow), fitted an arrow to the string, and pulled it back as far as it would go. If he missed, he would surely kill Catandra.

"He sighted carefully, held his breath, and let go of the arrow. It zinged through the air, and there was a loud THWACK and a short scream from Catandra. The entire village was silent.

"Then the apple parted into two pieces and fell off Catandra's head to the ground. The arrow stuck hard into the caterpillar. Only a few hairs on Catandra's head (she was my mother) were mussed, and those by a feather on the arrow which was having such a great time flying that it forgot to pull in its fingers.

"The drooling dog was very disappointed. He had been looking forward to skewered cat. 'Okay, you can go,' he growled.

'But I see you had two arrows. I allowed you only one shot.'

"'Oh, that,' your great-great-grandfather purred. 'If I missed with the first arrow and hurt Catandra, the second arrow was for you!'

"'Seize that feline!' barked the dog. But it was no use. Your great-great-grandfather's bravery so inspired the mom and populace that the cats drove all the dogs out. Cats ruled peacefully in The Catacombs in Catalonia from then on."

As it should be. Another saucer of milk!

All the folks agreed it was a good story. Many of the children were inspired the next day to make bows and arrows from the lower branches of the fruit trees in the courtyard (children were prohibited from leaving the house, and the adults were too scared), until Mom and Dad banned the practice.

Mom, who had served catfish with Catalan saffron orzo for dinner before the cat's tale, had Dad help her set the after-tale table for a catawba raspberry sherbet and Crema Catalana, which everyone, including the cat, lapped up. Only Princess asked Dad why he was wiping his eyes.

He Gets By With A Little Help From Man's Best Friend

The cat, enormously proud of himself, and pleasantly full after two saucers of milk and Crema Catalana, found a cushion in the weak sun rays the next day and curled himself up. No amount of pleading or teasing could get him to talk again. As the sunlight moved, the cat repositioned himself around the big room to follow the dim rays and tepid warmth.

The rest of the gathering drifted here and there to some private tasks, remembering the agreement to assemble again later for more stories. The Aunts and Uncles (honorifics for age, no actual relationship required) had their own homes, and lives and finances, and fretted at their inability to tend to those matters, at missing their daily habits, and even at having to sleep in unfamiliar beds. They would not risk their children to travel home, they said, with which solicitude they hid their own fear of venturing outside.

Outside, the wind howled and the dark cloud remained, with an unlucky sparrow or two falling suddenly from the sky. Princess shivered, and helped Mom prepare dinner; her job was to smooth out the chocolate frosting on the chocolate cake. At this task, she was assisted by the pudgy kid, wish granted, who religiously accompanied her to the kitchen.

"Is the pudgy kid a boy or girl?" Princess wondered about her playmate. She could be a pleasantly plump-faced girl of eight or so, or he could be a slightly husky boy with a broad face. There was no clue in the appearance.

"'Cousin' doesn't say much. Even with a bearded hag, 'grandma' lets me know the sex," mused Princess; "I know that even the smallest, thinnest, wasp-waisted, least hairy of the uncles, for all his dance and falsetto and bustling about the kitchen, is underneath a man. But 'cousin' doesn't tell me a thing. And I can't remember her, or his, name, for the life of me. I guess it doesn't matter much."

The pudgy girl, perhaps, managed to get as much icing into his, perhaps, mouth as was put on the cake. And the dancing uncle came by, looked at Princess, the cake and the pudgy kid, and said, "What a fabulous job you two are doing!" and took the cake out of reach of pudgy, who had grabbed a fork and was thinking of sampling.

"Billie, come here," Mom said, looking at the pudgy kid. "You can lick the cake bowl. You," she said to Princess, "have the frosting bowl." As Princess twirled her finger through the thin film of frosting left, she said triumphantly to herself, "'Cousin Billie,' now I remember; she's a girl!" But then, finger in her mouth, she stopped and said to herself, "But maybe it was 'Billy.' Hmm. No help there. I guess it doesn't matter much."

After dinner, all the people staying in the house came, sooner or later, into the great room. They looked at each other to see who would offer a story. Dad had told Princess that she shouldn't tell a story they all knew, like the ones Princess had sung and danced to since the company arrived, but should tell one that was rare, or make one up herself. She decided to listen to some others' stories to learn what a proper after-dinner tale sounded like.

But at first it was difficult to get a "proper" story, because Uncle Ax wanted to tell a story. Most families have an Uncle Ax, even more so then when drinking water wasn't safe ["Fish fart in it," Princess giggled] and everyone drank wine or beer or mead or even heavier stuff. Uncle Ax was a souse, which means he drank more than he should, and usually acted like he had. He was always giving Princess an unwanted hug, smelling of stale wine, sweat, and as vile with tobacco as a 1910 Grand Central Station men's room cuspidor.

Uncle Ax stood up, unsteadily, and swayed as if the gusting wind outside buffeted him inside. "I'll start," he said.

"Uncle Ax, recite the rhyme you told me about, 'This young lady dressed in a vest, which couldn't quite contain her....'"

"Lance, be quiet," some Auntie shouted, and the running boy stopped suddenly. However, the sot (another word for "souse") didn't take the Auntie's warning and started a sort of poem called a limerick:

There was a young lady of Poughkeepsie,
Who kept herself uncommonly tipsy.
She'd drink through the day
And into the night,
But when offered a drink, say, "just a lil' bitsy."

A collective relieved sigh was heard from the parents in the room. Uncle Ax continued, "Here's another one."

A young man by the name of Friar Tuck,
Was seen in the rain and the muck.
He was asked, "where ya going
In your black mukluks?"
"To get me," he said, "a good..."

"Shut up, Ax," the parents warned, but he finished, "*pickup truck.*"

"Tell a real story, a decent story, or sit down," one Auntie said, and there were murmurs of agreement among the adults, although most of the kids wanted more limericks.

"All right," Uncle Ax said. "This happened to me when I was drinking too much [an "Oh, lordy, some things never change" was heard] and I was poor and living on the streets."

A Little Help From Man's Best Friend

I entered the town, I think it was in Persia, without a dime to my name, in tattered clothing thick with the dust of the road. I hadn't eaten all day. I was so poor I was sobering up. My last meal was the crust of a sandwich someone else had thrown away.

I tried begging, but a tall soldier, dressed in a fine uniform with a long sword, grunted at me and put his hand on his sword. I moved along into the market, looking for some unsold fruit thrown out, or the trimmings of a piece of pork or beef, but no luck. And the merchants, when I came near their stands, stood right in front, so there was no chance to grab anything.

A loud procession came into the marketplace. First, there were young men dressed in finery, shouting, "Move aside. Rajah coming through." Then came a fancy carriage, except without wheels; eight burly men carried the windowed litter. More retainers followed behind, all in splendid clothing and, I noted jealously, all looking well-fed. Some large dogs, big black Labrador retrievers, ran alongside the carriage. I followed the carriage, together with about twenty other people seeking favors from the Rajah, and managed to get through the gate to his mansion before it was barred.

All the followers were ushered into a long hall, the walls and floors of which were covered in brightly colored rugs. We were told to sit and be quiet. About an hour later, the Rajah, about 15 servants, 4 dogs and several beefy men dressed in black, who seemed to be the Rajah's advisors, came in.

The Rajah sat on a majestic seat; he towered over us and looked down. Several servants presented food for the Rajah and his advisors, and nearer to us, they set down four golden bowls for the four dogs. Each bowl was filled to the brim with tasty steak and pieces of cooked chicken and goat. My mouth was watering; I wondered if I could jump out and steal a bowl, or make a fool of myself and pretend to be a dog, bark and eat on my hands and knees from one of the dog's bowls.

As if he understood, the nearest dog looked at me, straightened his tail, and wagged it in jerky motions. He moved to the other side of the bowl so that he blocked the Rajah's and his servants' view of me, and, I swear, that dog invited me to eat from his bowl. I inched forward, which was easy because I smelled bad and people would sneer, move away and then pretend I wasn't there.

I grabbed a piece of steak; it was warm and juicy and tasted like heaven. The dog nosed his bowl towards me, letting me eat it all up. When it was empty, he pushed the gold bowl even closer, and then pushed it behind me; I understood he wanted me to keep it.

I glanced around, but nobody seemed to be paying any attention to us. I put the bowl under my filthy shirt, backed myself to the rear of the crowd, and left the mansion with only a scornful and disgusted glance from the guard at the front gate.

That dog's bowl was so valuable that it allowed me to purchase a wine shop in my home village, the shop I still own. ["If you've got a talent, use it," the Whisperer said.] I have prospered and become well-off due to that dog's favors.

In fact, I went back to the village some years later in an attempt to right my wrong and repay the Rajah. Where there had been a great house was then just ruins, with an old, feeble man poking around them, looking no better than I had looked those several years before.

I asked where the Rajah was. The man replied, "What is it to you?" I told him my story, and my desire to make things right and repay.

"I'm that man, that former Rajah," he said. "That night, when we discovered that a golden bowl was missing, I accused my vizier, a learned wizard but a proud and dangerous man. He fell into a rage at my suggestion and placed a curse on my house and family.

"True to his prophesy, my only son died soon after, and the house burned to the ground during my son's funeral. No one would do business with me for fear of the curse, and I was soon ruined. Now you see me as I am, without riches."

Feeling guilty, I offered him twice the bowl's worth, right then and there, and to pay for an inn so he would have a soft bed to sleep in. He shook his head, gray hair atumble, and refused.

"I live a poor life now, but with my faithful daughter. She loves me deeply, and each night I sleep well. I don't have money to rage about, nor do I have to impress anyone. I can do no better than this for my few remaining years." He shook my hand and shuffled off.

I followed him without his knowing to see where he lived: in a small stone hut only a few hundred yards from his former manor.

When he left the next day to poke at the ruins, I slipped his daughter a few silver coins. She would take no more, saying, "We have all we need," although it did not seem as if they had anything at all.

As I went home from the town that night, a dog howled at the moon without stop; I heard it for miles.

Uncle Ax sat down, heavily, almost breaking the chair, and sobbed.

That was the end of his tale. Dad, his brother, went to him and hugged him, crying himself for a different, related reason.

Dinner had been franks for the kids, with pease pudding, and German shepherd's pie for the adults. While Mom took over comforting Uncle Ax, Dad served the after-tale snack of masghati and great Danish pastries.

Introduction To Moses For Nonmosicians

Princess was giddy. Everything seemed funny to her, even the mundane. She had spent much of the day playing with her toddler brother, tickling and teasing him until he turned red from his nonstop gales of laughter, and Princess was infected with the funny bug now. She remembered that after Uncle Ax collapsed into his chair at the conclusion of his story, the Whisperer had said, "Give him a saucer of wine." Princess thought that was so funny she laughed until snot came from her nose.

The running boy, Lance, suggested the children have a race. "Headstrong, that boy," said the Whisperer, which started Princess giggling, although she didn't know why. It was even funnier when the boy's mother said, "Lance Legstrong, stop fidgeting!" and Princess sang to herself, "Legstrong was headstrong but strongly held in a headlock." So, when there was a knocking at the door, Princess went to get it so she wouldn't keep laughing in front of everyone.

But even the door knock seemed funny. Rather than a simple, "knock, knock," or a big "bang," the sound came to Princess as "boom, shaka-lacka, boom, shaka-laka" as she skipped to answer. She looked through the peephole, and that's when she first saw the Rabbi. It was a middle-aged man, perhaps a few years older than Dad, but looking far more aged. He was dressed in black, with a big black hat with a wide brim, dripping wet, on his head. He was standing next to a bag almost as tall as he was.

"I am the Rabbi Ibraham Tayers, a peddler," he said.

"Okay, wait," she answered. She sought out her mother and said there was a man with a beard at the door, and with a sack. "Hmm, too early for Saint Nick," said Mom, and Princess started giggling. Mom went to the door and told the man to get inside, pulling on his sack to hasten his entrance.

The man clothed in black came in, shook the rain from his coat and took it off. Underneath, he was dressed in a simple black caftan. He took off his big hat, but underneath was a smaller cap, which set Princess giggling again; she had a sudden image of a cat in a big tall hat, and when the cat took off his tall hat, underneath was another cat, smaller, also in a big (but smaller) hat, underneath . . ., and so on. It was so funny she dissolved into a gale of laughter.

"A few verses short of a Torah, that one?" asked the man, but Mom just shrugged at him. Following the last guidance of the town crier, before he was reduced to sobs and then silence, she made the visitor wash his hands and face, while she counted to twenty, before she led him to the great hall.

"I am the Rabbi Ibraham Tayers," the man said to the assembled residents of the house. "I am an itinerant peddler. Whatever you want, I have, at a price. For instance, I have this magic log," and he pulled a big colored log out of his bag, "which, if you burn it, will dissipate the black cloud. Only 2,000 shekels! For you, such a nice family, only 1,750!"

The assembly shook their heads incredulously, speaking over each other that it must be a fraud. The Rabbi looked around, spread his hands, and made a moue.

"You doubt?" he inquired. "But I am here, no?" he added. "And healthy and hale," he shouted to prove his strength. "Perhaps I know something?"

Mom looked at him sharply, asking, "Does it really work?" He looked at her, deep into her blue eyes, and saw her soul. He looked away, shook his head, and said, "No, of course not. But I have everything else."

"Rabbi Tayers, do you have a hairbrush?" asked someone.

This man was named "Rabbit Ears?" Princess completely lost it, laughing so hard she had to hold on to a chair, but even then, slowly sinking to the floor, finding it hard to stop long enough to breathe. The Rabbi looked at Mom and asked, "How can be little girl too long in the sun when there is no sun? Perhaps a bissel chicken soup?"

The Rabbi got busy selling his wares, a hairbrush here, a pair of shoes there, some pots and a Weber Barbeque for Mom, some hunting knives, plows and harnesses for the men, a few hot water bottles and lots of patent medicines for the Aunties: whatever they asked for, he pulled from his sack. Princess stopped laughing and just stared, wide-eyed.

She looked at him more closely and noticed his long beard was streaked with gray. Streaked? Rather, almost lined, some vertical, some gently curved. Suddenly, it seemed like a zebra! She started laughing again, and he looked at her and asked, "Nu? You see something funny?" She swore to herself that the stripes moved just like a zebra running, so she stifled her laugh and shook her head.

"No one wants this nice hourglass?" he asked, holding up something with a thick top and bottom and thin waist, filled with sand in the top, slowly leaking sand to the bottom. "Accurate to a few minutes every hour, and turns itself over when all the sand runs through. No?"

He opened the sack and dropped it in. Princess counted all the way to 17 before she heard it hit bottom, so she stared again at the man. The money purse at the man's waist had grown large.

"How about some gifts for the keiki?" he said. "For the boy goy," he said, "toy flyers, jew's harps and pea shooters, and these bouncing balls." He handed them out, the flyers being made of a few pieces of thin wood, some of which went through the others, and if you threw it right, it glided across the room. "And for the goyals, hair ribbons and bracelets and candy mints."

Princess waited for the pudgy cousin to come forward to see which type of gift she, maybe, or he took. But pudgy said,

"I want both," singing, "One for tomorrow, one just for today!"

Princess got a bow of crimson ribbon, which would unravel whenever she put it in her hair, but stayed just fine if she treated it like a ring and wore it on her middle finger. Everyone settled down, although Princess still had to suppress a giggle or two. Rabbit Ears!

"We have a custom of telling stories to pass the time," said Mom and Dad.

"Oh, have I a story," the Rabbi said. "It's a story we often tell in the Spring." A glance at the windows and a shrug substituted eloquently for the unspoken "if it ever comes." "It is true and a story important to my people."

Princess started giggling. "My people": it sounded just like "my peephole," which was where she first saw the Rabbit. Oh, it was all just too funny.

The Rabbi started his tale then, even though it was before dinner. He didn't know the custom.

"'Rabbi' means teacher. ["No," thought Princess, "it means 'bunny.'"] I have taught this story to all my six sons and four daughters." ["Ten kids? No wonder he's an itinerant peddler," said the Whisperer.]

And so began The Rabbi's Tale. ["No, the rabbit's tail," said Princess to herself, unable to stop her mind.]

The Rabbi's Tale

Very long ago, my people [a quick glance at Princess], the Jews, were slaves in a land far from home, in a place called Egypt. ["You can't gyp a Jew," said the Whisperer. It was a dark time, indeed.] They were forced to work building gigantic burial places for the rulers, the Pharaohs. ["Jews in Fair Oaks? Who'd have thought it?" wondered the Whisperer.] They had to carry and move huge stones, were given almost no food, and had to live in straw huts.

Worse, they were told to worship only the Egyptian gods,

rather than the one god of the Jews.

One day, a Jewish woman gave birth to a boy ["Mazel tov," said the Whisperer.] She didn't want the boy to grow up a slave, so she made a boat of reeds for him, kissed him tenderly, and pushed the boat into the Nile River, hoping it would carry the infant far away to where he could grow up in freedom.

But the boat only sailed a few miles. There it was seen by one of the Pharaoh's married daughters, who waded out and pulled it to shore. She was childless and believed the baby was a gift from Ra, the Son God, in answer to her prayers. She named him "Moses." She raised Moses as her own.

Moses was accepted at the royal court for many years, although he felt he didn't fit in. The other boys played bocce ball and raced chariots; he liked to read. They teased him and bullied him, and gave him wedgies, even though he only wore robes.

One day, when Moses was about fourteen, a captain of a ship bringing spices from Phoenicia pointed out, "He doesn't look like the rest of you. He looks more like your slaves." His adoptive mother disagreed, "Phoeny, he doesn't look Jewish!" But the Pharaoh, wanting to keep the royal line pure, banished Moses from the palace.

On Moses' way to the poor side of town, a sage bush burst into flame, and a voice filled the air. "I am the God of the Jews. You must lead them to freedom. I will make it happen, but you are my vessel. You will be their leader. You will demand that the Pharaoh release the Jews from slavery and let them leave Egypt." ["The man's mission is manumission," freely quipped the Whisperer.]

Moses cried out, "Why me? Why now? Why do you demand this of me?"

"Don't be a whys guy," said the voice from the burning bush. "Do what I command." The bush burst into colored flames and then showed the original Abbott and Costello "Who's on First" skit, followed by highlights of the recent Cairo 500, a long chariot race. Duly impressed, Moses pulled himself together and determined to lead the Jews to freedom.

He spent many years with the Jews to learn his own people's customs and laws, and about their God, while he grew into a young man. Then he told their leaders, a warren of rabbis, "I will confront the Pharaoh and tell him to let my people go."

"Yeah, I wonder why I never thought of that," replied one rabbi, whose back bore the marks of years of heavy toil and an occasional beating. "That should go well."

When the rest of the Jewish men went to work the next day, Moses went to the palace to see the Pharaoh, with only Aaron, his younger brother, to accompany him. Many of the palace guards remembered him fondly; as a boy he would slip them coins and oranges and ask about their families.

"Hey, Mo, how's it go?"

"Never slow; gotta go!" said Moses, high-fiving and exchanging secret handshakes. He went through to the Reception Room, a huge place, as stupendous as an emperor's ego, with Moses' sandals making a "flip-flop" and his walking stick a "click, click, click" as he crossed the room and stood in front of the Pharaoh.

"I am the spokesman for my people, and for the God of the Jews," he said, "and I demand that you LET MY PEOPLE GO," he continued in a capital voice. ("Funny, I still don't think he looks Jewish," said his adoptive mother from the rear of the hall; she missed him greatly and wasn't very objective.)

The Pharaoh called in his astrologers, advisers, priests and magicians. The Chief Magician was dressed in a black silk robe with stars and constellations, and long pointed shoes with a curl at the end.

"Why should I?" sneered the Pharaoh. "We have our own gods, who are powerful, and who will make mincemeat out of your god, and I'll eat mincemeat pie." As always when the Pharaoh made a joke, everyone laughed and elbowed their neighbors, saying, "That's a good one, no?"

Moses heard in his head the Jewish god commanding, "Throw down your stick." So, Moses cried loudly, "See the power of our God!" With that, he pounded his walking stick onto the floor, and then threw it towards the Pharaoh. The stick turned into a large viper with a bent neck, which slithered towards the Pharaoh.

"That's nothing," said the Chief Magician. He took off his silken belt from his robe, placed it on the ground, and muttered a weird incantation in a foreign tongue (which sounded much like, "This better work or my ass is grass," but nobody spoke English then), and said, "Behold!"

His belt turned into a huge black mamba snake, which, after a short eponymous dance, darted to Moses' stick viper; Moses' snake, a king snake, ate the Egyptian's snake. But that didn't impress the Pharaoh.

"No, I will not let your people go!" roared the Pharaoh. "For your effrontery, I will double their work and cut in half their food, and now they have to supply their own straw for bricks. Now, begone yourself!"

"You will regret this! Our God will call down upon your people and country a series of plagues, until you relent and LET MY PEOPLE GO. I will come back after each one to see if you wish to spare your realm from further plagues and suffering."

Moses and his brother left. Behind him, the Pharaoh's retainers were saying, "Way to go! That's telling him. Good joke, too, your most eminent royal everything," and stuff like that.

As Moses left with Aaron, a rumbling voice in his ear said, "You must listen and obey me. I didn't say to pound your stick; I said to throw it down. You almost broke the snake's neck!"

"Sorry, I was trying to be dramatic."

"That's my job. I'll give them some plagues they won't forget, and soon the Pharaoh will relent."

At this point, the pudgy cousin said, "I'm hungry."

Dad asked, "Should we take a break? How much longer is the story?"

The rabbi looked up, shrugged his shoulders, and replied, "Only a few thousand years to go. A break and a bit of food would be a mitzvah."

Most of the company went to the dining hall and sat down to wait for dinner. Princess went with Mom and Dad to the kitchen to help out. The Rabbi followed them.

"We Jews have very strict rules about what we may eat," the Rabbi said. "Many foods are forbidden to us, and there are more rules about which foods can be eaten at the same time, and during certain holidays, and exactly how to prepare meat. So, I'm sorry, I must ask, what do you plan to serve?"

"You're in luck!" said Dad. "Suckling pig."

Grade: A Big Red C

"Ach, no," said the Rabbi. "Treif. I cannot eat that. Jews have a saying: 'First, do no ham.'"

Princess would hear some of the ensuing conversation as she came and went from the kitchen, carrying clean plates and utensils out to the dining hall, following Mom's instructions. It sounded to her like:

"Some lobster?"

"Treif."

"Cheese omelets?

"Treif."

"Bacon? I guess that's just another word for ham."

"Right, treif."

"Seafood casserole? It has shrimp, mussels, and clams in a spicy tomato sauce, hmmmm."

"Treif, treif, treif."

"I'll try it," the pudgy kid said, seemingly appearing out of nowhere.

"Camel steaks?"

"Treif."

There must have been much more that Princess missed as she set the table. The Rabbi was still trying to find something he could eat.

"Perhaps," said Dad, "we could roast some of the venison. I nabbed a female deer only a week ago."

"Treif."

Princess, who had somewhat recovered from her giddy

spell, had to squelch a giggle under the sharp eye of the Rabbi and the gentle eye of the zebra on his beard, because in her head, her last Spanish lesson became, "Uno, does, treif."

"Pepperoni pizza!" the pudgy kid suggested. "Everyone eats pizza."

"Ach, no. Treif. Jews don't eat pepperoni or meat and cheese together."

"No cheeseburgers?" the pudgy kid asked, astounded by the Jews' discipline.

"What can you eat?" Mom asked.

"Ahh," the Rabbi replied dreamily. "Blintzes, stuffed cabbage, pot roast, falafel, kreplach." A pause. "What I wouldn't give for a Reuben sandwich. A good potato salad." Another pause. "Gefilte fish."

"I've never caught one of those," said Dad.

"You're not like that Hindu who passed through, are you? You eat cow?"

Princess almost lost control at "Hindu who passed through," but she managed to turn her giggle into a snort and a sneeze.

"Her joy seems infectious," muttered the Rabbi.

"Sit down, Rabbi, at the dining table. I know what to make," said Mom, always practical. First, she served most of the guests the suckling pig, which was finger-licking good, by visual, oral and digital acclamation. Then, only a minute or two later, she bought the Rabbi a plate with a large flattened disk of cooked ground beef, with a piece of bread below and one above, and a side of potato kugel.

"This is all good," Mom said as she placed it before him.

"Ahh, kosher," he said.

"Gesundheit," she replied automatically. The Rabbi took a bite of the sandwich and closed his eyes with joy.

"Vunderlekh. So kind of you to make special for me."

"You can eat hamburger?" the pudgy kid asked, as Dad rolled his eyes but kept them in his head. The Rabbi jumped up, spitting out food. "You lied to me? You told me a big whopper? This is pig?"

"No, no," said Mom. "It's 100% beef. It's just called 'hamburger.' Come to the kitchen; I'll show you."

The Rabbi, remembering his look deep into her eyes, said, "You don't have to. I believe. But the irony: I, a poor Jew, eat with gentilemen and women for the first time, and I eat 'ham.'"

In later years, after the Rabbi returned home, he served the same sandwich in his village, but just called it a burger, or the "big whopper." It was so liked that even a traveling prince tried one, and then had it served regularly in his castle, from which came his title upon ascending the throne: the "Burger King."

After a loud and resounding series of burps and grunts and belches signaled that the meal was over, and Mom and a few Aunties made quick work of the dishes, the company assembled again in the large hall, and the Rabbi resumed his story.

Rabbi's Story Continued and Concluded

Now, a plague is a terrible thing. You wouldn't wish it upon your worst enemy, but our God did. Only a day later, the River Nile turned red; the water became blood. Even the wells and springs ran with blood, not water. Moses and Aaron went to the Pharaoh and said, "See the power of our God! LET MY PEOPLE GO."

But the Pharaoh sneered. "The Nile is cleaner now, and the water tastes better than when it was fouled with Spring silt and cow and camel dung. ["And fish farts," giggled Princess.] And our women's lips look luscious. Besides, bright red pasta matches the sauce perfectly. You'll have to do better than that." The Pharaoh, who bathed regularly, was as red as a boiled lobster.

"Treif," said Moses.

Soon, it began raining hard, what we call "cats and dogs." But it was frogs. Frogs everywhere, hundreds and thousands of frogs. Not Parisians, but frogs from tadpoles, jumping, playing leapfrog, getting into food, tunics, and pockets. A real mess.

But Moses' "LET MY PEOPLE GO" was met with a firm, "No way! Egyptians love frog legs, a real delicacy. Thank your god from me." Indeed, some frog legs did seem to be kicking outside the Pharaoh's lips.

"Treif," said Moses as he and Aaron shuffled out of the palace, careful not to step on the frogs, which were slippery.

The third plague was lice and fleas, which are tiny animals, parasites that live on people and suck blood and cause many small itching sores. Still the Pharaoh, although scratching everywhere (ordering his servants to scratch those unreachable spots), was unmoved and refused to LET MY PEOPLE GO. Actually, Moses and Aaron were glad when this plague ended, because even though the lice and fleas started out only on the Egyptians, they soon spread to the Jews, who didn't have servants to curry their hair and pick off the parasites.

Next came a plague of wild animals and flies. Through the streets of Thebes ran jaguars, elephants, hippopotamuses and bison, while in Memphis down Beale Street and past Graceland raced yaks, wolves, lions and tigers and bears.

"Oh, my!" said the Pharaoh to Moses, but the Pharaoh refused to LET MY PEOPLE GO. "We haven't had so much meat to eat in years. Catching them gives my army something useful to do beyond harassing Jews. And, swarms of flies? That's normal for the Nile in Spring. We can stand that for a while." ["Time flies," said the Whisperer.]

The wild animals had barely been cleaned up (the flies remained, but that was normal for the Nile in Spring) when, as Moses had warned the Pharaoh, more plagues came. Boils, which are large, terrible open sores, afflicted the Egyptians. The Pharaoh almost gave in, but his advisers said, "No. You will be forever known as a sore loser." The Pharaoh couldn't stand ridicule.

Next, there was pestilence on livestock, so there was no animal meat to eat, but still the Pharaoh refused to LET MY

PEOPLE GO [by now, the entire family chimed in]. Perhaps there was a remaining stock of yak meat.

Soon after, the God of the Jews used the heavens: hail, lightning and thunder pummeled down and rocked the earth for days, causing crops to wither and drown in the fields, and making all Egypt sound like front seats at a heavy metal concert. But the Pharaoh, safe in his palace, with food stored in huge urns, refused to relent.

When Moses demanded, "LET MY PEOPLE GO," he shouted, "Whaat?" and said, "Begone with you. The slaves will have to work whatever the weather."

The next plague—of locusts—also failed to persuade the Pharaoh to LET MY PEOPLE GO. The locusts ["A kind of grasshopper, Grasshopper," the Rabbi said to a young cousin who had raised her hand] were everywhere, sometimes blotting out the sun, and crawled into ears and noses, so the Egyptians could hardly open their mouths without eating an insect. But the Pharaoh was unimpressed. With Moses standing there, he ordered the Chief Magician to get an old oldspaper, and black robes and curled toes went away, and soon came back with a scroll.

"Let's see, yes, last Summer's oldspaper."

This was in olden times, so long ago there were no newspapers, only oldspapers, and the back issues were "old oldspapers."

"See here. Second papyrus. Headline: 'Plague of locusts predicted for next Spring,'" read the Chief Magician.

"So... take... your... brother and... get out... of here," shouted the Pharaoh (still a bit deaf), speaking slowly because he had to spit out locusts between his words.

"You trifle with powers beyond your imagination," warned Moses. He spread out his hands to the skies, and total darkness descended. There was no sun and no stars, no twinkling of a planet, not a streak of a meteor. It was as dark as if one were a mile underground in a mine. You could strike a match, and "psst;" it would ignite and burn you, but still be dark. Stoves and fireplaces shed only dark heat and energy.

"Let him deal with that," thought Moses, and he grabbed Aaron and they stumbled out of the palace, almost knocking themselves silly hitting walls and low doorways.

"Next... time... brother... wait... until... we're... outside," suggested Aaron, as he walked blindly into a sharp-sided statue, spitting out some locusts.

Two days later, the Pharaoh sent for Moses, and a day or so later, his messenger found Moses. Back to the palace (where ropes had been installed to guide people), and again, LET MY PEOPLE GO.

"The slaves may go," the Pharaoh relented, "but the whole of Egypt belongs to me, so they may take only what they can carry, no goats or sheep or chickens or pigs."

"Treif," muttered Moses at the mention of 'pig.' He conferred with Aaron, then addressed the Pharaoh.

"They will starve if they can't take food."

"Let them starve; that's my offer."

There was no mediation or ADR in those days, and only one ancient tome on how to negotiate, *The Art of the Deal* ["Treif," everyone muttered in unison]; it advised never giving ground. So there was an impasse.

The final plague was so cruel it was almost unthinkable. A thick dark cloud, which the Jews called "the Angel of Death," passed over the land. In every Egyptian household, the first born son, that is, the eldest, choked and died. The Jews were warned to put lambs' blood on their doorways, and the Angel of Death passed over those houses so the Jewish sons were saved.

Mournful wailing spread over the land. The Pharaoh asked his advisers, "Is my son safe?" They assured him that he was, that the Pharaoh's gods were as powerful as the God of the Jews. But when the Pharaoh looked for his son, he found him dead.

"LET THOSE PEOPLE GO," he sobbed.

"Let them take what they want. Let them leave Egypt and never return, except as tourists." His messengers had the word spread; it was easier now that the sun and light had returned.

Moses told his people, "Jews, move away from here." The Jews quickly got ready to leave. They packed up the babies and grabbed the old ladies. There wasn't even time to let their bread rise, so they had only unleavened bread, *matzoh*, today called "flatbread."

They loaded their wagons and drove their livestock towards the Red Sea, towards their promised home in the north. The Jews were singing, laughing, and shouting; they even forgave Moses for all the trouble he had caused them with plagues and extra work, the last straw and all.

After all his magicians and priests failed to revive his son, the Pharoah's sorrow turned to anger. He changed his mind, goaded by his Chief Magician, who said, "If you let them go, you'll be forever remembered as a loser."

He summoned his army and, mounting chariots pulled by swift, large horses, the Pharoah at the head of his cavalry raced after the Jews, intending to slaughter them. The Jews were trapped between the Red Sea and the bloodthirsty Pharaoh and his army.

Moses told the Jews to drop everything except what they could easily carry. The shoreline was soon littered with wagons, stoves, couches, kitchen tables, encyclopedias, anvils, and the like. Moses raised his arms, hands wide apart, and the waters of the Red Sea parted just far enough to allow the Jews to pass through in single file (grabbing a fish now and then), herding their animals through as well. They were several hundred yards into the Red Sea when the Pharaoh's chariots arrived.

The Egyptian horses slowly picked their way through the discarded bric-a-brac and entered the tunnel through the Red Sea's water. But after they were in only a short way, still well behind the Jews, the chasm disappeared, and the waters closed down on them. It wasn't deep enough to drown them, but the horses shied and would not go forward, and the chariots became mired in the mud, and the Egyptian forces had to give up and slither back.

The Jews were finally safe and freed from Egyptian bondage. They gave a mystic Hebrew two-handed, one-fingered farewell salute to the Pharaoh from the other side of the Red Sea.

After crossing the Red Sea, my people wandered in the desert for 40 years before finding their promised land and sacred city, Jerusalem. That's a distance much less than 500 miles. But Jews are a patriarchal society, which means the men, officially, made all the decisions. The men simply would not ask for directions.

But that's another story.

The Rabbi sat down (he had been pacing during the story), and the cat, seizing the opportunity, curled up in his lap, with the zebra gently stroking him until he purred. Mom thoughtfully brought to the Rabbi the dessert she had whipped up of chocolate babka and rugelach.

A story or two more was told that evening, but without capturing the guests' imagination in the same way. To the Rabbi's delight, shouts of "LET MY PEOPLE GO" were heard from the children over the next few days, although Mom and Dad were less thrilled at the kids' attempts to inflict plagues on their playmates.

Easter Rhyme

Dad, up at about dawn to get the nonexistent early mail delivery, saw a solitary man — the first since the Rabbi — come down the long hill, to the flat on which the house stood. The man was dressed for an arctic winter, and had to pull a scarf away from his face before he could talk.

"Remembrance curtains on every block in town," he said, "and memorial candles in virtually each house's door sconce. Never seen it this bad before. Safe enough, though, if you stay inside." He banged his head with one hand, demonstrating that he realized his own situation contradicted his advice, reset his scarf, and resumed his trudge. Dad went through the house and gathered eggs for breakfast from the roost just outside the kitchen.

Later that day, Princess heard, or maybe she just had a feeling, that someone was at the front door. She looked through the peephole and saw white. She opened the door. But did she? In any event, in the next instant, a tall white rabbit was inside, towering over her.

"I am the Rabbit of Verona, but everyone just calls me 'RV.'"

"Are you real?" Princess asked, not knowing what else to say.

"No," said the rabbit, but when Princess looked sad, she added, "I am as real as St. Nick, real as a free lunch, real as grandpa's grasshopper stories, real as a unicorn, real as the hero in a romantic novel, real as love at first sight, real as witches and warlocks, real as Harry Potter's scar, and really upset you would ask me that!" And RV bowed, took Princess' hand and let Princess feel her ears.

Princess brought RV to the kitchen to meet Mom, but Mom just asked Princess, "Are you doing anything? Can you help me in a while?" Princess started to say, "This is RV," but Mom said, "Run along now. I'll call you when I need you."

As RV passed Lance, however, he jumped up, and even jumped in the middle of his jump, shouting, "Wow, what a whopper of a white whabbit!"

The other children soon crowded around, vying to touch her, saying,

"How soft; nice fur; so smooth!"

RV said, "Gather round, my runaway bunnies, and I'll tell you a scuttlebutt, as rabbits' tales (and tails) are known. They're shorter and cuter than mouse or dog tails."

The children formed a circle around her and listened. Only children, no adults, were sitting in the circle, listening to the poem. Only children could see the storyteller or hear the words. Alexa, who was a teenager, wondered why the kids were so quiet, apparently doing nothing. She watched, and, in a while, was startled to see and hear the rabbit, but as soon as she said to herself, "That can't be real," RV vanished to her.

'Twas Good Friday before Easter, when all through the house,
Not a creature was stirring, not even a mouse.

"That's not right," said Mama Mouse, who was indeed stirring a pot of carrot soup and cutting onions to add.

"And what about us?" asked the cockroaches. "Nobody
thinks of us!"

The finest of clothes were hung on the line with great care,
In the hopes that by Sunday they would dry in the air.
The keiki were resting, finally asleep in their beds,
While heroic deeds and funny pranks enraptured their heads.

And Mom in her mumu, and I in the nude,
Were awakened by noises, so late and so rude.
My brain was still foggy. I was fighting a flu,
So I was slow to hear the hullabaloo.

I went to the window, my feet bare and cold;
Almost fell on my face: on a Lego I rolled.
I opened the drapes, and threw up pale green,
I hoped to the heavens it wasn't Covid-19.

I rubbed my eyes hard, to focus my sight.
It was dark and still the middle of the night.
The moonlight had pierced the dark clouds for a bit.
And what did I see? A huge white rabbit!

So slow did it move, at first I thought it a rock,
'Till it turned and exclaimed, "Eh, what's up, Doc?"
I heard it chomp on a carrot, two, and then three.
"You stop that," I cried. "Come down and make me."

I looked all around for something to throw,
But Mom took my hand saying, "Just let it go.
"She's but checking the garden.
She'll be elsewhere next eve.
Her work will be done;
Colored eggs she will leave.
The children will chortle, they'll race 'round the space,
Poking their hands into each hiding place."

And then in a twinkling, I heard on the roof
The splatter of an egg, and a, "Hey, you big goof,
Stick your head out again; give me a chance."
Another egg splashed. That broke my trance.

I raced down the stairs to confront that hair-raising hare,
But she didn't run away, just gave me a stare.
Up close I could see she was much bigger than me.
So I heeded Mom's words: I'd just let it be.

Her feet: how they thumped.
Her ears: long and straight.
Her nose: it just quivered,
Mouth: full of carrots she ate.

She held her furry fore paws ["But that would make six!" com-
plained a young cousin] just like a fighter,
So I abandoned any thought of trying to smite her.
The stump of a turnip she held tight in her teeth,
While rhubarb and carrot greens littered beneath.

She had a white fluffy tail, and ears that made her so tall!
I felt just like poor Alice, when she was "just this small."
She calmed down when she saw I was no longer a threat,
Said, "I'm the Easter Bunny."
And that's how we met.

A wink from her eye, and a twitch of her tail,
Let me sigh with relief, sure that peace would prevail.

She spoke right to the point, a trait I hold dear.
"How many kids you got living in there?"
"'Bout a dozen, right now," I said so she'd hear.
"I'll hide my eggs now, on Sunday they'll cheer."
She bustled round the courtyard and into each room,
Leaving things I saw not, then away she did zoom.

But I heard her explain, before she faded from sight:
"On Easter morning they'll see them.
For right now, please sleep tight."

The children laughed and applauded the Easter Rhyme, especially when the rabbit said, "Easter is next Sunday. How many of you like candy?"

"Me, three," said the pudgy cousin, even before anyone else could say, "Me" and "Me, too."

At the end of their questions ("Do rabbits have eggs?" "Can you fly?" "Do the eggs come out colored?" "Who framed Roger?" and the like) the children smiled happily at each other, and when they looked back, RV was gone.

A+ Stories And Grasshoppers

Another day. A few fights among the children, several resulting from other kids' attempted plagues of worms. Adults' biting references to decades-old grudges. Dad muttered *sotto voce* something about 'Evil Cloud, eviler crowd.' Mom, taking a break in late afternoon, sat in her favorite armchair; the cat, as always, came to warm her lap.

Outside, an empty street. Rust-colored clouds everywhere overhead, with a mist often turning to rain. A soft thud as a spasming bird hit the tile roof. Inside, the day dripped as slowly as crystallized honey from a thin spout. Relatives prolonged their afternoon naps. A few people, old and young, worked on stories, hoping for temporary celebrity.

Dinner, then story time. A feeble first story by an adult bragging about swindling an antique dealer when purchasing a desk, while another Uncle, knowing he was far older than the desk, discretely kept quiet.

Finally, it was Princess' turn to tell a story. Dad hushed the gathering and glared daggers at the kids, who continued to poke each other, whisper, and giggle.

Princess' First Tale

This is the story of the wind and the rain. No, sorry. The sun and the wind. From A+ Stories.

One day, in the sky, the sun and the wind were talking.

They made a bet. There was no prize, just a bet to see who was stronger.

A man was walking down below. He had a coat on. The bet was who could make him take the coat off.

The wind went first. He blew and blew, and even threw down some rain as well. He blew so hard the man could hardly stand. But no matter how hard the wind blew, the man wrapped his coat around him even tighter. Finally, the wind gave up. "He'll never take that coat off."

It was the sun's turn. The sun rose in the sky and was bright and warm. Soon the man stopped, and took his cap off.

"That doesn't count," said the wind.

"I'm not done," said the sun.

The sun continued to shine. Soon, the man wiped his face with his handkerchief. The sun shined some more, and the man unbuttoned the coat's top button. The sun continued to shine, and the man finally took off his coat, folded it, and lay down to sleep.

The sun won the bet.

Dad says the moral is you can get more done by being warm than being windy.

Princess' Second Tale

This is another story Dad tells me from A⁺ Stories. It is the story of the lazy donkey.

Once upon a time, there was a man who had a donkey. The man's job was loading up the donkey and using him to carry things from town to town.

One day, the donkey was loaded with sacks of salt. The donkey complained it was too heavy, but the man made him go.

They came to a river, and the donkey slipped in. Most of the salt melted away into the river, and when the donkey got out, his load was much lighter.

The next day, after many bags of salt were packed on his back, the donkey fell into the river on purpose to make his load lighter. The man was very angry with his lazy donkey.

The next time, when the man loaded the donkey, the load seemed much lighter. Yet anyway, when the donkey came to the river, he slipped in on purpose.

But this time he was carrying sponges. They filled with water, and his load was much heavier than ever before. The man made him carry it into the village anyway.

My Dad says the point is that cheaters will lose in the end. He also says the point is don't be a donkey. But [she giggled], he doesn't say "donkey."

Princess' Third Tale

This is a story from Gramps. He tells me grasshopper stories.

Benny was a grasshopper. There are so many grasshoppers, most have names like "21" or "aabadabac" [just saying the letters one after the other]. But by luck, Benny's name came out "Benny."

He was very proud of his name. He thought it made him important, better than other grasshoppers.

"With my name," Benny said, "I should live with people."

So, Benny followed a young boy to his home, a modest ranch house with a wooden sign on the porch showing the family name: Jets.

Benny flew right behind the kid. The boy opened the door and slammed it behind him. Benny flew into the closed door, hit it hard and fell to the ground. The boy's dad came out and stepped on Benny without even knowing.

That was the end of Benny.

I don't know the point of the story. I asked Gramps. He said, "It's not polite for stories to point." Gramps's pretty weird sometimes.

Princess told these stories herself, with background sound effects by the pudgy cousin, a whiz at orally reproducing every-day noises. [Remember, readers, to add those sounds to your performances!] For the first two, she just recited the story, just as written above.

For the last story, she started by saying, "Alexa, play!" Alexa, one of the older cousins, played some chords on her guitar, and Princess danced like a flying grasshopper while she told the story. Princess loved dancing.

Princess had gotten a lot of help with her stories from Mom and Dad, and the Rabbi. Dad suggested the A⁺ stories and told them again once or twice so she could get them straight. They all listened while she practiced each story many times. The third story she chose on her own, and honed it with the Rabbi's help.

The Rabbi was still there, although after finishing his story, he had hefted his sack and opened the front door. There was a flock of dead robins near the doorway. Mom grabbed his coat and pulled him back. She said he couldn't leave while the Evil Cloud remained. He started to say, "I got here fine … ." but Mom looked straight at him and demanded, "Promise!" He could not resist those eyes.

At first, Princess had thought the Rabbi was pretty funny: funny strange, not funny "ha-ha." She was almost afraid of him. He was *so* hairy; his crazy beard and his face: mostly hair up to his nose, with thick, red lips only sometimes peeking through, like the fat worms you uncover when you pull up a weed. He had even more hair down the side of his face.

And his pack! Sometimes it seemed to have moved from one corner of the room to another; she knew it sometimes chortled, or made sounds like a stream running over pebbles, or rippled like animals were chasing each other inside.

She only began to like him after the cloud message. The morning after the Rabbi finished the Red Sea story, she and Mom and Dad were on a balcony looking at a place where the dark cloud seemed to be thinning a bit. Then it seemed like white letters were forming in the sky.

Dad joked, "Will it say 'Surrender Dorothy?'" Princess knew that phrase was from a story called *The Wizard of Odds*. But letters actually did appear. Mom, in a wondering voice, read the words: *"HAM, WRITE YOUR MOTHER, SHE WORRIES."* The Rabbi muttered something to himself.

"Ham?" Dad said, "Is that for you, Rabbi?"

"Ach, yes, from 'Ibraham'"

What little Princess could see of the Rabbi's face blushed. Then Princess looked at his beard; it too took on some red color, becoming more a tiger than a zebra. Soon the stripes became more like big polka-dots, and the beard became a leopard; then, the spots shrank to a cheetah. It started changing again, and Princess thought that for an instant it looked like the gingham dress she was wearing, but then the spots became stripes, or streaks of black on the gray, or vice-versa, and she couldn't even see the zebra. Finally, she looked up and saw the Rabbi looking at her.

"What?" he asked, since she had been staring. She couldn't answer. "Katz got your tongue?

"I talk to you, you listen; you then talk to me. You talk to me, I listen; I talk to you. Simple, no?" the Rabbi said, and Princess nodded in agreement, although she really didn't understand. But seized by a funny thought, she asked, "Your nickname is 'Ham'?"

"Treif," he said. "Sometimes verse."

"What could be a worse name for a Jew than to be called 'Ham'?" asked Dad, but he didn't stay for the answer. Princess was left alone with the Rabbi.

"Well," she asked bravely, "what did they call you?"

"You know."

"No."

"Munchkin, what do I say if people mention 'ham'?"

"Treif," she answered.

"So you see!"

Princess felt sorry for him, seeing him as a young boy with a beard and sidelocks, wearing a big black hat, being teased by his friends' shouting, "Treif is coming, run!"

"But only when I was a kid."

Since he had confided in her, she told him, "You know what I called you, to myself? 'Rabbit Ears'" She waited for him to say "treif," but he was quiet, so she said it again, "Rabbit Ears!"

He looked at her, finally comprehended, but said instead, "Ach, no. Kosher."

"Gesundheit," she said.

"So now instead I'm 'Rabbi,'" he said, "which means 'teacher'; you, special, can also call me 'Rabbi Tayers,'" which to her delight he pronounced pretty much like "Rabbit Ears."

"So that's settled. What shall I call you?" the Rabbi asked. Princess knew he had heard Mom calling her, so he knew her actual name. Her brother called her "Sssthsss," a wet bunch of sibilant esses, probably meaning 'Sis,' but that wasn't right for the Rabbi.

"Shall I call you 'Princess'?" he suggested. She looked at him to see if he was teasing, but he was waiting for an answer.

"Yes, that's perfect!" she smiled, raising the interest of the cat for a sleepy second.

She and the Rabbi had practiced her stories all that day and the next. Princess had danced and sung for the family many times, but those were words from well-known songs. She was afraid she would be too afraid to talk in front of the crowd, and she'd forget the words for her stories. She wanted to be respected as a talented young girl, not just a cute post-toddler.

"Not to worry," the Rabbi said. "Just rub this," and he pulled a small flat rock from his sack and handed it to her. "It will give you the gift of gab. It's a Jewish talisman, a glock, a magical charm. It's a Bernie Stone."

"It will help me talk in front of people?"

The Rabbi nodded enthusiastically. "You'll talk like a narcissistic shiksa on her fourth cup of espresso," he answered, squelching a memory of a bad date.

Gramps and Nana weren't there to witness Princess' triumph. At the prior Dog Moon gathering, Gramps, after he had advocated electing the sheriff, with only the dancing uncle in his corner, had chastised the Moraga contingent as "smug, self-obsessed, over-educated aristocrats fearful of knowledge or tolerance, not worthy of the crust on the pies my daughter bakes for you." Mom and Dad felt it was better to postpone their visit to a subsequent moon. Mom was worried now, smartly not silly, about them, having had no word from them for quite a while.

The other kids were practicing their school songs. The younger crowd from the Dewy Eyes Elementary School sang: "*Dewy, Dewy, Dewy. Yes, we do, we do, we do,*" which made the Rabbi exclaim, "Treif." The older kids, the snobby cousins from Moraga, a moated palace inside a gated section of a walled city on an inaccessible island, sang to the tune of an Australian folk classic: "*Joaquin Moraga, Joaquin Moraga, you'll come a walking to Moraga with me.*"

Older teenagers and young adults were conspicuously absent from the gathering, having declared conflicting engagements when the Dog Moon get-together was discussed, but actually relishing the unchaperoned time they would have. Their currently trapped parents were conflicted: relieved that Gramps wasn't indoctrinating their kinder with radical ideas (no notice had been given of his absence) but worried, almost horrified as time passed, at what havoc was likely being wreaked at their unguarded homes.

From the general applause, Princess felt she was a great success. Mom and Dad were proud of her. The Rabbi's beard had the finger-circle "Okay" sign. Only The Grouch was unappreciative, sneering, "A$^+$ stories: soppy fables."

Princess, who enjoyed the praise without gloating, started working with the Rabbi on another story to tell. She should make one up herself, he suggested; that was the next big step. He prompted her.

"How about the Tin Man in the Dorothy story? What did he want?"

"A heart."

"Did he have one once and lose it?"

"Maybe. Maybe to a beautiful young girl," and Princess

danced and twirled to be that girl, while the young pudgy cousin, kneeling with arms outstretched, sounded out the bass line from *Heart of Gold*.

"Ah, what was the Tin Man like when he was younger?"

And so on, with many questions, which he called the "sarcastic method," the Rabbi had Princess make up small bits about the Tin Man, and concatenate them until she had a story that no one had ever told before, all of her own (although everyone knew how it ended).

The Rabbi was ever-patient when she worked with him. She loved his treatment of her as the most important person in the household, rather than the adults' usual distracted attention: talking to her for a minute, then looking for an excuse to leave.

They had lunch together; she: bacon, lettuce, tomato and cheese on white bread with mayo; he: corned beef on rye with thick horseradish mustard and a huge sour pickle. ("Can I have a bite?" asked the pudgy kid.)

"It could be verse," he sighed; indeed, his lunch was poetry.

So Many Tests Before Lance's Parents Wed

On top of the Aunts' and Uncles' worries about their children's missed schooling, their own households' safety, financial affairs and the like, the Moraga contingent felt the prolonged stay with Mom and Dad was, well, beneath them, beyond even the humiliation of having to wear the same gown twice. Moraga was top-of-the-hill in every sense, from altitude to attitude, and Mom and Dad were, well, halfway down the hill, plebeian, acceptable for an annual visit and short holiday stay, but.... Thankfully, there were few passersby who saw them there. A drunkard with a wine shop; no servants. How does that rank compared to royalty?

Mom was concerned over the Moraga relatives' high expectations for their children. She had noted to the pudgy child's mother how impressed she was by her child's oral repertoire, but Aunt B., first asking if Mom had seen Irving, dismissed the talent out-of-mouth as a ludicrous phase that B.B. was sure to soon grow out of: "a passing foley" she called it. Passing fortuitously, the pudgy cousin added a short drum roll and a high-hat and rim shot. But the different backgrounds came out in their stories.

Lance, the running boy, another Moraga scion, was thin and long-legged. He was also fidgety, unable to stay still for a moment. If required to stay in one place, his body nonetheless had to move, so he would shift from foot to foot, vibrate, wave his hands, and his face would twitch and jerk, so he looked like he was trying to swallow a live and furiously fighting goldfish.

If you sat near him at the table, you were sure to be coated with bits of his meal, flying from his fork or mouth, and occasional sprinkles of his drink, as he didn't wait to swallow before talking. He didn't think of himself as clumsy, but any object on a table or mantle near him would dive to the floor when he came close.

Lance stood up this story time, a rare pre-dinner occasion, knocking over the stool he had been sitting on while tapping his feet to music no one else heard, and announced, "It's my turn. I'm going to tell a story about how my dad married my mother." ["And they lived happily ever after," said the Whisperer, who was elbowed by Lance's mom, Lucy.]

He jumped and swayed and sprayed and made horrible faces while telling the story, but he did get it out.

So Many Tests Before Lance's Parents Wed

Once upon a time, a long, long time ago ["Lance!" objected his mom], there was a man who had a beautiful young daughter. He was a wealthy man, and noble. ["Count de Monet," was the stage whisper.] He wanted his daughter to marry the best man in the land, so he set up a contest to choose whom she would wed.

Only the sons of kings or princes or lords were allowed to apply; the Father didn't want his daughter to marry a commoner, although she would always have enough money from him. And, he wanted his son-in-law to be brave and strong and fast and smart. He was rich and a lord; he felt he could afford to be choosy.

First, he had the thirty or so suitors (as he called the young men who vied for his daughter's hand in marriage) write an essay: *Why I Want to Marry Lucinda*. Several suitors, whose swords were sharper than their minds or pens, simply gave up right then and went home, because they could hardly write, except to right a wrong, perhaps. [Lance twitched at his joke, upsetting a few tumblers halfway across the room.]

The Father didn't care much what the essay said, so long as it seemed that the suitor could write reasonably well and think a bit. He dismissed several more suitors whose essays hardly went beyond, "She's a rich [Lance paused a second] ostrich," or, "My dad told me to vie for her hand." After his winnowing, five candidates were left.

He did not consult Lucinda about having the contest, nor listen to her protestations that she wanted to marry a man she loved, not someone picked by her father; nor did he care about her stamping her little feet and calling him names. However, he did let her read the essays from all the suitors.

Several were drivel; perhaps decently written drivel, but lacking anything insightful or romantic. Dad remembers that one of the essays started: "Behind every great man is a strong woman. I plan to be a great man. I want Lucinda's strong behind. She will bore my children."

Lucinda snorted and laughed while reading most of the essays. One, however, went to her heart.

"I saw you one day, in a meadow in the woods, picking flowers for your hair, which didn't need them at all. You were far away, but I could see your radiance, and was entranced at the way you glided along the path. I wished I were a fern that could reach out and touch you. Then you walked away, and despite my vow to myself that I would someday find and marry you, my day turned from sunshine to bleak despair." [Mutters of "lovely" mixed with a "treif" or two.] Lucinda's heart tilted towards this lad, though she didn't know which one he was.

The remaining suitors, to stay in the competition, next had to kill a dragon. Five went out; four came back after a few days, bragging about from two to five dragon slayings. A pious churchgoing lad dropped out of the contest.

All four bore marks of a fierce fight: burns on their clothing, ash on their foreheads, blood on their swords, but luckily none was badly hurt. [Lance was here overcome by a series of brutal twists and jerks, thrusting his arms out and screaming, which Princess realized was his acting out a man fighting a dragon, although it wasn't clear which role he was playing.]

Lucinda's father said she could meet her potential husbands after the next contest. To pass that and gain a short audience with her, the suitor had to move a 500-pound rock, the old foundation stone for a demolished castle, at least two feet.

The first to try, a husky, burly lad of twenty-two who, rather than shaking the hand of the other competitors when introduced, had lifted each high into the air by his neck and thrown him 10 feet, said, "Child's play."

But, alas for the lad, not his game. Try as he might, he couldn't get a good grip on the stone, and once he did, standing on the stone, he couldn't lift it. So, off he went, cold-cocking horses in anger as he left.

"Phew," said Lucinda, "that was a close call. I'm glad I don't have to marry him." She couldn't believe he was very romantic, and wasn't attracted to him despite his brawn.

The second suitor, knowing that if the burly kid couldn't lift the stone, he had no chance, got a sledge hammer. He was going to break the stone into pieces. After ten, twenty blows, the stone didn't crack, although the ringing in the ears of all the onlookers didn't go away for days, well after that suitor had.

Lucinda and her father, as well as most of the villagers who were watching, pretty much counted out the next young man. He was of average height and not muscular, almost slight in build. There was a quiet air about him [here, Lance tried to stay as still as possible to illustrate, but of course his feet kept tapping and his hands flapping], and he often brushed his long dark hair out of his face. He wasn't handsome, though he was far from ugly.

He called for a long sturdy post, a bushel of carrots, and

a thick log. The villagers, intrigued, brought him a few posts, from which the youth selected the longest one without any knots, and they also brought a stupid dog, because they misunderstood him with the sledge hammer's ringing still sharp in their ears. Soon, however, they brought an unsplit log about a foot across and two feet long. A few villagers had bunches of carrots; sensing his need, they drove a hard bargain.

Finally, the kid was ready. He dug a small hole under one edge of the stone, just big enough to allow the long post to fit under the stone for a half foot; the other end would stick up high into the air. He put the post across the big log, which he pushed near the stone. Then he reached up and grabbed the post and hung from it. The stone lifted up a few inches where the post was under it.

He told one of the villagers to stick a few carrots there, all aligned with the post. Then he dug another hole about 6 inches further along the stone on the same side, and had more carrots placed there. He did this all along one side of the stone, and then repeated the same routine on the opposite side.

Finally, he dug a deeper and longer hole under one of the untouched sides, moved the post and log over to that side, and again put the post in the hole and over the log. When he hung from the post, the stone slid forward about 9 inches; the carrots acting as rollers.

Two more times digging holes and hanging from the post, with the villagers enthusiastically helping (charging double for the second bundle of carrots), and the boy took a bow. The Father conceded he'd passed the test.

The final contestant started to dig another hole, but the Father said he couldn't use the same trick. He got twelve men of the village to move the stone back to its original place. As a special gift, he let them keep the muddy crushed carrots.

This last guy was stupefied. Although he was tall and long-legged, with a muscular torso and thighs, he knew he could not lift the stone. The quiet young man came over and whispered to him.

"You think that'll work?" was heard.

At "not much to lose in trying," the remaining untested suitor fetched the sledge hammer, picked up a few of the thinner posts that the carrot-kid had rejected, and whittled sharp ends to them. Then he sat down with his feet on the stone. He inched forward until his legs were bent, with his knees up, and the heels and soles of his feet were flat on the edge of the stone. He reached around and drew a line right behind him in the dirt.

He picked two of the sharpened posts and, using the sledge hammer, drove them into the earth close to each other on the line he'd drawn until they didn't move when he leaned on them. Then he sat down in the position he had been in before.

With his back pressed firmly against the anchored posts, he used his strong leg muscles and pushed with all his might, grunting and sweating until his knees were almost straight. He managed to inch the stone forward almost a foot. He scurried closer to the stone, bending his knees again, and marked his line again. Only 10 minutes later, he also was declared a winner.

Lucinda met first with the lanky man. He bragged about his dragon killing and his stone moving. He'd gone to school and was fully literate, but he didn't like to read books. He never stopped talking to listen to her. But he did promise her a beautiful mansion with servants and a deep vegetable garden; she was uncommonly fond of turnips and other root veggies.

The other boy was quieter, almost shy. To get him talking, Lucinda asked about his dragon feats, believing all young men liked to talk endlessly about that. Instead, he asked her, "Have you ever seen a dragon?"

"Well, no. I live a sheltered life."

"Okay. Ever see a dragon skin?"

"They say dragons explode into flame and then turn to vapors when killed."

"Quite convenient, wouldn't you say? You don't see them. There's no proof anyone actually killed them. All you get are rumors of a dragon attacking a far-away village, and alarm-raising men wanting to be paid to keep you safe from them."

"What are you saying?" she asked, wide-eyed.

"Honey," he hazarded, but she didn't object, "there are no dragons."

"What? But you claimed to have killed two!"

"And the others claimed even more. We lied. Men are pigs."

"But the burns? The cuts?"

"We couldn't come back from a mortal fight with a fire-breathing dragon looking like we're dressed for a prom, could we? We faked it."

"Oh. What about the dragon feet they sell at the fair?"

"Not real. Probably dried bear claws." ["I love bear claws," the pudgy kid said, and there was a general murmur of agreement.]

"Dragon teeth? I have a dragon tooth necklace."

"Fake! No such thing. Stop draggin' this out," he said to her. At that joke, Lucinda fell for him, heavy, but he caught her and kissed her.

"What about dragonflies?"

"They don't but they do," he said.

"Dragon fruit?" and they started laughing.

"Snap dragons? Dragon roll? Dragon and phoenix?"

"Now I'm hungry."

And she went to dinner, together with both remaining suitors, the Father, and about 20 court retainers and other guests. The carrot kid sat at the far end of the table. Lucinda saw him wink and heard him say as she ate, "You are far away, but I can see your radishes."

The final test, the Father announced at dessert, was to be a long foot race. The tall suitor was confident he had this contest in the bag. Soon, dear Lucinda would be his. In fact, the Father, thinking the shorter quiet boy lacked manly attributes, purposefully chose that task, its outcome inevitable. Lucinda would marry the lanky one, who was also of higher noble rank.

The quiet kid was also confident: positive he would lose. There's no way to fake being fast, he knew. "I'll give it a try," he thought despondently. "Maybe that tall guy has some undiagnosed heart condition." But his bags were packed to leave before the race started.

The race course was three miles around the sides of the valley, ending in the village. The runners could be seen for the first and last quarter miles, but tall trees blocked the view of the rest. The Father posted some marshals here and there to guide the suitors through the course.

The signal was given, and the race was on. The tall man quickly went out front and kept running, loping easily. The carrot kid followed, but was laboring before he was fully out of sight.

Nearing the end of the race, lanky looked behind and saw no one following. He slowed down and crossed the finish line. The villagers were cheering. His arms were filled with a beautiful young woman, his bride-to-be.

He and Lucy, my mom, were married later that week, and in due time I was born ["Seven months later," was the whisper]. That's the story my dad tells of how he wed my mother.

"Wow. How romantic. So your mom was Lucinda?"

"No," answered Lance, shaking his head violently. "My mom is 'Lucy.' Lucinda cheated. She went about a mile onto the course and hid in the forest.

"When carrot kid came by, she shouted, 'Shorty, shorty, cut across,' and took him on a path she knew to the other side of the valley. He crossed the finish line three minutes before my dad. She had bribed the marshals with a promise of free beer for the village for the entire weekend. That's why they were all cheering."

And the running boy ran out of the room, down a hallway, and through the entire house before coming back and sitting down.

Lance's mom smiled. "Men are pigs," she said fondly.

"Dinner," Mom announced. The smell of roasted loin chops, carrots, turnips and radishes filled the room as the kitchen door opened, with a plate for the Rabbi piled high with falafel, and a mid-table appetizer of sushi also visible.

Heavy Metal
Love Story

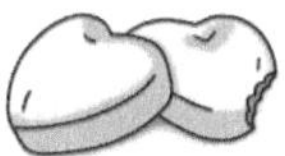

As Princess passed through the house helping Mom out, some-times taking towels or clean sheets to rooms, she would hear bits and pieces of conversation.

"So, that carrot kid helped you beat the stone test?" the Rabbi asked Lance's father.

"Yes, he gave me the idea. He seemed happy to help me," Lance's father answered.

"Hmm, a boychik mensch, no?"

"Oh, he said he hadn't met Lucinda. If I didn't move the stone, he'd be the only suitor. For all he knew, she was a skank, or a twit, or a bore."

A bit later, she heard some adults talking about the Rabbi. "He's a hairytic," said one. Princess didn't know the word. It seemed unkind, but rather accurate.

"We're all of the same faith, aren't we?" one asked.

"I'm an Antipastist!"

"Universalist Utilitarian, here."

"High Rastafarian Catholic."

"Pots and Pantheist," said the pudgy cousin's father.

"Wicca."

"You know that Hindu who passed through? He's my guru."

"Third and Sixth Day Adventurist."

"Church of Mammon and the New Orleans Saints."

"Epistlepainian."

"Budist," said a stoner.

They huddled together to see if there was anything spiritual they could agree upon. There was: the Rabbi should go; he was a hairytic.

Princess warned Mom there was something afoot against the Rabbi.

A delegation of relatives soon came to her. They explained their case: the Rabbi was a bad influence on the kids; he gave them gifts of toys to play with; his pack was strange; they owed him money; he was a hairytic; what about that message in the clouds?

Mom listened carefully, and seemingly agreed. Princess was crushed!

Then Mom turned to them and said, "It's too bad. The Rabbi was basically taking care of my daughter. When he goes, I'll not have time to bake the bread or cakes, or prepare the breakfasts, lunches or dinners or after-story snacks. Which of you wives or hubbies want to take over planning and cooking the meals?"

There was a hushed silence as the inquisition consulted its collective stomach. They put their heads together. Gastronomy decapitated orthodoxy.

"Well," the synod decided, "we can be tolerant, ecumealable."

"But he better not try anything," said an older uncle, who had a reputation as a perv.

Princess had for weeks practiced her next story, the story she had made up. The Bernie Stone was perhaps a bit thinner, but with the Rabbi's calm encouragement, Princess felt she could perform and, she hoped, dazzle.

When she started at story time, the Rabbi sat still, smiling, nodding his head, now and then mouthing a word like a stage prompter, but usually Princess couldn't make it out through his moustache. His beard was more articulate; if she got stuck, it formed a picture of where the story went next. The pudgy cousin also helped with squeaks, oilcan bubbling, soft breezes, sounds of a ballet, a steady "tick tock," and the like.

"This story is one I made up from *The Wizard of Odds*." [Lance jumped up, shouting, "He got that name when his hot air balloon crashed down on the Emerald City Casino, breaking the bank!" "That's the kid's version," tinkled the Whisperer, "actually he micturated on the casino: *The Whizzer of Odds.*"]

Heavy Metal Love Story

One night, when Dorothy, the girl from Kansas, a post-ata-co-lipstick this-toppia [Princess knew she didn't get that quite right, even after practicing it the way the Rabbi broke it down; he said it wouldn't matter; no one would realize her mistake; nobody would even understand it if she did get it right.], was sleeping (they were camping next to the Yellow Brick Road) [a sinuous gold river ran through the Rabbi's beard], the Scarecrow turned to the Tin Man.

"Tell us the rest of the story," he said. "I'm a dummy, but you're too smart to have been out in the rain without your oilcan at the ready. What really happened?"

So, the Tin Man told the true story. [Princess became the Tin Man.]

I was young once, just a tin can, so to speak. I came from a good family, well read, close relatives to a linotype machine. In fact, I was named after a debonair detective in my father's favorite novel series. Dad also probably read to me everything written by Hergé, a series I loved.

"I thought...," the Scarecrow started, but the Tin Man continued.

No, my family name is "Puter." we lived in the land of the Good Witch of the South, in Tinnessee.

I had a heart then, a very special heart. Like those in the towers of village squares, it had four separate clockworks; inside my body [Princess punched her chest, as the Tin Man], they didn't need faces. It was loud inside, a regular tintinabulation. But with such a heart, I could love.

And love I did with my big and multichambered heart.

My first crush, still as a child, hardly yet knowing my metal, was on a bronze-colored Matchbox '67 Chevy Camaro; what sleek lines and beautiful chrome!

I carried her with me wherever I went. But I loved too strongly; my crush was too heavy. [Here, the Princess as Tin Man pantomimed squishing the little toy car, looking surprised, and pulling her hands apart and letting it fall, broken. Then she danced a bit because she had gotten through the first part of the story.]

My next love, when I was older and going to middle school, was a Tonka Truck, the type with a spring drive, so if I pulled it back along the ground, it would race forward. I couldn't wait for classes to end each day so I could go home and spend quiet hours with her. ["He's loved the axle powered and the alloys," the Rabbi mused.]

Of course, she did not return my love or whisper sweet nothings to me as I did to her. It took me several years to tire of her, and even afterwards, with her in my mind, I often would pick up trucks.

With all that ticking and tocking inside me (the clocks were not quite in sync), I wanted to be a musician, but my hands weren't supple enough ["And he had a tin ear," said the Whisperer]. Being a doctor or lawyer was closed to tin men, even those from the best families.

I was strong, however, so I became a woodcutter. I was the best woodcutter for miles around. I could cut a tree in a few strokes that would take a man an hour or so. I made good money; I built a house and put on a metal roof. I joked it was my parents.

But I was lonely. I had only a few good friends: a schizophrenic named Clark Kent, whom I liked because he was a man of steel. And Mercury; he was a slippery guy, with moods hot and cold, rising and falling. But until I was a fully grown man, I never had a flesh and blood love.

One day, a young woman came running wildly through

the forest, screaming, pursued closely by a huge wolf dressed in an old lady's nightdress. I stood still, and just before the wolf caught up with the girl, I chopped off its head.

For me, it was love at first smite. The girl was beautiful, enchanting, and moved like water. All my clockhearts tolled the hour when she looked at me. With a sweet voice, she said, "Oh, thank you, thank you! He was going to eat me."

"Was she Little Red Riding Hood?" asked the Scarecrow.

"Oh, I don't know," the Tin Man answered, "she had lost any cap running through the woods."

It was true. I was transfixed by her hair, which fell in waves down past her shoulders. She was a platinum blonde.

"Be still, my silly corazón," I said to myself, but it beat louder than a telltale heart.

For months, we had a great relationship. She would lay next to me with her head on my chest, and we would enjoy the sun, or the rain; it mattered little to us. But she was human and graceful, and I metal with only stiff joints; it was a tinker's chance it would last.

I do believe she loved me for a while. She was a dancer, and she would perform for me in the woods, with leaves and even sunlight twirling above her head as she flew and leaped and pirouetted. Her copper bracelets (which gave me a rash) would flash, and even the squirrels and orioles would watch, jealous of her grace.

Soon, I sensed a change. She grew demanding.

"You've put so many human woodcutters out of business. One of them needs a new heart. Can you spare one?"

That seemed fair to me. And for her, I'd do anything. So, I let her take one of the clockworks out.

"It's quieter now; that's better," she said.

It wasn't but a month or two later when another woodcutter, she said, had eaten a bad mushroom and had digestive heart failure. I let her take another clock, joking that our song lyric was, "*Take Another Piece of my Heart.*"

"No, that's your song," she said, but she didn't tell me hers.

It was only a week or so later that she came to me, very excited, more lovely than ever in her flush, radiating cheer.

"I have such great news!" she exclaimed happily. "The world-famous Moscow ballet is in town. I auditioned for them, and they want me to join in their performance tonight! Please come to watch me."

Of course, I said, "Okay." I wanted to see her dance in costume, in a fancy setting, more than anything. And I did like listening to orchestras, especially the brass sections.

"But," she said, "you're too loud now. And the oboe player just played his heart out; he needs yours. It's perfect. You'll save his life and be fit to sit in the audience."

So, she took a third set of clockwork, leaving me with just one left as a heart. In exchange, she gave me an orange. I suspected something was horribly wrong; her words lacked any tenderness.

"Let me lie next to you," she said softly, half of my heart wrapped in her scarf, the rest of my heart in her eyes.

"You mean 'lay'?" I said jokingly, but she made no reply.

The performance was brilliant. It was *The Nutcracker*. [Here, Princess danced for about 10 minutes while her own audience refreshed their drinks. The Rabbi's beard showed a conductor with his baton raised.]

I was spellbound by it all. My love's role was as a sugar plum fairy. The *Dance of the Tin Soldiers* thrilled me. The audience, on its feet, demanded four curtain calls.

Afterwards, I elbowed my way into her dressing room (my axe was left at home), where she was surrounded by admirers. She looked at me, maybe snickered to a few of the men near her, and announced, "They've asked me to join!" ["She a Bolshoi chick; he a Menschchik; they have dielectrical issues. This can't end well," the Rabbi quipped silently.]

I was ecstatic, but also dumbstruck. It was her dream come true. It was my nightmare become real. She would be leaving!

I saw her only once more. It did not go well. It was a damp day; I had my oilcan nearby and used it freely.

"I've come to say goodbye. And ask one more favor."

"What? You know I love you. I'll do whatever you ask." I wept; my heart, what little was left of it, was breaking.

"The orchestra's conductor is ill. I need your heart to save him. He sponsored me. He's vital to my ballerina career."

I started crying freely, not only from my eyes, but from every juncture in my body. I could feel the joints start to tighten with rust.

"I guess *piece of my heart* really was the lyric that defined our relationship," I sobbed as she reached inside [Princess demonstrated that there was a small door in his chest right where his heart was].

"No," she said. "A tin man doesn't need a heart. Our relationship's real refrain is, '*What's love got to do with it?*'"

I cried even harder, at losing her, at the loss of my dreams, at her cruelty (and at the irony: Tina, who popularized the song, was one of the few of our kind to succeed in show biz).

Rust was overtaking me as she turned away to leave. I begged her, "If you ever loved me, even a bit, oil my joints and leave the can near me. I'm crying so hard."

She just snickered, moved the oilcan even further away, and skipped down the forest path without looking back, my heart in her hands.

But I heard her sing, with a snort, as she departed:

Love!
What's lube got to do with it?

Telling the story to the Scarecrow, the Tin Man now had tears running down his face. The Tin Man carefully oiled himself and then blew his nose loud and long, sending the Cowardly Lion scampering away, shouting, "Elephants! Elephants!"

"I've never trusted any humans after that," he said.

The Scarecrow looked at him sharply and asked, "What about Dorothy?"

"Dorothy? She's a human? She said she was from a can's ...."

Dorothy, hearing her name, woke up right then, silencing the Tin Man.

And that's how the Tin Man lost his heart.

Princess did an arabesque, a pirouette, waved a thank-you to B.B., and bowed. Lance promptly tripped over her.

The Rabbi's beard had a faint silhouette of a heart.

Mom served a post-story pick-me-up of anticuchos and deviled duck hearts, but only a few of the more venturous relatives partook. A plate of heart-shaped chocolates in tin foil, however, disappeared faster than The Tin Man's belle walking away in the forest.

The Long-Haired Princess

The household had settled into a routine as the days of the Evil Cloud stretched on. The high points of the day were the meals, and story time, usually promptly afterwards.

During the day, the children found ways to occupy themselves, mainly playing games like hide-and-go-seek, tease the younger kids, chase each other around the entire house until you collapse into giggles, and at the adults' stern direction, drawing and painting. One of the Moraga kids had invented a sort of jig-saw puzzle: he would search the wastebaskets for torn up letters written by the teenagers (and adults attempting adultery) to their sweethearts, and then diligently and laboriously piece the letter back together. If it set an assignation, he and a few friends would hide beforehand, make funny noises and recite parts of the letter, until the parties threatened them with fantastic miseries and deaths. A reconstructed letter's displays of emotions were repeated to the author in mocking voices.

No one yet knew what had caused the Evil Cloud, or how it could be dispelled. There was speculation: someone had insulted a vengeful wizard; an experiment at Hogwarts College of Alchemy had gone disastrously astray; it was retribution for mankind's evil ways, etc. But the murder of crows made it clear that there was still something deadly around.

Also, the cloud was now announcing in huge white letters, preceded by thunder and ended by lightning: *Stay at home.*

Don't go out. Shelter In Place," with a random commercial, like "*Parchessi's Pizza: We Deliver.*"

"Deliver?" Dad commented. "Who would deliver anything now?"

"Ach, the Evil Cloud started in my shtetl," the Rabbi explained. "A few people seemed unaffected, or had seizures and wheezes and then got over. They would take messages and goods from here to there in their tumbrels. ["A shtetl service," murmured the Whisperer, transported by her wit.] We call them 'uber drivers.'" Dad, then pulled away by Mom to help in the kitchen, made a mental note to follow up with the Rabbi on how the Evil Cloud came into being.

The adults, most of whom had expected to be at the residence only for an overnight, for the annual holiday celebration of the Dog Moon, were probably more bored and put off their routines than the children, who, lacking expectations, took the unexpected in stride.

Mom and Dad were always busy; beyond taking care of the toddler, who, for all they knew, might be fully grown before he ever went to school, they were doing virtually all the domestic chores like cooking, cleaning, laundry, gardening, checking the traps for rabbits, feeding the pigs and chickens and goats and sheep and horses and donkeys. There was a multitudinous range of tasks needing to be done.

The guests, Dad snorted, did their best not to get in the way. Even mild-tempered Mom suggested that the cat, acting as a live clock by his regular changes of napping spots, was infinitely more helpful than the relatives.

An exception to the general uselessness of the guests was the Rabbi. If Mom noted that the dining hall or another room needed scrubbing and dusting, the Rabbi would say "treif," haul his pack into the chamber, lock the doors, and several hours later the room would be sparkling clean.

There were a few other bright spots. Alexa gave music lessons, both singing and guitar, for the several kids who asked.

Uncle Irv, the reputed perv, offered to teach classes, but there were no takers. A red-haired boy's father announced he would teach wrestling to anyone interested. The Rabbi was willing to teach anything from basic reading to trigonometry and bioethics, but except for Mom and Dad, the other parents forbade their children to associate with him. A few of the adults and older children did attempt to provide some ongoing education, but proved to know little and lack the patience to teach; they ended up just reading aloud to inattentive students.

Nerves were frayed and tempers short, and quarrels and cuss words frequent, not always apologized for. "Cabin fever." Propinquity breeds contempt. Mom's luscious meals were all that kept the pack from turning savage. That and story time with its chance for glory.

The desire to show off at story time, both for young and old, was what kept the tinderbox from igniting. Many hours were spent thinking up and practicing stories, with soliloquies infiltrating the home and bouncing off walls and ceilings. There was a spirited competition for who would perform, which was settled by a nod from Dad. The stories, or at least the memorable ones, were getting longer, more complex, and somewhat stranger as time went on.

Alexa was less snobby than most of the Moraga crowd; beyond her musical mentoring, she would deign to talk with and even pat the heads of the younger, less privileged kids. Noblesse oblige.

She finally got the nod. She moved a straight-back chair to the front of the great hall, the story room, turned it to face the audience, and told her story while sitting primly, keeping her hands in her lap except for occasional emphasis. Pudgy kept the sound effects muted to maintain the mood.

The Long-Haired Princess

Once upon a time, in a kingdom not far from here, but which can't be reached anymore, there lived a princess.

Kingdoms then were small, so a princess, although rare, was still but one of a dozen or so throughout the land. There were probably a few other princesses within a day's hard ride.

And not all princesses were of the same noble status. Some families would trace their lineage back so far that their castle's hallways had portraits of bronze-age ancestors, and even missing links or one-celled amoeba, bearing the family coat of arms. ["Amoebas got no arms," limbed the Whisperer.] Others were of more recent vintage: nouvelle noble, so to speak. This princess was of the latter type and had a wet mark against her as well.

Yes, it was never forgotten when a family traced its heritage back to a prince (even if later a formidable king) who had been a frog. Even though these situations usually arose from black magic, with no fault or responsibility of the family, aspersions and a stigma followed the family forever. In Rapunzel's ohana, it was a grandfather who had been raised from the amphibian.

Worse, rather than just being cursed and having the spell broken by a kiss within a few years, in Rapunzel's ancestry there had been dozens of generations of frogs and tadpoles who labored under the hex, croaking to passing princesses. Eventually, an undiscriminating princess kissed Grandpa Kermit (honestly, not her first frog), and Princess Leia soon became a queen, warts and all.

You can well imagine that with this background, the family was somewhat protective of its princess. Grandpa and grandma had died some time ago, and King Crab and Queen Sighs had only Rapunzel. So, they catered to her every wish and whim; she had her own cat, Henry, exempt from mousing duties.

Rapunzel's room was a fourth-floor cold-water walk-up, although with an open window looking out from the turret's wall.

Her pampering did not extend to matrimony. As was the

custom, she was betrothed as a young girl through a matchmaker to a prince who was not then even an adolescent, in a kingdom which they knew only by the intermediary's recommendation.

That wedding was still in some hazy future. In the present, Rapunzel was a stunning girl of about sixteen, whose fantasies were all about handsome knights who would wander by and fall in love with her.

But generally, visitors and passers-by were less romantic. There were peddlers of gewgaws and knickknacks. Rapunzel would choose a few items, like ribbons for her hair, and tell William, her devoted doorkeeper, to pay.

One day, an old hag, looking like Ms. Dorian Gray's portrait in a hospice, came by selling spinning wheel spindles and apples. Rapunzel met with her, wondering which of the warts on her nose it was polite to look at, and refused to buy her wares, exclaiming that she was aware of the evil tales about this witch and her apples and spindles which caused princesses to fall asleep for years or generations.

"Ah, but you have heard of me," the hag replied vainly.

"Show her out, William, porter. Oh, Henry," she said to her cat, "I do wish something fun would happen."

Perhaps the witch had cast a spell, because something did. As Rapunzel was humming to herself, brushing her hair—she was rightfully proud of her long brown hair, so long she had to twist it into braids, and braids into coils ["She had coily hair?" quipped the Whisperer], so it didn't drag on the floor—a young knight came riding by.

"Hallooo," she called, and he looked up. Perhaps it was the spell, or just her gorgeous face; either way, he was bewitched.

"Hallooo, yourself," he responded smartly. "What's your name, young maiden?"

"No, it's 'Rapunzel.'"

"Well, Rapunzel, please come down so we can take a walk."

"Oh, my father would never permit that," she said.

"I'll come in!"

"Oh, no, William won't allow that."

After a bit more banter like that, and several failures of the knight's trying to throw up a grappling hook, they decided that Rapunzel would let out her hair. The knight took off all extraneous armor and, clad only in breeches and jerkin ["I thought that was a pickle," said the pudgy cousin], he stood on his horse's back, jumped up and grabbed a braid, and clambered up the wall, through the window and into her room.

He was tall and handsome, a deep drought of wine. Rapunzel, though, could hardly see him through her tears; it really hurt when he climbed using her hair, and she had a small bald spot. He tried to make amends.

"I'll treasure that lock always, my lady."

Rapunzel smiled at him, fluttering wet lashes. He was bleeding but paid it no mind. He wore a long sword, curved in an unusual shape. It hung from his waist, open, with only a length of leather against his breeches to protect him. In his climb, it had hit the tower's stones and several times knicked him (only commoners get "nicked") beyond the leather's reach.

They discovered they got along splendidly. She could see only his rugged good looks, and ignored his gawkiness. He was enamored of her hair, her pearly teeth, incendiary smile, and maidenly poise, and overlooked her habit of snatching flies in mid-air with a long tongue. Henry seemed to like him, which clinched the matter for Rapunzel.

He introduced himself as Reginald, pre-Count de Foissey. His father was a king. By right of primogeniture, his older brother, now the Count, would eventually become King, and then he would become the Count, shedding the "pre." Eldest sons inherited the throne and the kingdom, he explained. A younger son had a choice of becoming a knight or entering the priesthood.

Hearing sounds of someone approaching the chamber,

Reginald had to leave, and Rapunzel saw him ride off through her haze of tears as she cleaned up the drops of blood in her room.

Almost every day, Reginald would come by and shout, "Rapunzel, let down your long hair." Rapunzel soon learned that she could wrap her hair around a huge iron nail so that would bear the weight rather than her head. Rapunzel would tell him when she might be out walking, but Reginald could never see her then, because King Crab's men always chaperoned and shot their arrows before asking questions if strange men came near the princess.

So, they met only in secret in her room. She told him about her family's history, from when granddad was a tadpole. He told her how he came by his unusual sword, by conquering an infamous knight who had been unfaithful to his vow to a queen, and how the scabbard had been stolen; there was no one with the craft to make him another.

They both hinted, but did not discuss, that their parents were in charge of their marriages; they could only dream of a day when they would marry each other. Reginald found true the scuttlebutt that not even a Japanese geisha could kiss like a frog princess.

"Rapunzel, let down your long hair," he would shout.

"Hey, Doofus, come on up," she would reply gaily.

Now you might think that "Doofus" is a rude knickname (!) to call a knight, your hero, but Rapunzel would insist that it was short for "de Foissey" and not a comment on his tripping many times over Henry, her hair, and dust motes, endangering his and her legs from his sword.

It was that name she called him, angrily, after about the tenth time he had forgotten to bring a rope, and they were almost discovered; in his haste while defenestrating, he swung out from the wall, pulled her hair off the nail, and caused her to yelp in agony.

"Doofus," she shouted, as she threw both of her ivory-backed, jewel-inlaid, boar-bristled hair brushes after him, hitting him with the first, and hitting his horse with the other, causing a sudden gallop which dislodged "Doofus, ha!" on his way.

But he had been seen. The King was in a crabby mood.

"You may see him one time more, for ten minutes, to say goodbye," he declared. "I'm contacting Yentl to set the wedding date for one month from today. We'll soon join two kingdoms, and you'll meet the man you'll learn to love." The Queen sighed; at least her mother-in-law had chosen her husband from among thousands of toads. The King's messengers informed Reginald of his final meeting with Rapunzel.

Reginald scoured the local markets for a parting gift. Finally, he found the perfect one: both of the princess' hair brushes had been promptly stolen, and in a shady-looking and ill-smelling booth in the market of a town two rivers over, he found them. The merchant—so ugly he couldn't tell if a man or a woman, but with two large nose warts—wanted a king's ransom. Reginald had been away so long, dallying with Rapunzel, that he had little gold left. After bartering (he refused to sell his soul), they agreed he could have the brushes for his sword. He sat for an hour pondering, since his sword was his most valuable and esteemed possession, but love won out and he accepted the deal.

Rapunzel, on her end, was no less frantic about finding a gift that Doofus would always treasure, and would forever remind him of her. Upon a sudden inspiration, she sketched in full size his sword, from her memories of when it pressed against her in their parting embraces ["Or are you happy to see me?" teased the Whisperer] and sent out the King's messengers high and low to seek a scabbard. Those high were useless. Those low soon found a disreputable dealer in second-hand scabbards in a bizarre bazaar, who, peering at them above two large warts, demanded one pound.

"One pound? We'd have offered 1,000," laughed one royal gofer, not a smart shopper.

"One pound of princess hair!" demanded the hag.

Well, a pound of hair is a lot of hair. When the messengers returned with the news, they found that taking a pound would leave only a few inches on Rapunzel's head, just long enough for a bob, but not even sufficient for a Shetland ponytail.

Rapunzel, too, pondered whether to make the bargain, but finally said "Yes," both because it was the only perfect gift and also to spite her father and her unknown betrothed. William did the snip, snip, and soon a shorn princess awaited Reginald.

It was their first encounter outside her room. The King allowed the meeting to be in the royal garden; it was in the midst of lilies, irises, roses, birds-of-paradise and sweet-smelling lilacs, as well as a handful of watchful chaperones, that they met. They were prohibited from kissing, or embracing, or even touching: six feet apart at all times. They could only talk, but even that was stunted because, looking at each other, they were mutually dumbstruck.

"I brought you these hairbrushes," Reginald said lamely, looking at Rapunzel, virtually scalped.

"Doofus, you shouldn't have," she replied, accurately. "But I'll cherish the thought, and 'cherish' is a word I seldom use.

"And, for you, Doofus, I have this unique scabbard, which will fit perfectly," Rapunzel paused, "the sword you no longer have."

"Time's up!" shouted the King. He bundled Reginald off, giving him, as a pre-Count, an invitation to the wedding. He made sure that Reginald kept riding away until he crossed the far river.

Rapunzel, as could be expected from a proper princess, cried each day, morn 'til knight (!) until her wedding. She walked down the aisle without seeing or caring, and was uninterested as the groom came tripping to his spot. She was veiled and did not even see her fiancé, by then her husband, until after she said, "Well, I guess," and the minister said, "I pronounce you man and wife," as was customary then before women's lib.

"You may kiss the bride," said the minister. Rapunzel thought, "Like that's going to happen," and lifted her veil, keeping her mouth chastely closed.

But then it dropped open. Looking at her expectantly was her husband: Doofus! After a long kiss, which caused a chorus of "Get a room!" Count de Foissey, scabbard empty, explained.

"When I got home, my father was beside himself. I asked them both what was wrong. I learned that my elder brother had just died from an infected wound he got in sword practice with Kovid, his squire. An imminent wedding had been arranged for the Count de Foissey, and we didn't feel I could break the deal. I was halfway here before I realized you would be my bride."

They lived happily ever after and had thousands of children, six of whom were human.

Alexa pointed a finger at Lance, saying, "Don't move" while she placed her chair back in its place, with all waiting to see if anyone else had a story that knight.

Instead, Mom called from the dining room, "Come and get it," setting out plates of frog cake, a snack companion to dinner's earlier Toad in the Hole.

The Village Idiot

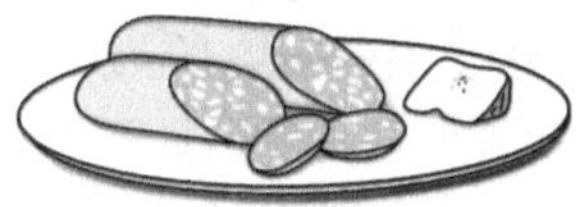

It had been a tense day. People were running cabin fevers of 103° Gesundheit, or among the Moraga snobs, 39.5° Centipede.

The older boys were reveling in a particularly vicious game called "Who can hit the softest?" An unsuspecting young one would be picked out and told that he could compete in a game in which being bigger and older was no advantage. They would play for some strawberries, or maybe a Rubik's Cube, which the Rabbi had given them to the bewilderment of all. The game's rule was simple: the winner was the one who "hit" the other the lightest. No hint was given as to how or by whom this would be determined in close cases, but that omission was too subtle for the young kid who jumped at the apparently even chance to win a game against the teenager.

"You go first!" the older boy invariably said, and turned his body sideways to take the hit on his shoulder. The younger kid would spread his or her fingers out, so only one would touch, and approach the shoulder slowly, imparting the barest possible touch, so slight that it would not have disturbed a whisper, or troubled a sunbeam, aroused a suspicion, or caused a thunderstorm across the globe. "I did it!" the youngster would say, in case the competitor hadn't felt the hit. He would then turn to present his own shoulder for the other's attempt.

Wham, Bam! He would receive a blow that would send him reeling across the room. "Whoops, I lose," the older kid would say, tossing him the prize and laughing nastily. The victim would generally keep quiet, or tell only a very close friend, either out of shame or a mean desire to see others suffer the same fate.

A less violent tactic was ruining Dad's new invention. Inspired by the kid's diligent attention for hours in piecing together discarded letters (now carefully burned instead), Dad took some carpets and paintings, attached them to a thin backing, and cut each into hundreds of differently shaped pieces. Both adults and youngsters liked putting the puzzle together from memory of the original pattern. The Moraga kids, though, quickly discovered that switching only a few pieces from one puzzle to another would stymie the players and eventually send them into explosive tantrums.

The adults quarreled over trivial issues. One Aunt berated The Grouch for his story's ending, yelling at him (virtually the entire house heard), "I better find out what those hatching golf balls turned into. And soon!" The Grouch replied, "And if you were my wife, I'd drink it." That made no sense, except that Dad, sipping tea, snorted it up through his nose and then washed his cup for twenty seconds.

The nod that night, from among five who had raised their hands, went to Brian, a teenager of about fourteen who wanted to impress Alexa. He glanced in her direction, saw her smile, and gained his courage. He had begun to stand when a hand on his shoulder pushed him down. The Grouch released him, moved to the front and began talking.

"I play golf." He glared at the woman who had accosted him earlier, then continued, "but I'm not going to tell that story.

"This is a story we studied in Fable Analysis 101, which is a course in universities in which myths are studied in a scientific fashion. The myths are broken down into small bits, which are given numerical values, which are then reassembled and added; the resulting numbers are put into denotimators and connotimators, which are then divided by the sum of the precepts, to prove elegant theorems of necromancy. ["Like the Hasids," thought the Rabbi.]

"The myths are also categorized as to the length of sentences and evaluated by the number of umlauts and diphthongs.

["I'd like to see the Whisperer in a diphthong," said Uncle Irv, a proven perv.] Attention is given to every part of the myth, except the story, the characters, and the moral.

"This fable was a favorite of my professor, who was so scientific that his will specified that he be buried with a thermometer and a sheaf of graph paper so he could record his temperature hourly in the thereafter."

The Village Idiot

The village blacksmith was named "Brick," and it fit him well. He was large, powerful, and stronger than a grizzly bear. In his hands, the blacksmith's hammer seemed like a feather; while most men could barely lift it, he would bet he could hold it with his arms outstretched as long as his adversary could hold his breath, and he didn't even care if the man cheated; he still won. But this story isn't about him.

He feared no man. He feared his wife, however. "Prissy," short for "Priscilla," was anything but. After Brick shod a horse, she would often carry the horse, who didn't want to scuff the new shoes, into the nearby pasture. When she was angry, Brick didn't duck thrown dishes or pots or pans; he had to avoid a flying anvil. But this story isn't about her.

Born into the village and left exposed was a huge infant, too stupid to die. He latched onto a passing milk cow and could not be dislodged until he could forage for himself. It was thought by some that he was the child of Brick and Prissy, for he did have three nostrils, like Brick, and earlobes almost down to his shoulders, like Priscilla. Priscilla's figure could easily have hidden a pregnancy. However, they denied being the parents, and there was no one in the village brave enough to dispute that assertion.

The orphaned infant grew up as big and dumb as a man can become, with no insult intended to the ladies. No attempt was made to school him, as he could barely speak. Ask him to spell "chrysanthemum," or tell you how many chestnuts were in the pocket of a man going to Dublin who passed six circuses, each with four monkeys who each had six fleas, and you'd get no answer.

He excelled at his job. He was the village idiot. I don't mean like a jester, who usually is a savvy person who plays the fool in order to give needed advice to a vain ruler when directly contradicting the ruler would cost one's head. No, he was dim, like only one LED Christmas light in a string of 100 was working.

It takes a village to raise an idiot, and Rock, for that's what he liked to be called—"Rock. Me," he'd say—had been the official village idiot since age 12. The position came with a hut and a small stipend, sufficient to keep him in food and drink, and the tatters which were his clothes. A small perk was the official hat, a visored red cap embroidered with the letters "V," "I," "L," "E," which Rock was told stood for "Village Idiot League Elite," but many felt "large enigma" or "excrescence" were more likely; perhaps most never considered whether it was an acronym at all.

His most formidable weapon, beyond his size and strength—he beat Brick at hand wrestling with both his hands tied behind his back, and occasionally, in order to stay in the sun, he would grab the boulder in the middle of the town square and turn the entire square 90° (or half a pie)—was his smell. He stunk. His stank was rank.

It was said with some authority that the reason there was a wide-open village square, rather than a crowded downtown, was so people could shop and gossip without coming near him. He stank worse than Brick's outhouse, worse than a backed-up sewer in the Sacramento sun, worse than a month of unwashed diapers. He wasn't bothered by flies because even flies avoided him. It was joked that raindrops shied away; certainly, social workers did. Perhaps it was something he ate.

He had but one steady friend, a bloodhound with anosmia; that means what it sounds like: his nose didn't work.

They would loll together. It was widely accepted that the dog was the smarter of the two, but unable to teach Rock new tricks.

The dog mastered one trick: upon command he would roll over. Rock liked to play "Throw Stick." Roll would bring him a stick, and Rock would throw it, and a half hour or so later, Roll would return, panting, and drop the stick covered with drool, and Rock would throw it again. Rock could play for hours, until Rock and Roll would simply fall asleep on each other.

They would howl at the moon together, and laugh at things that only dogs and morons could hear or see. They liked cat jokes: "How many times does a cat change its mind? Why did the cat cross his eyes?" And without an answer to the riddle, they'd laugh for several minutes.

Normally his official duties were light: scratch, fart, lay around on one side, then the other, throw a blind-drunk man reeling around the village square after midnight into his doorway, belch, tote steamships to the lake—stuff like that. Now and then, though, he had to fulfill the vital duty of the village idiot: fighting for the village's honor.

To prevent unnecessary bloodshed and mayhem, it had long been the country's custom that marauding bands, instead of engaging in open warfare, would challenge a village to a one-on-one combat. The band would select one of its own— usually a recruited champion with many victories on his pelt—and the village would send out its village idiot. To lose meant theft of crops, rapine, and maybe some houses burned down to make a point.

All the combatants were strong and courageous. But Rock had one advantage. His odor.

As an invader's goliath would approach Rock, the foe would find himself engulfed by a cloud of stink and start to cough, fighting for breath. Soon, he could fight only with one hand, the other occupied with keeping his nose pinched. Rock could easily dispatch a one-handed odor-blinded opponent, so usually won his fights without breaking a sweat.

Of course, if the fighter was truly heroic, like one Morekit was, and caused Rock to perspire, the increased body odor alone would overcome the opponent and secure the village's victory: a TKO by BO.

Only rarely did Rock need to resort to launching a belch (the opponent could see it coming, dark and tumbling and unavoidable) or, in extreme cases, passing gas. Rock's prodigious strength was used mainly to throw the defeated brute back to the retreating marauders.

Swords, arrows, knives and guns (not that there were any) and the like were not allowed for the fight. Sticks and stones were permitted, and name-calling, but that never hurt Rock.

On one occasion, a nomadic tribe sent forth a mere boy, tall and long-boned and strong, but only half the bulk of the other fighters. Unlike the others, he had brains. He came with a long piece of cloth, which he used to sling stones. ["Please, let it not be 'David,'" prayed the Rabbi.]

David, as he was called, said he wanted the sun at his back. Like most things, it made little difference to Rock. David also insisted the fight be at 6:00 p.m., when the sun would be low, and when a strong wind normally blew up the valley from the far-away sea.

The fight was Rock's first to last for more than a few minutes. Rock couldn't see David, as he thought it stylish to face the VILE visor backwards; the sun was blinding. David was upwind so he could advance near Rock without the malodorous fumes reaching him. Even Rock's burps and farts didn't reach David, although they felled several villagers and strained the area's ventilator supplies.

Blind and deprived of his long-distance weapon, Rock had to take on a smart challenger. David chose a round stone about the size of a marble and twirled the slingshot around three times, then let it fly. It missed, but knocked down a chimney about 100 yards behind Rock. David chose another stone, as big as a quail egg, and let that fly. It hit Rock square in the forehead. Rock truly didn't know what hit him and called out, "Louse bite me."

He pulled up a Sequoia and swiped it in David's direction, but only cleared an acre or two of ground for planting since David had changed position.

David next picked up a golf ball [The Grouch stared at his lady antagonist] and then slingshot that, hitting Rock square on the nose. Bop!

"Flea bite me!" Rock waved his tree up and down in front of him like a flyswatter, trying to crush the unseen enemy, but only created a few diamonds in old campfires.

David's next missile was as big as a hen's egg, and hit Rock right above his right ear.

"Mosquito bite me." Rock slapped himself, aiming for the unseen bug. He called out, "When you start fight?" honestly believing that David was a coward who might have run away.

Soon David was slinging stones the size of grapefruits, with sharp edges.

"Ha, Ha. Fight! No tickle," Rock laughed. There was a little blood on his face, where a fingernail had scratched when he slapped himself. "Start soon?" he asked, as the sun was beginning to set.

David saved his strength for a while, grappled with a stone the size of a basketball, and heaved that. He couldn't get it high enough to hit Rock's face, so it hit Rock square on his bellybutton, making Rock go "Oomph" and exhale gasses which almost felled David because the wind was waning.

Rock looked down, scratched his belly, cried out "Hungry," and noticed piles of stones at his feet. He kicked at them, and one caught David, rolling him away. When David regained his footing, he fled. His band was known thereafter as "The Lost Tribe."

Rock asked, "Fight start soon?" and ate a sheep or two, hoping those pupus would ease his hunger pangs. The villagers cheered, and the men came out to carry Rock on their shoulders back to the village, but thought better of it when they got closer.

But this story isn't about that battle.

There was one fight that Rock almost lost, and in which he needed help. It was several peaceful years later, as marauding bands, armies and hordes had learned to give the village a wide berth.

Rock was now a fully grown man. His VILE cap sat on his head like a beanie. He was over eight feet tall, weighed beyond 500 pounds, and had a full-size locomotive as a toy. The village building code had been upgraded to allow only stone houses, which could withstand his sneezes.

The village elders had, through much effort and the bribe of an increase in his stipend, taught Rock to do his Number 1 and Number 2 far from the village in the forest. Roll was getting old, as dogs age faster than morons, and could only play with Rock for a dozen or so throws before curling up for his nap.

Luckily for the village, Rock did not snore.

One day, a vast battalion of armored soldiers, seeking to conquer the world, came to the village and issued their challenge. They were confident because their champion, Antsea, was the product of the union of their water god and earth goddess. He was as big as Rock, furry like a bear; he looked almost like he was wearing a hirsute, to coin a word.

Antsea started by trying to impress Rock with his strength. Antsea stood with both bare feet spread, uprooted a tree, twisted it around many times, looked at it critically, then punched it hard, leaving a Jenga pile as tall as a church spire. Rock picked a piece out, and the pile collapsed, crushing an elephant.

Rock, getting into the spirit of showing off, ate a bushel

of garlic and a field of onions, dirt and all, and belched, dissolving the body armor of the watching army.

Antsea grabbed the nearby river, flapped it up and down like a rope, then snapped it twice; fish rained down on his army's lances so that each soldier had three to barbeque.

Rock set his own feet and, using his massive arms and hands, twisted his head around many times, as if he were winding up one of those new flying toys the Rabbi has been giving out. And then, holding his head still with his hands, he let his feet twirl. The resulting tornado brought to his villagers' feet stacks of cooked fish on platters of shields from the invader's horde.

Antsea seized the river again with one hand; with his other he punched a hole into a mountain, then threaded the river through, so it ran from top to bottom to top in a continuous loop. Rock was impressed, but only at the artistry; he was not awed by the strength.

Rock stamped his feet, then started jumping up and down, up and down, until the whole flat earth was moving in waves with the far ends reaching high up, then down low; he kept jumping until one end met the other and the earth became round.

"Bumbo," he burbled.

Eventually they began fighting in earnest, a cleared space about two miles from the village. Antsea had prepared himself by stringing his neck with a hundredweight of garlic, smearing his face inches thick with Camembert, Roquefort and Limburger cheeses, and sticking long hard salamis up each nostril to counter Rock's stink. Rock had prepared himself, as usual, by playing Throw Stick with Roll.

They fought for hours. Rock would sometimes seem to have the literal upper hand, holding Antsea up until his struggles diminished; then he would throw him down. Almost immediately, Antsea would gather strength and spring up ready to fight again. They grappled, and punched, and kicked, poked, nuggied and tore at each other.

At one point, Antsea held Rock and was about to tear him in half, but Rock said, "Hungry" ["Me, three," said the pudgy cousin in between pugilistic noises], and pulled out the two salamis from Antsea's nostrils and ate them, dipped in Limburger (he wasn't partial to Roquefort). Antsea had to stagger back from Rock's funk to pack his nose with cannonballs.

Rock caught Antsea in a half-nelson, which by brute force he turned into a double, then a triple-nelson, and brought Antsea to the circular river and held him under for five minutes, but Antsea was refreshed by the dip, broke the hold and fought with renewed vigor. Rock, to his own amazement, was beginning to tire.

"Nap?" he asked. Antsea, antsy to claim his victory, refused. He moved in for the kill. Brick, who had watched the entire match, rushed forward, shouting at Rock, but wasn't heard at first. Antsea grabbed the tired Rock, started punching him again and again, and twirled him around so that Rock slowly twisted into the dirt like an auger of bad times. Luckily, Rock managed to get a grip on Antsea's waist, and lifting him high above his head, he prepared to throw him down again.

"Don't, don't," yelled Brick.

"You're not the boss of me," thought Rock as he spun around, unscrewing himself. [The Grouch glared at the Whisperer, then at Uncle Irv, daring a comment.] His hold on Antsea became so tight that Antsea couldn't move his arms or take a breath.

"Hold him up," yelled Brick.

"Me no robber," answered Rock, moving to throw Antsea into a lake.

"No, don't throw him. Just keep on holding him. He gains strength from the earth, or from touching bodies of water."

The villagers nodded in understanding; Brick wasn't so thick after all.

"Huh?" responded Rock, who was. Brick was silent for

a while, trying to think how to get through to Rock, when Prissy almost pulled his ear off.

"Bet him!" she said. Brick was a bit slow on the uptake but suddenly understood. Braving the stench, Brick came close to Rock, who was still holding Antsea above his head.

"Remember my game? I'm holding my breath, Rock. Bet you can't last longer than I can," Brick taunted.

"E.Z., P.Z." said Rock with difficulty at uttering so complicated a thought. He held Antsea out at arm's length, high enough so Antsea's toes were still inches from the ground. Brick kept his cheeks puffed out and tried to look like he was suffering, all the while actually breathing through his tripartite nose.

After about twenty minutes, Antsea's struggles diminished, and soon he hardly squirmed at all. As the sun set, he seemed to shrink to the size of two or three ordinary men.

Brick exhaled loudly, pretending to give up and release his breath.

"Win!" Rock bragged. He started to put Antsea down, but Brick yelled, "Throw!" Roll wagged his tail and barked.

Rock threw Antsea so high, and so far, that Antsea can still be seen today: he's the man in the moon.

"Hungry," said Rock.

"That's our boy," cooed Prissy to Brick, giving him a love tap which prompted a further revision to the village's building code.

The Grouch abruptly sat down, and no one in the room moved for a while, until Mom said, "Devils' food cake with chocolate syrup and raspberry jam in the dining room," which caused a sudden people jam at the doorjamb.

The cat was nowhere to be seen.

The Woman Who Bested The Genie Twice

Another dawn coughed asthmatically into existence, foreboding a low noon and sickly sunset. No mail for Dad; no news from home for the Aunts and Uncles. Outside all was eerily quiet: no people shouting; no wagons creaking; no clip-clop from horses' shoes on cobble-stones; no street urchins' raucous laughter. No chirping bird songs, just avian sneezes and dirges. Nevertheless, hours passed and story time impended.

Because his opportunity had been stolen by The Grouch, Brian was acknowledged to be the next story teller. He was a quiet youth, with dark hair and eyebrows, but otherwise a fair complexion. He was at that awkward age when his opinions were automatically rejected by most adults, yet children viewed him as too old to trust with childish thoughts. He was barely past being a mere boy.

Alexa was his first crush. His mom was amused that Brian talked like he was the first to discover that girls were intrinsically different from boys and deserving of ultimate attention.

His mushy letter to Alexa, ripped into small pieces before he chanced delivery, had been reconstructed and was now repeated at odd intervals around the house; some of the voices were good mimics of Donald Duck, Yoda, President Kennedy, and Barbara Walters.

Alexa was unaware she was the intended recipient of his romantic thoughts because the letter was addressed to "My beloved," followed by several hearts and flowers, which gave the mockers range to improvise. She had sensed Brian's interest and was flattered. She had not yet learned to exploit the power young women can have on young, and older, men.

Brian purposefully selected a tale that he thought would appeal to her. He had practiced telling his story, using Princess (the name was adopted through the house) as his audience. It was a simple, direct story with no frills; he timed it at about eighteen minutes, short enough so his shirt shouldn't get too drenched with nervous sweat. He was apprehensive; this was his big chance to impress Alexa.

Seeing his distress, Princess told him, "Hold this in your pocket. It's a charm which makes storytelling easier. Make sure to give it back when you're done!"

Dressed in his best shirt ["Isn't that what he wore for Easter?" sneered one of the Moraga parents], Brian turned a chair around and leaned forward on its back, which helped conceal his shaking knees. He had a frog in his throat due to his agitation. With the Rabbi's help, they got it out, and Jeremiah hopped away, singing *"Joy to the world."*

Uncle Ax waved to the frog, explaining, "A true oenophile. He has an account at my store." Several of the other men winked at Jeremiah as he left, having helped him drink his wine.

With the unfamiliar word "oenophile" reeling in his brain, Brian patted Princess' charm and returned his hands to the chair; he discovered his shirt was already drenched. He began again.

Before a word came from his mouth, a sing-song chorus began of "My beloved [whistles and lip smacking], star of the morning, cannot imagine a day without you, ecstasy to hold your hand," excerpts from his letter. The teasing ended with "passi, passi, passi." Brian had torn up his billet doux before finishing the valediction, intending it to be "passionately yours." His fair complexion was fairly close to fiery red.

"Cut it out," warned Dad.

Brian looked everywhere, except at Alexa, and began.

The Woman Who Bested the Genie Twice

This story is set in the future, when wondrous inventions are part of daily life. Women are considered men's equals ["A step down from now," said the Whisperer] and could become doctors, lawyers, sheep farmers or even priests [mutters of "hairytic"]. Infants are still given names at birth, but since a marvelous invention, called Max, keeps track of almost everything, most people, when older, would take on fanciful names of their own choosing, and even vary them from time to time.

The heroine of this story used the name "Rosanna Danna," because she felt it mellifluous and funny. [Brian paused a second, bewildered, since the story he had practiced had "Amanda," so close to "Alexa," as its heroine. He was compulsively rubbing Princess' charm. He hadn't a notion what "mellifluous" meant.]

Although it was a time dominated by science and technology, belief in the ancient magic still persisted. Proper incantations by a shaman could bring rain; gamblers still talked to the dice. Rosanna Danna was dimly aware that not all was sane and rational, by jokes about a black cat's crossing one's path, superstitious jabbering about Friday the Thirteenth in an elevator whose stops skipped from 12 directly to 14, and the like. But as a pediatric nurse with aspirations to be a gynecologist [neither Brian nor anyone listening had a clue what that was], she was usually no-nonsense, all fact and reality.

She was dressed to the nines, which was the floor of the hospital her ward was on. Under her scrubs, she had a white silk blouse and black pants in the style of the day: custom-made from a video of her sent in with the order; the pants fit like a second skin at the hips and derriere. A crimson belt gave color around her waist. At work, she wore no bracelets, nose ring or earrings, since they could be unsanitary, and her young patients would often grab them.

She loved her work, spending most of her time with

the children, dictating notes on her patients as she walked through the corridors, with the ubiquitous Max tracking her utterances and adding them to the appropriate charts. [Brian breathed a sigh of relief; it seemed he had regained some control of the story.]

I know you would like to know about her love life, but she was married. [That wasn't in the practiced version, shy Brian knew.] Her husband was chief hydrologist for an organic kale aquafarm which supplied all the best restaurants in the city. He had been the primary caretaker for their daughter while Rosanna Danna earned her scrubs, but daughter was now off at college, writing her Ph.D. thesis on neurological networks in nematodes. Hubby was in his early 50s, while Rosanna Danna looked about ten years younger (twenty, to her own eyes).

On her lunch break, Rosanna Danna went to a few antique shops searching for a good reading lamp for a living room table, a birthday gift for her husband; hubby had been complaining that it was too dim to read easily on the couch. To stay current with the latest fashion, it was important to fill one's house with antiques.

She soon found a halogen lamp with a switch, a far cry from the newest LED intellilights, which lit if the room was dark and someone in proximity said the lamp's name and commanded "Light." The one she had in the bedroom was named "Bud." When the lamp was balky, it sounded like she had overindulged in cheap beer. The antique lamp, though, listened to no one; its manual settings were "low," "bright," and "brightest." How quaint!

She took the gift home, planning to wrap it the next day. In her country, that was a special day, celebrated everywhere by joyous revelry. Not because it was her birthday, but because it was Eccentric's Day, which came every four years, and was not a Monday or Tuesday, or any of those calendar days, but a day wedged in between. It traced its inception to the need to align the solar calendar, which pegged a year at 365 days, with a full revolution of the earth around the sun, which took an additional quarter day. Another day was added every olympiad in mid-summer. People could get away with almost anything on Eccentric's Day, sort of like Mardi Gras, or an entire day of the clock's striking midnight on New Year's Eve, or anytime in Las Vegas.

The next morning, Rosanna Danna prepared to wrap the present. She polished a little spot at the base of the lamp, where the price tag had been, and went to the kitchen to pour a cup of New Age Holistic AntiOccident Herbal Tea, part of the Buy American campaign, thinking of a snack to eat while she sipped. When she returned, a large man, dressed strangely in a turban, vest and harem pants, all of the same smooth cotton fabric, was standing in her living room.

She didn't bother to ask who he was, she just yelled, "Hey, Bud," and when he turned, she pushed her hip into him, tilted him off his feet, stood back and let him fall heavily to the ground. The light in her bedroom switched off.

"That was fun," the man said, readjusting his turban. Rosanna Danna then rushed at him, and when he put his arms out and took a step forward to protect himself, she grabbed his hands and casually flipped him over her shoulder.

"Wow, that shakes the dust out!" the man said. He was darkly handsome, with defined muscles under his vest, brown eyes, and smelled of falafel.

"I am Mudhammid Ali, a genie. You cannot hurt me, for I am a child of lesser gods. I have been stuck in the lamp for ages, and you have freed me. This is your unlucky day."

In one smooth motion, Rosanna Danna pulled out her iPhone35, a handheld device, snapped several pictures—a sort of instant painting—and a video—a sort of instant memory with motion—and sent them to all her contacts: a list kept by the device of all the people she knew—so the pictures and video would show up on their devices. They thought she was showing her living room and the new lamp, since genies, like vampires, don't register in mirrors or pictures. Soon, her iPhone beeped with early birthday wishes sent to her, which the device could receive either in text or a recorded voice message.

"Get out of here, you sicko. Don't threaten me," Rosanna Danna answered bravely. She was a tough cookie.

"Let me explain. I am a genie, or more properly, a 'djinn.' It is my fate to be sealed in lamps, to await by chance a person who rubs the lamp three times while craving halvah. That's the only way I can get out. Normally, under the Code, I must reward my liberator by granting three wishes, if a test is passed. After that, I am free to enjoy myself for a hundred years before I must be confined again."

Rosanna Danna tried to deny any fondness for halvah, but to demonstrate his powers, from thin air the djinn produced a heaping plate, and she couldn't stop herself from taking a piece.

"Really goes well with that tea," she conceded.

"Then why is it my 'unlucky day'? I should get three wishes," she inquired.

"Yes, normally. But I had waited so long I lost my temper and uttered my father's name in vain. Following the Code, in expiation I vowed to slay the person who released me, on the same day, in his honor. He's old school. I must keep my word. But don't worry, you have several hours to live. I want to explore for a bit."

Mudhammid Ali put a spell on her, so all Rosanna Danna could do was eat halvah. In a twinkling, he flew around the city and country, seeing what had changed in a few millennia. He came back dressed still in the same fabric, but in an orange aloha shirt, with dark red pants, torn at the knees in the chic style; his turban now had a navy-blue tail, which trailed behind to his shoulders. The loud colors worked well with his dark complexion. He released Rosanna Danna from the spell. "I am 'Engine-Engine-Number-Nine,'" he declared.

"Prepare to die." He was humming *Casey Jones*, but sang when he reached "*the engine just gleams.*"

Rosanna Danna stalled for time. "I thought you were 'Mudhammid Ali.' And what's with the get-up?" she inquired.

"I really like your modern notion of choosing your own name," he replied. "My new name comes from 'N-Djinn,' which is my religious faith. I am a Muslin," he explained, pulling at the fabric of his shirt. ["Ah, a man of the cloth," said the Whisperer reverently.]

"Yeah, right. How did you pass all those years while confined in the lamp?" Rosanna Danna asked, trying to get him to talk. Men were generally garrulous about themselves; they were all pigs.

"Well, as I explained, I did go a bit stir-crazy. Usually I passed the years working on sudoku."

"You had a book of sudoku? How did that fit into the lamp?" she prodded, desperate to keep him talking.

"A *book*? There is more than one?" he screeched incredulously. She realized she wasn't dealing with the earth's smartest inhabitant.

"Yeah, well. I don't believe anything you say," she said snottily while helping herself to more halvah. "Genies don't come out of halogen lamps; they come from old-fashioned oil lamps, for one thing."

"We try to change with the times," the former Mudhammid Ali replied.

"Yeah, right. It's all an incredible load of duck feathers. You must be a hundred times as big as that lamp, and your muscles look rock hard; I can't believe for a second that a huge, strong, handsome man like you could fit all of yourself inside that itsy-bitsy lamp." She was playing to his vanity. She stared below his belt; that always made men stupider.

"I can, too," he said, but he was basically preening under her compliments.

"No way! I bet you're just a lot of talk, like most men,

all lies," she said, fluttering her lashes, licking her lips and moving her eyes from his dark orbs, to his pecs, and then to his crotch.

"I'll show you!" he bragged. And he twirled, becoming slowly more of a vapor than a solid object: a thin spinning whirlwind, the bottom of which touched a hole in the base of the halogen lamp, and with a sighing sound, the vapor entered the hole until nothing was left.

"See, lady?" the djinn said from inside. Then, a few seconds later, woefully, "You tricked me."

Rosanna Danna plugged the hole with halvah, and put the lamp in the closet. She searched online for another gift to give her husband on her birthday, as was the custom. A light which clipped onto the pages of the book being read was delivered by two-hour drone. She celebrated Eccentric's Day madly for the next several hours, pushing the djinn from her mind.

A short pause was called here. Dad was afraid Brian would collapse from dehydration, so heavily was he sweating, and so thoroughly was he soaked. Dad brought him a pitcher of water and a few towels. After drying and wetting, Brian still looked quite anguished, not only due to performance anxiety, but because he couldn't seem to control the story; it just rambled out of his mouth. He continued:

The next day, Rosanna Danna used her iPhone35 to contact her work; she said she had a headache and couldn't come in. Since about half the staff, suffering from Eccentric's Day excesses, were making the same excuse, no one suspected she was fibbing.

Rosanna Danna reasoned to herself that, by that Code thing, Mr. Engine Ali, whatever, had to kill her on the day he was first freed. Since this was the next day, perhaps those three wishes could be hers. She was a smart cookie, yet her belief in science and reality was taking a back seat for a while to the prospect of the ultimate score.

She appreciated the risk. Ropes, guns, tasers, laser ionizing personal vaporizers, Chinese handcuffs, none of those weapons might work against the djinn. She would have to rely upon her wits. Wits against wizardry; which will win?

She ate a lean breakfast of only a mandarin orange and an apple, having counted calories from the halvah, with more to come. She shopped, and came home with a bag of goodies any kid would have loved. Hubby had left for work, where he was peacefully sleeping off his own Eccentric's Day revelry. With her vision of unlimited wealth or power, or both perhaps, or more and more... she overrode all the possibilities which ended in disaster and determined to go forward.

Rosanna Danna dressed in her most provocative outfit, remembering how pliable the djinn had become when she flirted with him the day before.

At this point, Brian paused, almost dislocating his jaw, fighting not to give the detailed description forming on his lips of her clothing, which included skin hugging this-and-that, an indecent top, and Fetch-Me heels, or something similar. He gulped convulsively from the pitcher and continued.

Rosanna Danna put the lamp on the table, and prepared to rub it, while visions of halvah danced in her head. On a sudden impulse, she plugged it in and turned it on. An unearthly howl filled the room, infusing her with a fear of wild, ancient spaces and malevolent spirits; she unplugged the lamp. She understood why the original owner hadn't kept it.

She rubbed the lamp. A thin vapor, like the beginning of steam from a kettle, leaked out, slowly gaining size, becoming less transparent, until the djinn was standing there again.

"Jeez, lady," he proclaimed, "that really hurt. We really didn't think through the switch from oil to electricity very well."

He was dressed as he was when she last saw him, but his turban was about six inches higher, as all his hair stuck out as if running away from him. He gathered himself together, pulling in stray wisps.

"I am Engine-Engine-Number-Nine! Prepare to die!" he bellowed, pulling out a long, curved sword, perfect for beheadings.

"Calm down, hunk," Rosanna Danna cooed. "You had to kill me yesterday, remember? Now it's too late. I checked the Code."

There was a long silence. Engine-Engine-Number-Nine pondered. She had a point. A vow was very specific. His vow was to kill her the same day she released him. Now what should he do? She said she checked the Code. Hmm. Did she know how to interpret it? He probed.

"What do you know about the Code?"

"I know it governs your behavior and that you are in breach of it. Tell me more about it," she fluttered, putting on the teasing mode.

"As you say, the Code governs the lives of the N-Djinns."

"Tell me more. I really want to know. Why are you the 'N-Djinns'?" Rosanna Danna licked her lips again, but this time to catch a stray crumb of halvah; Engine-Engine-Number-Nine was never without.

"Okay," he said, explaining slowly, since this stuff was known to grade school kiddjinns.

"A long time ago, when djinns populated the earth, before the ascent of humans, there were many different Muslin factions; eventually the sects were named from A to Z. [Uncle Irv was elbowed simultaneously from each side, so he kept quiet.] The most important one, with the greatest scholars and accomplished magic arts masters, was sect N, my faith.

"Tired of the division and animosity between the different sects, and the frequent wars among Muslins, a great convocation was called to iron out the varied beliefs and adopt one set of rules. It met for several hundred years, a result less of the significance of the differences between the sects' tenets, than the widely held conviction that any compromise was impossible because there was only one truth.

"Eventually, it was decided to give authority to a small group, a committee of only three, of which one was from our sect; although diminutive, he was the most revered scholar and, although an Nmam ('mam' is what we call a minister), he was universally trusted.

"The small group included as well as the notorious dissident, Omam Abdollar Ichan, who would dispute his own hunger with himself until he fainted from piety. Finally, to represent the reform and modernistic Muslins, the in-sects, the notable fiery-haired windbag Char'les daar Wyn, the Orange Djinn of the Specious." Engine-Engine-Number-Nine genuflected while saying these sainted names. "The scribe was Chris' the Moor. They met for several years, somehow maintaining the absolute secrecy of their discussions and running up charges for food and entertainment which floored the bigger convocation with its excesses.

"After three years, they presented an agreement which was adopted by the entire congress, with only the exception that proved the rule. That became the Code."

He stopped, lost in pious thought, but maybe it was Rosanna Danna's perfume, "Purple Haze," getting to him.

"Who voted against it?" she prodded.

Still lost in reverie, he replied, "I think, Ichan." Slowing coming to himself, he repeated with more certainty, "I think Ichan. I think Ichan." He continued his explanation of the Code.

"The compromise N-Djineered by our revered was called 'The Little N-Djinn D'Accord.'" Engine-Engine-Number-Nine stopped, as if he was finished.

"And what was the Code they came up with?"

"You must know that! The Code," and here he became solemn and recited in bold, centered words:

Act Towards Others As You Would Have
Them Act Towards You,
With Exceptions.
And No Meta Wishes.

He muttered a quick prayer on saying the holy commandments. "Because of that, we sometimes call the Code the 'Towards.'" [The Rabbi snorted involuntarily.]

Rosanna Danna thought to herself that the Code wasn't too original, but perhaps it was novel way back when.

"'With Exceptions'?" she asked. "How would you know when to act as you want others to act, and when it was an exception?"

"Because the Code is so short, and yet filled with meaning, our learned faithful, especially some Imams and Nmams, for centuries have debated and commented on the Code, filling massive books with strictures and advice to guide us." Engine-Engine-Number-Nine still was using his "how come you don't know this" voice.

"The two sacred books of interpretation are the Mishmash and the Allmud." [The Rabbi was helped back into his chair by Princess.] The djinn kneeled again.

"Oh, that's wonderful. You are so smart," she flattered him. He lapped it up like a cat with buttermilk.

"So, back to business," he said sorrowfully. "Lovely lady, prepare to die." He lifted his sword up high.

"No, no," said Rosanna Danna, not showing any fear but patting his arm. "That was yesterday. Today, I'm just like any other halvah addict who rubs you the right way," she purred.

The djinn brought the sword down, but not on her neck.

"That would make it easier," he agreed. "I'm in dutch with dad either way." He thought about it while wolfing down what was left of the halvah. "Okay, we'll do it your way."

"So, I get my wishes?" she asked hopefully. "Can I wish for

more wishes, or that my wishes don't turn out with unfortunate side effects?"

"Of course not!" His tone signified they were stupid questions. "'No meta wishes,' according to the Code."

"Oh, yeah, that's what it means. All right, what about my three wishes?"

"Not quite yet. You must pass the riddle test."

There was a long pause. Each of them looked at the other expectantly.

"Well," they both said together.

"I'm waiting," said Engine-Engine-Number-Nine.

"How can I solve the riddle if you haven't asked it?" Rosanna Danna protested.

"Lady, it's your job to make up a riddle I can't solve. You get a bonus wish for a true riddle. Remember that I have centuries of practice solving riddles," he bragged. "Few beat a djinn. You don't see a lot of people around making wishes that actually come true, do you?"

She had to admit she didn't know anyone that fortunate.

Rosanna Danna thought for a while. Offhand, she felt something simple, like, "How many fingers on your left hand. No looking!" might be complex enough to stymie this mook, but her vanity made her want to come up with a tough riddle, and also earn that fourth wish forthwith.

She thought for a while and announced: "I have a daughter. I'm twice her age and half her age."

"It needs to end with a question," complained Engine-Engine-Number-Nine. "It's a riddle."

"Okay. 'I have a daughter. I'm twice her age and half her age. How'd that happen?' It's a true riddle; I'm going for the bonus."

"Under the Code, I have an hour to solve the riddle," the genie stated, improvising.

Rosanna Danna opened her shopping package and took out a yo-yo, walked the dog, and handed the toy to him. He spent some time practicing, then, with an effort, returned to think about the riddle, humming *Casey Jones* without realizing it. "*Just gleams*," he sang softly.

"Have you ever done crossword puzzles to pass the time in the lamp?" She handed him a book of Monday puzzles, the easiest. He quickly got 1-down: "Where the sun rises," writing "east." He was stumped by 9-across: "Hawaiian flip-flops." (The answer is "slippahs.")

"I like this," he said, then remembered the task at hand.

"You adopted her!" he said confidently. She couldn't figure out how that would solve the riddle. Now she was feeling sure he would fail to find the solution.

"No, I'm her natural mother. But anyway, try again."

She handed him a harmonica after blowing a mean riff. He took to it well, and later, during his years of freedom, performed that song with a band called "Blues Traveler."

Rosanna Danna continued to give him toys from the bag every time he tried to work on the riddle, also stroking his arm and whispering "hunk" and other dolces. Soon, the hour had passed.

"Lovely lady, I give up," the djinn conceded. "What's the answer?"

"Five," she said with a laugh, then continued. "I was born on Eccentric's Day, so my birthday comes every four years. My daughter is now 24, and although 48 years have passed since my birth, I've had only 12 birthdays. So, actually, I'm twice her age and half her age."

"But lady," Engine-Engine-Number-Nine began to object, and then had to admit that such trickery was perfectly acceptable for riddles.

"You beat me. You pass the test. I grant you four wishes, but no meta wishes!"

"Yessir, I stuck that one!" Rosanna Danna proclaimed triumphantly, pumping her wrist and arm like a hammer.

"Now, genie, scamper away. Enjoy your freedom. Come

back when I make my wishes."

What wishes did she make? That's another story, but she did become a renowned gynecologist.

Brian wiped his brow, wrung out the towels and, without daring to look at Alexa, sat down. His shirt stuck to his body. There were cries of "Bravo!" mixed with Porky Pig's saying, "passi, passi, passi; that's all, folks."

"Cut that out," said Dad.

The cat was nowhere to be seen, despite the plate of halvah and dates soaked in rum, which Mom brought in.

Aye, Earn Pirates (The Black Spot)

Another day at the house, with nothing unusual. Mom and Dad finally got the kids involved in doing some tasks, by conditioning either presenting or even practicing stories on helping out. That gave Mom a few minutes in the late afternoon to sit in her favorite armchair, where she waited, futilely, for the cat to warm her lap.

With the word play of the recent tales, the kids quickly dubbed their work "punishment detale," but volunteered for some jobs ("I'll lick the plates before you wash them," offered the pudgy kid) and put in a child's half-hour on general tasks each day, not counting the time spent blackmailing adults whose letters they had reconstructed. Their parents were at first proud that their offspring were contributing, although they certainly didn't themselves want to deprive Mom and Dad of the virtues and rewards of hard work.

Mom had noted offhand to Dad that, for the size of the gathering, there seemed to be a lot of love notes found and reconstructed by the kids. Dad noted that most of the Aunts and Uncles had grown up together, camped together, been in school for years together, and while young had hung out in the same cliques after school and in summer. Throwing them together for this long had revived the vivid emotions of first dates, first loves, jealous boy- and girlfriends and other youth angst; suppressed for a few decades, puberty randiness was escaping. Dad remarked that he was surprised they didn't have pimples. Acne at an age of aching knees.

The dark cloud remained deadly. A messenger pigeon was sent out to a pigeon fancier two towns over; two hours later, a different pigeon returned with a message, "Your bird DOA," and promptly gave up the ghost.

"Shelter in place" continued to be Dad's Law. So long as the food and the drink ("and the drink," added Uncle Ax) held out, while outside dead animals abounded and dire messages were stenciled in the skies, the in-laws declined to be outlaws.

Today's cloud message, with thunder and lightning, was: *"Now Aren't You Sorry You Laughed At Me?* Shortly after that: *Tom Paine's Bakery. Sourdough our specialty. Pains au Chocolate. Blackbird Pie. We deliver."* The rainbow was a nice touch.

After the usual delicious dinner—pulled pork tacos filled with radishes, lettuce and salsa, with cream-filled churros for the relatives, a side of brisket and some borscht for the Rabbi—the crowd slowly assembled, patting their stomachs and belching happily, in the great hall for the evening stories.

There was a yelp with a shout of "I lose" from a pair of stragglers coming in from the courtyard. The dancing uncle was heard to challenge the loser to the game, "you go first." The red-headed kid hurried into the hall, followed a few seconds later by a tear-stained six-year-old comforted by the dancing uncle.

At his request, Dad was given the nod, but since he couldn't see himself, there was a long delay until someone brought a mirror, and he realized his nod was for himself.

As I said, a normal, boring day with nothing special happening, and certainly nothing wrong.

"This story actually happened only a few miles from here, in a pub I used to visit before Mom showed me how much happier I'd be if I stayed home."

Despite his buttering her up, Mom was signaling to Dad from the door of the kitchen to come help her.

"Well, I'm needed. Uncle Ax knows all about this, so I'll let him take over. Brother, this one's yours. Tell them about Barnacle Bill and his tavern."

Uncle Ax got up, if swaying back and forth a little higher than when he was sitting down is getting up. He tottered forward, let Lance trip over him, and addressed the group with breath guaranteed to sterilize their faces and hair.

In a sing-song voice, he began:

There once was a sailor, with only one leg,
Called Barnacle Bill, the captain's first mate,
Known for demanding, on the very first date,
"I've lost one of my legs, but come touch my peg.
I'm Barnacle Bill the Sailor."

"NOT THAT ONE," shouted the Aunties. "Dad said tell the story about the tavern two towns over."

"Oh. Treasure. Buzzard. Black Spot," he muttered to himself.

The Black Spot

A few towns over, in Loadeye, there used to be a tavern, which replaced a tanning studio. Before that, Simple Simon's Mud Pies, a Tourette's Syndrome sufferer's psychology practice, and an outlet of the nationwide franchise BugWay Sandwiches had all failed at the same location. I think because of that, when Barnacle Bill, the sailor, bought the building, he named his tavern "The Black Spot."

Barnacle Bill had been a sailor. In fact, it was hard to say his name without adding "the sailor." He would entertain his guests and customers with story after story of his life on the seven, or seventy – he wasn't quite sure – seas, mainly as a pirate.

He invariably dressed like a pirate. Bandanna on his head, loose-fitting blouse crossed by baldrics to hold weapons, large cuffs of leather, a belt seven inches deep ["What Ax just drank, I think," said the Whisperer accurately], outlandish pants of silk with slashes and holes here and there, and huge boots, with iron nails showing, and each with a big buckle of crossed bones, chicken I think; the boots went halfway to his knees. Crude tattoos which changed from day to day. A gold earring on one side and a gold ear on the other. He kept a knife in the baldric, and would often slam it into the table for emphasis, or dare patrons to put their hands down for stabberscotch. And a full black beard, of coarse [Ax mumbled something too faint to hear], which hid his mouth.

There was always good wine at his place. He had an account with my shop. That's why I'd drop in now and then ["on the same day," added the Whisperer] to clink a glass with him.

"Why there's a sight that makes eyes sore," he'd bellow at me. "What brings your sorry aft here?"

Now, on a ship, the front is the bow, and going towards the rear is "aft," and all the way aft is the "stern." ["Get on with the story," someone directed him aftly.] That was Barnacle Bill, the sailor: always nautical talk.

Barnacle Bill, the sailor, when I came in, would signal to the bartender to treat me well. "Don't comp anything for him. Run his tab. We'll deduct it from his bills." He'd shake his huge fist at me and tell me one of his sea stories.

"On a whaler, if we ever ran across a sack of landlubbing blubber like you, scalawag, why, we'd teach you to scamper up the mainmast like a monkey, by slicing at your legs while you climbed. We'd leave you up there as the look-out. Yes, matey, the men would shout 'look out' as the harpooners practiced, with you as the wailing whale. Let me Ax you a question."

Now, that's a lame joke I've heard all my life, so I'd pay it no mind. I'd retreat to a corner, sit down and slowly sip some wine, and watch him jolly all his customers. I'd join in the pretense like it was a pirate hangout, and I'd pinch and kiss the serving wenches.

Barnacle Bill [he started], the sailor [he added automatically], had this weird stuffed bird, I think it was a stuffed buzzard, which always sat on his shoulder. Barnacle Bill, the sailor, would pretend he was a ventriloquist and use the stuffed bird as his dummy, but I could see his lips move. He was proud of that ugly bunch of feathers, and upon meeting people he'd have the damn thing say, "I'm a parrot." Later, he was buried with that buzzard.

Barnacle Bill, the sailor, only had one leg. When he walked, it was "thud, whack, thud, whack, thud, whack." It was especially loud that day, when he was tapping his peg leg to music. For the only time I remember, there was a guy playing a guitar and singing at The Black Spot.

Was he telling about the treasure he'd hijacked from another pirate, hidden, and used to buy The Black Spot? Hmm. Maybe. No. Now I remember.

He was telling one of his pirate stories about Twisted Sneer Adderly, a man of all trades who never lacked a ship.

"Not a pretty man to begin with, while in his early twenties, sailing as the blacksmith with Pink Beard, on the gay ship *Pestilence*, a rope had been left sloppily coiled on the deck; a misstep, and his right leg was mangled, soon cut off. He was called 'Twisted Sneer One Legged Adderly' then.

"Not long later, in a fight against the *Evangelical*, a bolo took off his right hand. For a while Twisted Sneer Hook Hand One Legged Adderly stayed healthy. I heard he was a cook on the *Salmonella*, but didn't see him for a few years.

"In Cartagena, I hired him to be ship's sawbones and carpenter, even though he had only one eye by then. But a sudden huge swell while he was sawing a coffin cost his good arm. Twisted Sneer Patch Eyed One Armed Hook Hand One Legged Adderly could still read charts and plot courses by the stars, so I kept him on.

"He earned his keep, I'll give him that, until a small mosquito bite became infected. We gave him all the rum he wanted, but eventually, we couldn't save the leg."

Barnacle Bill, the sailor, would glare at everyone at his

table, waiting for the inevitable questions. The first was always: "Did you call him Twisted Sneer Patch Eyed One Armed Hook Hand No Legged Adderly?" It took the more soused patrons a few tries to get it out, and Barnacle Bill, the sailor, would wait patiently until they got it exactly right.

"Naw, there wasn't enough left o' him for a name that long. We called him after his new job. 'Cannonball Adderly.'"

Barnacle Bill, the sailor, would snort and laugh so hard snot would run down his face and shirt, and he'd lean back and cry, "*Mercy, Mercy, Mercy*," echoed by the bird, until someone else interrupted with the other obvious question.

"How did he lose his eye?"

"I asked him that," Barnacle Bill, the sailor, would reply. "'First day with me hook!' answered Cannonball."

Barnacle Bill, the sailor, would again succumb to paroxysms of laughter. His bird would sit there on his shoulder, calling out the obscenities Barnacle Bill, the sailor, would mouth as Barnacle Bill, the sailor, rocked back and forth.

Every night, he would tell gory stories of what pirates did to captives, or to one another. When I looked at the bartender for confirmation, and another drink, the bartender would run his hand across his throat to tell me they only slit their throats, I guess, and the rest was just exaggeration.

The guitar player, Clarence, no Creedence, that's it, wasn't too bad, and quick on his feet. Seeing what a dump the place was, he'd quickly made up a song about being in Loadeye, playing before a bored, drunk crowd.

Uncle Ax hummed to himself for a while, trying to find the tune. He burped. "Ah! That's it." He smacked his lips a few times, pretended to drink some wine (he had no glass), wiped his mouth with his sleeve, whispered, "*fishes in the deep blue sea*," and continued, singing only one line:

Oh! Lord, I'm stuck in Loadeye again.

I remember the song well because he sang it twice. On the first time, somewhere into the third verse, one of the patrons, a local named Hal•Linden, waved his hands. I think he put two spells on Creedence, one with each hand.

Creedence started choking. The serving wenches pounded him hard on his back, to no avail. He started turning purple.

Someone shouted, "Give him a beer!" The bartender came over, said, "No! Plain water is best," and holding his head back, poured some into Creedence's mouth and forced him to swallow by holding his nose. Creedence swallowed, sputtered, heaved up the water, but recovered, breathing again.

With tears in his eyes, he hugged the bartender, saying, "I was dead there; thanks for bringing me back." He looked around for Hal•Linden, and not finding him, started from the beginning and sang through, ending with:

Oh! Lord, I'm stuck in Loadeye again.

He sang a few more songs. Damned good, as I said. He packed up his guitar, sat at the owner's table arguing for a while over his pay, and then left.

It was only an hour or so later he died, did Barnacle Bill, the sailor, right at that table. I think his brain gave out from all that drink ["And his," indicating Uncle Ax, "goes on?" wondered the Whisperer]. His fist was clenched, and I think with his last breath, he was trying to bequeath the tavern, because his final words, I heard them, said almost like he was strangling, were:

"The Black Spot."

Brother, how did I do?

Uncle Ax acted like he was finished. Dad had come in a bit before Uncle Ax reached this point. Dad was shaking his head slowly, a bit bewildered. He wanted to know the whole of what Uncle Ax had said since the part he had heard wasn't the story Dad had wanted to tell.

That's not an easy task, to figure out what had already been said. Dad didn't have, like now, a copy of the story to read. There was no recording.

If you can figure out how Dad could review Uncle Ax's recital, now's the time to speak up. Otherwise:

There was a delay.

Finally, Dad took over.

You're quite an observer, Brother Ax. A few corrections, though.

Barnacle Bill [with an effort, he went on without "the sailor"] had both his legs. You knew that: you described his boots. He did walk with a limp, though, so there actually was a "thud, whack, thud, whack, thud, whack."

There were no serving wenches in The Black Spot. There was only Barnacle Bill, the sailor [it slipped out], and the bartender. The bartender, in crossing his throat with his index finger, wasn't indicating what happened to the captives; that's the universal bartenders' sign for he's cutting you off from any more drinks.

And, the bird was real. Real ugly, yes, but an actual bird. Maybe a small parrot, 'cause it talked.

Barnacle Bill, the sailor [it slipped in], wasn't introducing the bird by throwing his voice, he was bragging to the customer about himself: "I'm a pirate."

And that bird was pretty darn smart. When Barnacle Bill, the sailor, told the story about Twisted Sneer Patch Eyed One Armed Hook Hand No Legged Adderly, it was the parrot who took over in a pirate's voice to say at the end, "First day with me hook!"

In fact, the main reason Barnacle Bill, the sailor, hired Creedence, who on sight he detested as a redneck, was that the bird kept insisting, "Polly wants a cracker."

That fellow Hal·Linden, yes, he was a local, a local nuisance. He worked for the music industry. When Creedence was singing, he slapped on his guitar case a Nay Say letter and a Nay Play letter, one from each hand, each demanding Creedence pay $500 for using the song in the tavern.

Brother Ax, most importantly, you also left out the part that makes this a story rather than a Yelp tavern review.

Barnacle Bill's [by adding the "s," Dad avoided saying "the sailor," but to no avail; a chorus of "the sailor" interrupted him anyway, with one "passi, passi, passi"] favorite story was about the buried treasure he stole from Black Bay Area Rapid Transit. No one knows how he got that name; perhaps he chose it himself. And woe to the sea scum who tried to shorten it; a "Black Bart" could get the gangplank or, if Black Bay Area Rapid Transit was in a generous mood, ten days duty winding the dog watches.

As Barnacle Bill, the sailor, told it:

"Now, that was a fearsome pirate. He commanded a four-master he named *Sweet Georgia Brown*, the former naval vessel *Queen Latifah*, which he had captured.

"Black Bay Area Rapid Transit was the scourge of all shipping from the Caribbean to the Caribbean and back. Even the scurviest pirate on the *Sweet Georgia Brown* (the bird would squawk *'jump overboard and drown'*) was festooned with diamond necklaces, jewels, ruby rings, and gold buckles; it put the *Pestilence* to shame. You couldn't walk a mile on a beach near his hideout without tripping over a dozen "X"s, marking buried treasure chests.

"I did decently as a pirate, but was only a cat burglar compared to Black Bay Area Rapid Transit. I would bravely take on a twenty-two gun Spanish three-masted barque carrying gold. He would take on the entire Spanish Armada, all 130 ships, odds be damned. I might sneak behind an island and surprise my prey. He would haul his ship up into a cloud and splash down suddenly beside his intended prize, blasting away with all his cannon. He didn't care that his cannonballs were five years beyond their 'use by' date.

"He was notorious for his cruelty, even though it made

for more work and bloodshed, since the sailors, well my swabby, even the rats on the ships he attacked would fight to the death rather than be captured. Why, I once saw him take a young captive, a blameless man of only about twenty-two, the type I would impress into my crew, and that cutthroat captain forced him to eat Spam." That bird on his shoulder would agree: "Awk, forced him to eat Spam."

"No one sane would dare cross that vicious brute. Black Bay Area Rapid Transit swore on his mother's grave (and he put her there!) that he would track down any walking mud-pile who stole from him, shortchanged him on rum, short sheeted his bunk, or dissed him in any manner. Before he killed that doomed fool in some excruciating way, Black Bay Area Rapid Transit ("Awk, Black Bart" hazarded the bird) would deliver an omen so that the poor buzzard bait would know he'd been found, and live in hellish fear.

"Black Bay Area Rapid Transit used a heart-shaped small stone, black, of course. It was known throughout the pirate world that receiving that Black Spot portended imminent horrific death. The warning scheme was common among pirates; Pink Beard used a pink polka dot lace handkerchief, perfumed highly. I always intended to use a live crustacean, but never had the occasion.

"I did okay as a pirate, as I said, but I wasn't getting rich. I certainly wasn't going to ship aboard the *Sweet Georgia Brown* to make my fortune ("Awk, *they all sigh, and want to die, aboard Sweet Georgia Brown*"). So, being the depraved pirate I was, I decided to do a little bit of beach combing.

"One night, when the moon was fast asleep and the fog so thick it muffled the sound of my oars, I rowed myself – I would trust no man other – to that sandy beach near Black Bay Area Rapid Transit's hideout. His crew of blackguards, rogues, cutthroats and brutal globetrotting villains were mainly on board the *Sweet Georgia Brown* ('*She knocks 'em dead when she lands in town, awk*'), so only the already dead constituted a skeleton crew on the island. No one heard me. I thought I was lucky.

"And I continued to believe I was lucky. I hadn't gone 30 paces before I tripped over a 'Y,' some illiterate savage's attempt at an 'X.' I could hardly haul the chest to the boat, it was so heavy. I used the oars to lever it in. My luck held: the dead men crew thought my curses were from their parrots. I rowed away unnoticed.

"I transferred the jewels and gold – doubloons and tripleloons – into a few sacks and threw the chest overboard. I carried the sacks one-by-one into my room in the fo'c'sle ('Gesundheit, awk') without attracting notice. It was more loot than I'd captured in all my years flying the skull and crossbones.

"I'd dispatch the first mate to the poop deck, whether he had to go or not, lock the door to my cabin, and enjoy the feel of the riches sliding through my fingers. I let a few months pass, faked my death in a fight, and disappeared.

"Eventually I wound up here, far from the sea, where no one would seek me. You sea ("see, awk") before I left, I learned that my luck wasn't all good. The treasure chest I disinterred belonged, of all the missing-limbed and one-eyed limeys hauling the keels of scuttled pirate ships, to that murderous Black Bay Area Rapid Transit himself, damn his doomed soul ("sole, soul, sol, caw. Sorry! awk"). There was no way he could know who took it, though ("Awk, *they all sigh and want to die*").

"I purchased this watering hole with that loot. That's why I named it 'The Black Spot.' I've plenty treasure left, so I don't fear the future. That is, unless I get a Black Spot."

Barnacle Bill, the sailor, would then laugh so loud the bird would put her wings over her head, and he'd gasp out "*Mercy, Mercy, Mercy*" (with the bird in counterpoint), bang his hands on the table, snort and snot, pull out his knife and ask, "Anyone for stabberscotch?"

The customers would sit transfixed, and never notice they were overcharged for their ale.

Now, the day he died, he told that story maybe once or twice, insulted the guitar player a few dozen times, refused to pay Hal•Linden's fees, and was having a fine old time. So it was a shock to us to notice he had been quiet for a while. He was at his usual table, looking down, and was stock still. He was pop eyed ["the sailor man," said all]; his face was ghastly pale, and his coarse black beard was white, though he'd dyed it only that morning.

I was the first to get to him. He was rigid, like rigor mortis had set in instantly, although only minutes before he'd been hale and hearty, even bawdy and boisterous. I sighted down to what he had been staring at: it was his left hand.

His fingers were so tightly closed I had to pry them open. Then there it was, clenched in his palm: a small heart-shaped token, midnight black. The Black Spot.

Dad let this scene filter through the minds of the audience. This was quite a different take from Uncle Ax's. After a pause to let his listeners appreciate the weirdness of what happened, he continued.

Now, if that weren't strange enough, there was the matter of the bird. The bird was still on his shoulder, uglier than ever, her claws clinging tightly to his baldric; but she, too, was stone cold dead. That's why they buried the bird with Barnacle Bill, the sailor.

A wolf howled at the moon, or maybe at another wolf ["Should have whistled," said the whistler]; it's hard to say from miles away.

One of the other Uncles spoke up.

"That's all true, by the way. I knew the guy. I was there that evening.

"But there's more, and less, to the story.

"Barnacle Bill was no sailor. I went to high school with him.

Before owning The Black Spot, William Barnes was a milk-man, or as his cart said, an 'Organic Grass Fed Dairy Products Residential Delivery Service.' The closest he ever came to the seven seas was his report card.

"There was no pirate loot. One day, when his wagon was fully loaded, he ran over his foot. He walked with a limp ever afterwards. He was insured, so he sued himself, claimed it was malicious, and bribed himself into a huge settlement; that's how he paid for the tavern. All that pirate and 'Black Spot' malarky was just imaginative marketing, like his name.

"And the bird. Yes, there was a live, speaking bird. I sold him that crockadillapig. It was a myna bird, not a parrot. I got rid of her because she was old, about twenty-two ["Then it wasn't a myna," said the Whisperer], had scaly mange, and hated me. That bald-headed feather duster would never sit on my shoulder, 'cept to peck my ear. When with me, she spoke only to echo my wife's scoldings. She took a liking to that Barnacle Bill, the sailor, though.

"One last thing. That thing in his hand when he died. I have it still. It was black and heart-shaped, all right, but it wasn't any Black Bart ["Black Bay Area Rapid Transit," the audience cor-rected him] pirate's Black Spot. It was Creedence's guitar pick."

Not even Mom's heart-shaped dark chocolate truffles could break the gloom and confusion this story provoked.

The cat was nowhere to be seen.

Time To Be Schooled

Gather around, children.

> *Gather 'round children, and you shall hear*
> *Of the midnight bout of diarrhea*
> *Out of the bed and onto the floor,*
> *A twenty yard dash to the bathroom door!*
> *Ooops, too late. Dad, the mop!*

I know this isn't story time. So that your young minds continue to develop, I have been told to provide some instruction during this long quarantine with no school, compounded by a failure of other education efforts.

Yes, you did get some education in the stories about sailing ships and a bit about levers. But apparently, that's not enough.

You there, with that strange thing in your hair, that looks like the prow of a ship. What? It's not the prow, it's the bow? You asked your older sister for a bow, and that's what you got. Sorry. It's cute, I think.

You, there, what's your question?

[pause]

That's a good question. The answer is "no." Another question? [paws] Again, no.

Yes? You there! The Dubs, oh, sorry, Wilhemina. Speak up, please, I can't hear you. Oh, you're the Whisperer's daughter. I see.

I should repeat the question before I give the answer, you say. Yes, that will make it clearer when the story is read.

The kid there eating a sandwich. Do you have a question? Oh, not a question. You find it strange – "off-putting," you say – listening to a voice coming out of nowhere. I'm sorry.

You there, you'd like to draw a picture and put it on the back of a chair, so it seems like a real teacher? Okay, good idea, go ahead.

…

That's not a very nice picture. I don't know if it is a good likeness. It is a very well-drawn picture of the back end of a horse. Someone, please draw a head, and put it there instead.

…

Very funny. Yes, a "head" is the nautical – sea – word for "toilet." Put a head there with eyes and ears and nose, okay?

…

No, don't just put eyes and ears and nose on that toilet.

Yes? Alice asks if that means I don't want them to think outside the bowl. No, no, please be creative.

…

Thank you, although it would be hard for me to talk with that thing in my mouth, or to hear you with those, whatever they are, in my ears. But, let's go on.

A lot of the stories have had puns. What? Yup, as in "pun-ishment detale."

A pun is a play on words that sound the same, or are very close, but have different meanings. Sometimes, a word itself can have several meanings.

Like just before with "bow," a type of knot, usually of ribbon, when in one's hair. Spelled the same way – What? Okay. – "B," "O," "W" – but sounding different, is "bow," the front of a ship.

And again, the same spelling – yes, "B," "O," "W" – and the same pronunciation as the ship's bow, "bow" is when you bend forward at the waist. With that meaning, it also has the meaning of accepting praise, as when, at the end of a play, the actors "take a bow."

Yes? He wants to know if that custom came about because the actors had to duck flying fruit if the play was bad. Perhaps, but I think it has been a sign of respect.

The girl in the green dress. She asks, "Will that be on the test?" Let's not worry about that now.

So, we already have several meanings for "bow." Another word spelled differently — Yes? Okay. "B," "O," "U," "G," "H" — sounds like the ship "bow," but has the meaning of a tree branch, as in:

Rock-a-bye baby, on the tree top
When the wind blows, the cradle will rock
When the bough breaks, the cradle will fall
Mother will catch you, cradle and all

What if she misses? There is an alternate ending:

Rock-a-bye baby, on the tree top
When the wind blows, the cradle will rock
When the bough breaks, the cradle will fall
Down will come baby, cradle and all

And you have "bow" as in "bow wow," from a dog, of course. Yes, Lance?

No, Lance. I don't approve of putting babies in trees. Yes, like the song says, it's dangerous. Well, tell your Dad whatever you want, I'm not advocating child abuse. I think the nursery rhyme comes from an old custom of hanging cradles from tree branches to let the wind rock the baby.

And if you take the pronunciation of "bow," as in the ribbon in the hair, there's the word "beau" — Okay. "B," "E," "A," "U" — which means one's honey or male sweetheart. And if you add an "X" — What? Okay. "B," "E," "A," "U," "X" — it's the plural for male sweethearts.

No, a 'BFF' still has only one heart, but there are BFFs.

And the same spelling and sound is a name, in "Beau Geste."

Yes? Uh huh? No, I don't know what "passi, passi, passi" means.

And pronounced like the sweetheart "beau," but spelled like the ribbon "bow" – Right. "B," "O," "W" – is the bow of a violin or of a bow and arrow.

Going from the "bow wow" "bow" – "B," "O," "W" again – of a barking dog, there is the meaning of "bark" as the outer covering of a tree. Both "barks" are spelled the same way. Okay. "B," "A," "R," "K."

You can also use "bark" as a verb, to mean to remove the bark, like skinning a tree. Yes? Okay, it is a bit weird that the same word means both having and removing the bark.

On the beanbag, you. Yes, it would be a pun to say, of a dog scratching bark off a tree, but not the one he was supposed to, that he was barking up the wrong tree. That phrase usually means choosing the wrong one: like a dog at the bottom of a tree barking at a squirrel, but the squirrel's already gone to another tree.

Princess? No, I don't know if the squirrel's in the tree with the baby in the cradle. Where are you going? Oh, to check. Let me know!

When two words with different meanings are spelled and pronounced the same, they are "homonyms." If they sound the same but are spelled differently, they are "homophones."

You, young man with the red hair, why are you leaving? No, that has nothing to do with a "gay agenda." The prefix "homo" here just means they sound alike. No, not the gays, the words. The "homo" is used as in "homogenized milk," meaning it's the same all through, without cream on top.

Oh, your dad won't let you drink that kind of milk because of the gay agenda. Well, that's a parent's right, I guess.

And there's even another meaning to the word "bark." Going back to our sea words, "bark" is also a type of sailing ship with three or more masts. This type of bark can be spelled a different way. Okay. "B," "A," "R," "Q," "U," "E."

Anyone have some other examples, even from today's talk? In the back.

Very good: the word "waist" means one's middle. Another word has the same sound – what's the word for that? No, not "gay-like." It's "homophone."

What's a homophone for "waist"? Anyone? All right, think of: "That kid didn't waste any of his sandwich; it all went to her waist." What's your name? Billy? Billie? You said you answer to either? Okay. No, I wasn't really talking about your sandwich in particular. Oh? You're not particular about which sandwich you eat.

In a story, you can insert sound-alike words to make the story funny.

Sticking with the sandwich theme, you could say, for a pun, in *The Black Spot* story, that Barnacle Bill (the sailor!), when he was stealing the treasure on Black Bay Area Rapid Transit's hideout island, he walked on the sand which is there.

Billie? Billy? Yes, that would ruin the sandwich.

Green dress girl, why are you squirming? No, you don't need to raise your hand, just go.

Not all of you!

Who can think of some other sound-alike words with different meanings?

Mary? You can't think of one? Okay, Mary, when a man loves a woman, and he gets down on his knees, what does he say? Yes, he might say, "this hurts," but let's be romantic. No, that's not an Italian hairytic.

C'mon, Mary, he says, "Will you ... me?" ...

Someone else? Yes, that's it. "Will you marry me?"

Don't cry, Mary. I'm sorry. I didn't mean to hurt your feelings. I wasn't making fun of you.

Irv, junior? What do 'Peter,' 'Dick,' 'John,' 'Willy,' 'Tiny Tim,' 'John Thomas,' 'Johnson,' and 'Rod' all have in common? Hmmm. They're all names for boys. No? Irv, junior, *don't* answer your own question.

Irv, junior, don't you belong with the older kids? Oh, you don't have anyone to blackmail, so you're here with us. Well, don't show off.

No, Lance, that certainly won't be on the test.

How about I give one more example, and then you all come up with some sound-alike words which can help make puns for funny stories?

The space between two sections in a church, or shelves in a store, is called an "aisle" – Okay. "A," "I," "S," "L," "E" – while a piece of land sticking out of the water is an "isle" – Okay. "I," "S," "L," "E," – which word can also be used for "island." Can anyone think of a homophone for "isle"?

Yes, red-headed boy? No, I don't think your dad said he was proud to be a homophone; close, but no cigar.

A homophone – a sound-alike word – for "aisle" and "isle." I'll give you a hint.

...

I did give you the hint. Yes, I did.

All right. Now it's up to you to come up with some funny puns. I'll give you a few minutes. Then you'll tell each other what you thought up. That's the only test.

...

All right. Let's hear what you have.

"Katz got your tongue?" Good one; the Rabbi said that.

"After he put his hand through the window pane, Tom Paine was in pain." Okay, good thinking. I like it. You added a name for a triple pun.

"She stove in the stove." Excellent.

"The lady plumber didn't fix the toilet line, so sue her." I'll accept that, although the other "sewer" isn't actually said. It's still good in a story.

"Fuzzy Wuzzy wasn't fuzzy, was he."

Okay, we'll end with that one. The whole verse goes:

Fuzzy Wuzzy was a bear.
Fuzzy Wuzzy lost his hair.
Fuzzy Wuzzy wasn't fuzzy, was he?

["That's a bald-faced lie," whispered the Whisperer's daughter.]
What's that, Alice?
You're tired of being cooped up? We all are.
School's out.

The cat was nowhere to be seen.

A Tupac of Spiders On The Brain

The children had played pirate for a few days, talking in gruff voices, dropping "h's" everywhere (Mom had to sweep them up), fashioning crude swords out of discarded wood and cannonballs from cantaloupes, wearing eye patches, and in general making Dad regret his choice of story. Lance busted his nose running (nose and him) full speed around the house, screaming, "I'm Two-Patch Lance!"

The adults were debating what had killed Barnacle Bill, the nonsailor. Those with an antipathy to guitarists or rednecks suggested it was a diabolical act by Creedence; Uncle Irv even suggested the guitar pick was poisoned.

Uncle Ax was nursing a hangover, which, like a kitten at a molly, was growing more playful every day. Mom and Dad tried to continue to be the perfect hosts, but lacked the perfect guests.

Notwithstanding their increased anxiety over their own lives' being on hold, the guests preferred that appellation and situation over becoming part of a community. They were accustomed to being lords and ladies in their own manors, and felt no compunction to soil their hands or chip their nails just because an Evil Cloud quarantined them with lesser folk.

Deprived of nights out at taverns, beauty salons or bordellos, marriages were tested, rarely matriculating, and resentment simmered. Assignations abounded. Children were harshly reprimanded for trivial reasons. Mom was excluded from the lashing out, solely in fear of possible culinary retaliation. Privately, but not quietly, the adults blamed their problems, and the Evil Cloud, on the Rabbi, overlooking their genesis before his arrival.

I've managed to get through. I can talk for only a moment, then they'll pull me back into narration. "The cat was nowhere to be seen" doesn't tell it all. They know where he is. They're pretending nothing is amiss.

The Evil Cloud stayed in place, as did the guests. Mice were getting braver, leaving little gifts in the kitchen at night, and even scurrying along the walls at story time. There were now several sets of Evil Cloud messages each day, with one always being some self-pitying cry. Today's noon message was: *Four Eyes Had Foresight, But You Were All Too Blind To See.*

That was followed by a new commercial: *Merry Mary's Maternity and Midwife Service: We Deliver!* The start and end of an ad were heralded by bright flashes of lightning.

The Rabbi spent much of his time alone, when not tutoring or playing with Princess. He stared often at his pack, shaking his head from side to side and saying the era's equivalent of "oy vey." After a brief conference with Mom, he declared he was all out of play knives for stabberscotch.

Princess was learning quickly under the Rabbi's unique tutelage. She had previously drifted at school, letting the other students answer questions. Her own questions, like, "How do birds fly?" had generally been rebuffed by simple answers, like, "That's what they were made to do." But the Rabbi would seize upon one, and they'd spend all day discussing it.

For the "how do birds fly," the Rabbi pulled a balloon from his bag and blew it up, letting it bounce around. (The other watching children, keeping a heresuitical safe distance due to parental interdict, were intrigued by the Rabbi's demonstration, but more impressed by the long fart sounds the balloon could make.) Toy parachutes above a candle continued the lesson on pressure and air movement. Finally, Princess and Rabbit Ears built an airfoil and experimented for hours (it took many tries) with damp wood and heavy huffing to show the different speeds of the smoke above and below the wing. The lesson was sealed into Princess' memory by his gift of several different toy gliders and airplanes.

Alexa hoped Brian would talk to her. He didn't need to try to impress her, she felt. His crazy story, so outlandish, reminded her of a Jim Stafford song about an immature boy teasing a girl by slipping spiders and snakes down her dress. Brian, aghast at how overboard his story had slipped, hung near Alexa, but was too timid to open a conversation.

The crowd all wandered into the great hall for another story. The children were given places up front, on the floor, with the adults on chairs or couches behind. Alexa, at that in-between age, let herself drift back from the children, and then be pushed farther back by the adults. That was okay, because she had her guitar, having agreed to play some background music if certain of the prospective storytellers got the nod.

The Whisperer's daughter, a wee wisp of a waif whose words wafted wearily, was the next up. Alexa perked up; Wilhemina Wahnita was one of her music patrons. She played a few cords, then changed to nylon strings so she could play chords.

SPIDERMAN

Hari Vishnu, that Hindu who passed through, became my parents' guru, and who knew? He told this tale I'll tell you. Now, you know, he wouldn't eat cow, so I asked him what all the beef was about that.

He was pretty old, I thought. I told my father that I thought he was pretty old, maybe 35. My father said, "That's not old!" So I said, maybe he was a gadzillion years old, and Dad said, "Don't be silly."

So, my parents began chanting something in Sandscrape, an Indian language. It sounded like chanting the name of the lad Hari Vishnu, that Hindu who passed through, now a guru, or whatever, 'cause it's in Sandscrape or something (it's all geek to me), to make them free, Hari Vishnu said, but of course he wasn't free, it seemed, but cost an arm and a leg, so maybe he was of the cult of Kali, which I hear uses its cultlery for more than eating....

Alexa only needed to play some simple notes behind this. Knowing the story was about a spider, she was playing a plain melody, which most kids would recognize as the tune to:

The itsy bitsy spider
Went up the water spout
Down came the rain and
Washed the spider out
Out came the sun and
Dried up all the rain
And the itsy bitsy spider
Went up the spout again

Her fingers could repeat that tune without her thinking, which was good because her mind quickly wandered. She was in the back of the gathering, and the Whisperer's daughter's words, soft at the outset like the breath of an ant, hardly reached her, so Alexa would lose the thread of the story. Luckily, she wasn't playing a hem, or it would have been ruined. And Wilhemina Wahnita just prattled on and on, in Alexa's opinion, seemingly sniffing every flower on the path instead of just getting on with the tale.

Rather than straining to hear, Alexa relied primarily on the pudgy kid's sound effects to gauge where the story had progressed to. She would take images from the words she heard now and then from The Dubs (as Alexa dubbed Wilhemina Wahnita), and sometimes just play with them in her head, or put them into her own silent story. At least she could hear her own story clearly. She worked out the story in her mind as her fingers wove a web on the fretboard.

"Rivetingly romantic. With a handsome hero. Who?" "Brian" came to mind, but although she was tickled by his obvious crush, she didn't want to commit to him, especially as he hadn't spoken to her much beyond, "Please may I have the butter," and, "Passi, passi, passi some peasies, pleasies." Maybe that was one of the mocking kids. She chose "Brandon" for her unspoken story, a name that seemed strong and somewhat tall.

"Brandon should come in riding a horse. That's always romantic." "But," another internal voice said, "that's also a cliché, the handsome boy riding in." "So what?" she answered herself, "it's not like I'm telling anyone else the story." "Well," came the reply, "why not come up with something original?" "Like, he rode in on a McLaren 570S Spider?" She pondered that picture for a period. "Yes! That's a great beginning. It establishes that he's reckless, wealthy...." "And wasteful. But who cares, so long as he's handsome?" "What does he want to do?" "Woo her, obviously."

... an Indian village of maybe only a few thousand people, because this was a long time ago; I think villages now have about a gadzillion folks in India, where there are cows, cows everywhere, but not a drop of beef. So, like I said, she was no beauty. Not a leper or an untouchable, quite, she didn't crack mirrors or anything, but with no dowry, because, as I said, her dad was pretty much a scoundrel and not even very good at that.

He sent word to her, undoubtedly by elephant. They have a lot of them in India; that's their version of "neither sleet nor snow nor monsoon rains." His message was he was held captive in a huge haveli, or halvah, I forget which, and she had to come. Please bring his ransom of 5,000 rupees. Which was a joke, because Kunverba Kathy Cakes Kushi Kuni didn't have ten rupees to her name, which you'd think was long enough for at least fifty.

Anyway, as a dutiful daughter, definitely dopey if you ask me, she prepared to follow the elephant back to the haveli, but just then, her luck of course, the elephant had to musth, right at that time, and ransack a few villages the other way. By the time Kunverba Kathy Cakes Kushi Kuni thought to look for a return address, she'd missed the evening flood and had to wait until morning, which was a local flood, so it took her all day to get there, and she had to endure some long smelly time packed into a small poleboat with like half a gadzillion Indians and chickens and pigs and monkeys, and of course, any cow who wanted to get on was given the best seat although they always tipped the boat over. You'd think they'd learn there had to be limits, as my mom would say.

Her father met her at the door of the halvah. His hoofs were hobbled with thick silk cords; he could take only half-steps, so he couldn't escape. He told her he'd been caught stealing, but only so she'd have a dowry, he explained. She was guilt ridden, although my parents say guilt is a counter-productive emotion which no good Hindu feels, although, if you ask me, they certainly lay a heavy guilt trip on me almost any time I disagree or disobey. Kunverba Kathy Cakes Kushi Kuni believed her dad implicitly, like, as I said, she was a dutiful daughter, definitely dopey if you ask me. I don't know how being caught stealing galub jamun, kulfi and keer helps her dowry, huh? Do you? He said it was a big mithaike. Even the silver candlesticks he pocketed: now wouldn't it have made more sense to take matching ones if a dowry was intended? But Kunverba Kathy Cakes Kushi Kuni lapped up his excuses, showing her dopeyness, in my humble opinion.

"If only she'd been born completely dumb, rather than just reduced to a whisper," thought Alexa uncharitably, thinking of one of the Marks brothers she knew at school, who used sign language. She decided to retreat into her own story, and trust her fingers to repeat the *Itsy Bitsy* notes. She felt *Itsy Bitsy* was a fitting name for The Dubs' story, given how Wilhemina Wahnita's recital tiptoed towards the finish.

Spider Man

... screeched to a halt, tires and his whole bod smoking ["That's enough of that."], and looked at her with those bedroom brown eyes, and said, "Hey, babe, want to go for a spin?" She ["You mean, 'I'?"] looked away for a second, judged that my parents wouldn't be back for an hour or two – my mom's shopping for shoes – so I said, "Sure." And away we went.

It took me a bit to figure how to get in the Spider, but once in the seat, it basically folded around me like a trusted uncle's arms ["Not Uncle Irv, that eight-armed perv," "Or Irv Junior," "Ug, he's gross"], and I felt safe and secure, even as Brandon brought the speed up to 100 mph, still in city traffic.

"You know how much this thing costs?" I shook my head; I had no idea. Also, trying to talk at 100 mph in a convertible, over the engine noise and wind sound and hundreds of horns and homies ["homies?" "I'll fill in a better word later."] screaming; well, it's not easy, so I didn't try. Besides, at that speed, you'd eat about fifty flies.

"Well, I won't tell you. That'd be bragging. But it's a beauty, isn't it?" he bragged as he deftly crossed a quintuple yellow line to pass a garbage truck, laid rubber, popped a wheelie ["Don't know many street racing terms, do you?"], did a 180° and slid into a space only about three inches bigger than the car.

"Which side of the street, babe?" I looked. On one side was Tropical Dreams, my favorite, with the best gourmet ice cream ["Wuss of a dad only gets sherbet." "Not when Mom's not with him."]. And on the other side: Lambert's, with equally good ice cream, different flavors.

"How about both?" I replied flippantly, to show I would be too much for him to handle ["Yeah, right." "Not bad for a first date ever."]. I forgave him for shifting at least five times with my left knee, although he was far too experienced to make such a mistake.

... guilt trip, her father went home, while she agreed to stay and work off his debt at 10 rupees each day. Which would take a gadzillion years: I worked it out. She still hadn't met the Maharadjadhiraja Bahadur, the big mucky-muck nabob of the haveli, which was just as well since she needed to practice a lot to get his name down; she wouldn't want to mess up on something like that.

Alexa, slow down!

Indeed, Alexa's fingers, connected to the wrist and forearm and eventually to her brain, which was thinking about hunks and 100 mph, had morphed from a leisurely *Itsy Bitsy Spider* to a full-on tarantella, so that Wilhemina Wahnita's Indian story had background music seemingly from an Italian wedding. *Itsy Bitsy* resumed, both musically and in The Dubs' narration.

She slept well. Indeed, it was the first time Kunverba Kathy Cakes Kushi Kuni had slept on a tempertantrum bed, the best, between silk sheets, with pillowcases of cotton candy containing captured cumulus clouds. She did remark to the talking silver service for forty-eight, most of whose voices were muffled, still in the chest, of which the serving spoons were in charge and most vocal, that there was one tiny hard spot on the mattress, slightly to the left of middle about where her hip – she was a side sleeper – met the bed. And the soup and dessert spoons, dinner and butter knives, salad and bacon forks talked to each other and marveled about how just maybe Kunverba Kathy Cakes Kushi Kuni really was a Kunverba of royal blood, wouldn't that be something, because who else – especially someone who had before only slept on the floor – would notice one grain of sugar placed beneath the tempertantrum mattress, under the box springs and frame, on the floor....

The Dub's voice had become so faint that all of the listeners, except Alexa who was only half listening, strained forward to hear; it looked like a mighty wind had been blowing the human trees in the great hall for ages, and bent them, like shrubs on sea-shore cliffs or bonsai plants, towards Wilhemina Wahnita.

Only random phrases reached Alexa, sitting the farthest away, as she willed her fingers to *Itsy Bitsy* and continued spinning her own spider web. She was greatly relieved that the pudgy kid's additions were only to The Dubs' story; her's remained private.

... lives in the new wing... can't see because it's outside...
... meet at dinner... picking flowers... spider plants...
... most ginormous spider she... dressed to the eights... "Who's your tailor?" ... which eye to look at...

And that is a fair question. Have you ever known someone whose eyes don't point the same way? It's called being "wall-eyed." If a wall-eyed person is talking to you and not looking right at you with one eye, then which eye should you be looking at to be polite and show you're listening?

Well, imagine the problem for Kunverba Kathy Cakes Kushi Kuni with Maharadjadhiraja Bahadur and his eight googly eyes all pointing in different directions.

... shy for his size... discussed books and poems... listened intently to her... didn't eat her chicken tandoori... basasmi, chicken tartare, ossen and mett... gadzillion flies... slowly fearing him less... one leg brushed her arm in passing... shivered and shuddered... ran away to the new wing all eight legs aflutter...

In Tropical Dreams, I tasted most of the flavors, skipping the sorbets, and settled on Peanut Butter Chocolate Fudge in a sugar cone, two scoops, and Brandon had Vanilla Bean in a cup, the first chink in my romantic image of him. Across the street, I tasted most of the flavors, skipping the sherbets, and eventually chose Peanut Butter Chocolate Fudge, single scoop ["Now you're watching calories?" "No, dinner with the parents."] and we talked about cars, racing cars, speedways, and him, at length ["Men are pigs."]. I noticed we had been gone over an hour, and he ran to open the car door for me, waited until my legs were in, and shut the door. He jumped over me into his seat. ["Can't be done in that sportster; he'd impale himself on the windshield." "Blue balls in a blue car." "You don't even know what that means."] We raced back, reckless and thrilling, just in time. He tried to kiss me, but I turned my head. I don't know why. So Brandon bussed my cheek. Even that chaste touch made me shiver and shudder. I ran to meet my parents.

I was with him all the next day. It was summer vacation, and my days were generally free, although I had to read a few books before school reopened, but there was plenty of time. ["As always, 'last-minute Alexa.'"] He was gallant, strong – no kidding, he lifted me over a puddle with one hand around my waist; I almost fainted – and the drives with him were incredible. We went along Highway Uno at about 150 mph ["Why not a gadzillion? Jeez."] with him never pausing in his talking, and still throwing in one or two shifts with my thigh every few miles.

He was a race car driver, naturally. He invited me to watch him race the next Sunday at Haltaminute Speedway, up near Loadeye. He had to go up Friday to get ready, so we had only that day and the next, Thursday, before the race. Brandon had charisma as thick as stage make-up, and I was quickly falling under his charm. He told me he was going to dedicate the race to me ["Like a knight."] and asked for a favor. I said, "Anything within reason." He said, "No, I mean a favor, like a lock of your hair, a token of your affection." I was touched. ["Sounds like it."] I cut him a curl; he put it in his wallet.

He drove like a banshee to Big Sir, where we had a scrumptious lunch. A tejano-cajun/zydeco rock band was playing, and we danced a bit, ending up with him holding me close. I could have turned to liquid ["And then he'd have to mop the floor."]. That old song sounded in my head, telling me not to be fooled by his face, or even his embrace; proof of his love is "in his kiss."

Thank you, Alexa, that was perfect.

The Dubs had just reached the part of her story where Kunverba Kathy Cakes Kushi Kuni was overcoming her revulsion about the enormous, hideous spider Maharadjadhiraja Bahadur:

They had danced. He was all feet, of course, but if she led, it came out okay, although there was that strange feeling when six, rather than two, arms are holding you, sort of like a one-guy group grope. She had shared with him her thoughts, her dreams, her favorite poems. He had been unfailingly polite, seemed to know by heart all the poems she liked, and could play violin and drums, even turning the score's pages, all at once.

He spun her a warm cap and the softest silk stockings possible, both of which would be a blessing here now, let me tell you, and even wove a dream-catcher orb for her to hang above her bed, so she could tell him more dreams, I guess.

Kunverba Kathy Cakes Kushi Kuni was wondering about the next step. Maharadjadhiraja Bahadur always ran away when she started to express any affection for him, like he was deathly scared, so she wondered how she could tell if he loved her. You know the song; it says not to be deceived by his eyes (even if eight?); if he loves you, as my mom would murmur, "shoop, shoop, it's in his kiss."

She pondered how she could break through his reserve, his fear of her. She told the serving spoons that she had deep feelings for him but didn't know how he felt about her. Was she just his 10 rupee per day companion, a paid escort, so to speak? Or did he reciprocate her feelings?

There was a cacophony from the silverware chest as several settings tried to speak at once, although even one full formal setting violates Covid gathering rules. One setting was short a dessert spoon, who had run away with a chafing dish.

The asparagus server wised her up.

"I think he likes you. But you must remember, many female spiders kill the male when they mate. He's not sure what will happen if he kisses you."

Quelle dilemma, as my mom often says, but she messes up phrases a lot, like when Dad rushed her to the ER after she said she'd cut herself with Occam's Razor.

She decided that she would buss the spider puss that very evening.

I decided that I would kiss my fearless hunk that very evening.

Fearless? Well, not absolutely. When we were eating lunch on Thursday, at the outdoor tables of Mugs 'N Jugs Sports Bar & Grill, a common garden spider dropped on the table from an overhanging tree branch. Spider driver jumped up, grabbed his napkin, and brushed the arachnid away, all in one motion. But it wasn't to protect me; I could tell Brandon was startled, and beyond that, scared. Why, I used to talk to such spiders in my vegetable patch ["Used to?"]. I thought it was funny and endearing to see a vulnerable chink in that man who talked endlessly about his ability and courage on the track.

He talked about zero cars, t-boning, splash and dash, and other racing terms, which I only half understood, thinking more about the kiss, the kiss. Right before I was to get out of the Spider, a half block down from my house, I turned to him and closed my eyes. He kissed me! It was out of this world. ["It wasn't so great." "How could it be when you don't know what you're doing?"] I knew it then: he loved me. I was his only girl.

I was at Haltaminute early on Sunday, because First Base, one of my favorite bands, was doing the pre-flag concert. Over the sound of engines being tested, and a hundred thousand ["almost a gadzillon?"] people talking, the band played a prophetic piece ["You know the ending?" "No, but I'll have to make it work."]: *Boris the Spider*, about a "creepy, crawly" spider.

He won! Brandon won the race! He took a victory lap, and as he passed my section, I saw he was holding high my lock of hair! In his comments in the Winner's Circle, he even said, "Here's to Alexa!" although he didn't explain his meaning.

That evening, while they were dancing a tango, more like an entango, if you ask me, and he was saying, "sorry, sorry, sorry" as he stepped on her with those extra feet, and she was pushing away those probing extra arms – he seemed all hands for a guy afraid of her – "men are pigs," as my mom says – she drew him in close, and voilà, she kissed him.

Now, to make sense of what happened next, you have to understand reincarnation, which at first I thought, until Hari Vishnu, that Hindu who passed through and became my pop's guru, told me otherwise, was what you did with what was left in a can of milk after you made pudding, or whatever. But that's not even close, by a mile.

Hari Vishnu, that Hindu who passed through and became my mom's guru, explained that reincarnation was part of some Sarah, perhaps his sweetheart, since I'm sure he never met my redhaired schoolmate of that name, whom I really miss right now because she and I would sit in the corner of the school yard together making fun of the boys. No, Hari Vishnu, that Hindu who passed through, said that every living thing had a soul, but I bet he didn't know Kevin, that jerk, and that the soul was infernal, so it would return in some other body, could be human, could be an animal, could be a bug, but I'm not sure about plants, or microbes, and I sure hope I don't come back as an eel, because they gross me out big time.

So Kunverba Kathy Cakes Kushi Kuni kissed Maharadjadhiraja Bahadur right on the ol' voilà. It wasn't so great, she thought at first, but that was because he was surprised and wasn't really ready.

When Maharadjadhiraja Bahadur kissed her back, focusing all eight of his wobbly eyes on her two, and putting his infernal soul into the kiss, why, she almost passed out then and there, but he caught her with two arms, wiped her brow with another using a handkerchief he'd spun himself, and fanned her with two arms, using that last one (he needed two to stand, don't cha know) to wipe his own brow, because he was worried. Even though she was pretty much out of it, "comma toes" they call it, she knew he loved her. She was his forever girl, forget that some Sarah.

And when she came to, they looked at each other and held hands, he changing from one hand to another every few seconds, which at first she thought annoying, but then felt it was tender, especially when he said, *"In my eyes, you're everything,"* making it clear it was in each and every one of all eight googly eyes.

But, just like a male spider, he suddenly died, right there in her only two arms, like he had been sprayed with Raid or something. That's not the end, though. Stay tuned, because....

Brandon had so much work to do after the race, with his crew and all the media, that I only saw him for a few seconds. He said he was pretty busy the next week because he was racing next Sunday as well, up at the Merced Speedway, which isn't near anywhere. Brandon promised to call on me if he possibly could. I was looking forward to improving my kissing style, and feeling that tingling in my toes I'd read about.

But curse my luck, my parents on that Wednesday insisted I go with them to Salinas, to visit some relative on Dad's side. I think he wanted to see me before he died, because he looked pretty close. I was bummed out, because I was sure that Brandon would be stopping by, revving his car in front of our house so I'd know he was around. So, I was in a mood wishing instant death on my parents and Dad's stupid ancient relatives. ["Now we see the true sweet you."]

Imagine my surprise when, stopping for dinner on the way home at the Salinas Mugs 'N Jugs Sports Bar & Grill, I saw a 570S McLaren Spider, bright blue like Brandon's, parked in the lot. That's not a common car, like an Edison. My spirits were picking up; what incredible luck!

Inside, though, my luck turned to muck. At a window table, Brandon was talking to a girl just about my age, with blonde hair and a gorgeous face, though

I hate to admit it. I only saw Brandon's back, but I could recognize him probably from just a finger. It was obvious he was buttering her up like toast, just like he had done with me only about a week ago.

I quickly steered my parents to a different dining room so Brandon wouldn't see me when he left. I was seething. I knew he'd never call on me again. I was more angry and vengeful than sad, but it was close.

I brooded a bit, then settled on a plan. I begged my parents for permission to go to the race at Merced, claiming, quite truthfully, a sudden interest in auto racing. I made all the travel plans myself, taking only a small box, suntan lotion, and a big broad-brimmed hat because the sun is fierce in the summer in Merced. A quick trip through the garden for a flower for my hat and an incidental, and off I went. I was so excited!

Before the race, waiting until Brandon was occupied elsewhere, I went into his crew area. The guard and the crew recognized me and simply said, "He's not here. Don't stay long because it's a restricted area." I took one quick look and sort of patted his racecar and left. I made sure I didn't have seats near the front row, although the chance he'd recognize me during a race was low.

Karma has a way of settling accounts for race drivers. Only a few laps into the race, on a straightaway, the easiest stretch, his car lurched a few feet, but that's all it took. He clipped another car's fender and started spinning, and a third car clipped his front. No one was badly hurt; the other two damaged cars stayed in the race, and the first one hit actually came in sixth. Brandon's car was totaled, however.

Brandon was kept in the hospital overnight for observation and released. I read his interview in the paper the next morning while I was eating breakfast. "It was my fault. A spider dropped onto my lap, and I flinched."

"Yes, Mom, I'd love some more bacon."

... as a Maharadjadhiraja Bahadur, he was a big nabob even to that some Sarah, and being kissed by a Kunverba only doubled it down. He came back to life in only a few minutes, but this time as a donkey, full grown. Kunverba Kathy Cakes Kushi Kuni, as a devout Hindu, not just one passing through, knew all about reincarnation, so she bravely kissed the donkey. Low and beneath, the donkey died, and

Maharadjadhiraja Bahadur came out of the reincan as a rabbit, which she dutifully kissed.

Well, to make a long story short [there was a general cheer], she kept kissing up and down the animal kingdom, every type of fauna there was. Took a lot of guts and stamina, and Chapstick, for her lips were fairly raw and blistered by this point, to get through the cockroaches, slugs and, yuck, eels, which freak me out, big time.

She almost gave up when Maharadjadhiraja Bahadur appeared as a chocolate Labrador retriever, thinking maybe she should settle for that, even if not human, and not risk another few hundred rounds of obnoxious lip smacking with who knows what gross animal, and some Sarah knows what she'd end up with, anyway. And really, think about it, what could be better than an affectionate, happy dog who thinks you're heaven reincarnation, and who goes out and brings back chocolate every day?

But she persevered, which I think is Sandscrape for kept on trucking. She was pretty relieved about kissing him in his various forms when he reached the cattle species, despite those huge tongues, because she knew, holy cow! a holy steer was pretty far up on some Sarah's list.

And in the end, there he stood: an Indian king: dark, tall, handsome and with a devilish grin in his eyes, but only two. As a Kunverba, Kathy Cakes Kushi Kuni took her place as his queen, or Maharani, or whatever. But on the side, she really got into selling lip gloss, under the trade name, don't cha know, of "Queen Kunverba Kathy Cakes Kushi Kuni's Kosmic Kandy Kissing Kreme," a portion of the proceeds from those sales provisioning poor Hari Vishnu, the Hindu who passed through, my parents' guru. And they lived happily ever after.

The entire crowd trooped into the kitchen, where Mom was serving ice cream.

Alexa finished her private story with the thought, "Perfect. Revenge is a dish best served cold."

The cat was nowhere to be seen.

The Cycle of Life

Notwithstanding an almost unanimous petition, signed, sealed and delivered, Dad refused to forever prohibit Wilhemina Wahnita, the Whisperer's daughter, aka "The Dubs," from telling another story. He insisted that story time was open to all, and any problem would be dealt with as it arose ["or it apetunia," said The Dubs' mother].

Princess' mail parent maintained his futile morning habit. Nothing delivered, of course. In the early morning rain, a driverless wain tumbled down the hill, occasionally shuddering to a stop before the wind caught the underside and started the cart rolling again. Dad morosely wondered whether it was the farmer, or the horse, whose death had liberated the vehicle. The Evil Cloud, he concluded, played no favorites.

When the children progressed from fantastic farts to water balloon battles, Mom rolled her eyes at the Rabbi, who declared his balloon supply was completely exhausted. The children safeguarded their remaining hoard, sufficient, should aquatic hostilities resume, for Mutually Assured Drenching.

A quarantine routine had been informally established. Punishment detale continued, to Mom's great relief. The Rabbi locked doors to the largest common rooms and opened them later to a sparkling chamber.

There were desultory attempts at education, although yours truly hasn't yet repeated a grade. The Rabbi continued to worry, while the Catholics worried their worry beads; and everyone watched for new messages in the dark skies.

Whoever was responsible for the miasma was still nursing a

grudge. Yesterday the whine was: *Choose Me Last, Huh?* There was extended discussion as to who it might be that was getting even with the entire world, but it was all speculation. Advertisements over the past week were from Fred's Express (*Big or Wee Delivery*), Righteous Hostelry (*No Sin In Our Inn*), and Busting Beverly's Bronco Breaking (*Tame As A Dame*), which last brought a smile to Dad and a convulsive laughing fit to Uncle Irv.

Mom continued her joy in cooking, and the adult guests were looking chubbier from the combination of gourmet meals and a steadfast disinclination to exercise or undertake tasks. Dad made the obligatory comment about fish and guests, but Mom cooed, "Suck it up." Princess was being tutored by the Rabbi, who was helping her build an electron microscope.

At story time, with tastes of crêpes suzette still on their tongues, the company assembled, and Uncle Irv insisted it was his turn. All the Aunts objected, but Dad noted the open floor rule applied to the Perv as well as The Dubs, so with muted protests and under their breath mutinous mutterings, the assembly awaited Uncle Irv's story. One Aunt stationed herself on his left, another on his right, ready to dual elbow him.

The Cycle of Life

This is a story my dad would have told me, if he knew it. It's about the great ghetto detective Schlagelock Homeys.

Those of you who recognize that name have probably read some of his earlier exploits, when his forte was locating missing persons. Perhaps my favorite account is *The Speckled Band*, in which, by pure power of wage deduction, he located an up-and-coming Harlem rap trio which had been missing for three weeks, figuring out that they were holed up in a motel in midtown Manhattan, mending from the measles.

And Doc Watson II, his famous chronicler ["chroniculi, chronicula" slipped out before the Whisperer could stop herself], narrated Schlagelock Homeys' solving *The Adventure of the Five Pips.* Those Kansas City parents were at wits' end with worry, woefully wondering the whereabouts of their teenagers, good kids each of them, all in the church choir. Following clues no clearer than crumbs, Schlagelock Homeys brought them home one glad-ass night to relieved relatives; the kids had just signed a contract in Detroit with Motown Records.

My personal favorite is the tale of *The Red Headed League.* Remember? The owners of that elite club (not a lot of red headed guys in the ghetto!) hired Schlagelock Homeys to find the only initiate who didn't renew after the free initial membership expired. The surprise ending: it wasn't a renegade ranga redophobe at all, but an orangutan!

The Adventure of the Dancing Men arose in a barbershop in Bedford-Sty, in Brooklyn. All the neighborhood remarked that the barbers and the customers danced oddly around the salon. Schlagelock Homeys figured out that there was a short circuit in the floor and the underfloor radiant heating had gone haywire, thus saving the soles of a heap of homeboys.

In my own college town, far from here, a Saluki used to live on the porch of a retired actor specializing in *Othello,* known affectionately as The Moor. When the dog went missing for over a week, The Moor hired Schlagelock Homeys. The sleuth tracked da dog down to a brownstone where several three-on-three jockstraps [the Aunts lifted, then put down their arms] were taking good care of him. The dog had wandered onto the court without a collar. Schlagelock Homeys returned him to The Moor's. Doc wrote it up as *The Hound of the Basketballs.*

This caper ["Get to it!" by general consensus], probably because it involved a white person who had the connections to squelch the publicity, is not included in any of the usual collections.

The prospective client contacted Schlagelock Homeys and arranged to meet at the chic new automat restaurant, the Lowdown, so no one would see Homeys near the client's home.

When Schlagelock got there, the client said, "Let's talk while we eat."

There were no cooks or waiters, or even order takers, to be seen. "Choose your entree by number," the client explained, "then a letter for the side dish. Then decide whether to have it baked by a chef the normal way, or cooked using the robotic convection microwave, which some people prefer. Finally, let them know if it's for eating here – say 'Inside' – or to go. I advise getting it to go because the portions are large, and that way you get a take-home box at the outset. I'm going to have the chicken cacciatore, number 21, with a stir fry vegetable medley, choice B, on the side."

There wasn't any soul food on the menu, so Schlagelock Homeys sagely and thymely said, "I'll have what you're having." He listened as the person in front of them waited for the loudspeaker to say, "Address me," and the man voiced his selections. Then his client, at "Address me," intoned: "two; 21; B; baker; street." They ate outside while the client revealed his problem.

"My name is Firestone Flint ["Hot, hot," breathed Alexa]. 'Flint' is the family name, of course, and describes my father wonderfully: a man quick to spark and flame. The 'Firestone,' my parents' joke, comes from when I was conceived. [Two elbows at the ready.] There were some goings-on between them in the backseat of a car, and one was impatient with the protection, and threw it out the rear window onto the street. *Ufff.* [Two elbows into his sides.]

What'd I say?

Anyhow, Firestone Flint explained his problem to Schlagelock Homeys.

"My father, Skin Flint, ..."

"He's a cheapskate?"

"No, that's his name, but at times it might describe him. Skin Flint, as I was saying, on my son's third birthday, gave him a strange gift: a broken tricycle. You could still ride it, but its front wheel was crooked, and the back wheels didn't track the same path, so it wasn't easy. One pedal faced up, the other down, and the handlebars had a sudden bend. So, you might think my father was cheap.

"But that wasn't the reason.

"I had an older brother, Gunnerson, or 'Gunflint' as they called him. Well, he wasn't really 'older,' as much as prior. I was hardly home from the hospital after my birth when he was killed in a tragic accident. No one saw it. All they heard was a musical repertoire from a semi's – a tractor-trailer's – horns, followed by an ear-blasting *cayuga* – it must have been when the driver saw he couldn't avoid Gunflint – and they ran out and saw the mangled tricycle against a tree and Gunflint with a severe laceration. Skin Flint took him to the Emergency Room, where they took his temperature orally, anally, digitally, in his ear, on his chest and on his forehead, but no matter how much they took, his fever got higher, and he died the next day. I never really knew him, of course, but I must have heard that story a hundred times. The cowardly truck driver fled the scene.

"The bike that Skin Flint gave to my son, Flint, for his third birthday was that very same tricycle. For reasons I can't explain, of all the gifts Flint Flint got that day – and we went all out for him – that was his favorite. He rode it a few feet, which was an accomplishment, tried the little metal ding-a-ling bell, but it wouldn't tinkle. Flint wrapped his arms around the handlebars, then, with almost a dazed look, he hugged my father on his leg, saying, 'Thank you so much. It's hyperfantastic,' a word all the rage in his pre-school.

"Now, my dad, Skin Flint, used to come over frequently to visit me and Flint Flint; he also liked my wife, Mrs. Flint. [One elbow, from the Aunt who saw his wink.]

"Doesn't she have her own name?" queried Schlagelock Homeys.

"Yes, I told you. 'Misses Flint.' Queer names run in her

family on that theme. Her big brother, whose name started it, is 'Bullseye'; another brother is 'Rydon.' Misses' younger sister is 'Magpie.' The teenager's name, it takes a bit of thinking to fit it in, is 'Miley.'

"A few days after Flint Flint's birthday, dad visited, and when I got home, Skin Flint was in a towering rage, waiting out front to yell at me.

"'What the devil are you up to, Firestone? You knew the importance of that tricycle to me. Gunflint's last moments of happiness were spent on that bike. It was, to me, the embodiment of his innocent soul. I gave it to Flint Flint to show I felt he was carrying on Gunflint's life, perhaps as a reincarnation. It was my way of saying I was willing to love him as I loved Gunflint. I had hardened my heart after his death.'"

"'Duh, tell me,'" I muttered to myself.

"'So, I give him, as the most important gift ever, that memento, that treasure, that embodied love and elegy, and what do you do? You go out and buy him a new tricycle just to show me up. What did you do with Gunflint's bike? Throw it in the trash?' He stalked away and hasn't talked to me since.

"Now the odd thing is, I didn't buy a new tricycle, and I have no idea how Flint got one. I asked Flint Flint, but he said it was Grandpa's gift. He rode around the block on the sidewalk, screaming in happiness, but saying some things he must have picked up from the Missus Misses, because I don't use that language in his presence or the presence of his presents."

"So, you want me to find Skin Flint's treasured junk tricycle? I don't do dumpster diving."

"No, no. Hear me out. That's not all. Flint Flint continued to love that tricycle, riding it blasphemously every day, and sometimes kissing it before he came into dinner. He named it 'Precious.' He wouldn't let anyone else ride it, and even seemed to push his friends away if they tried to touch it or ring the bell.

"And his behavior at home changed. He had been a gentle, well-behaved kid, pretty much skipped the 'terrible twos.' Now, he's made up for lost time. His favorite word is 'no.' And where he had been a kid who happily ate whatever was on his plate for dinner, now he was refusing boiled spinach and turning up his nose at Brussels sprouts. Misses Flint was heartbroken when he insulted her broccoli, kale, arugula and creamed corn casserole."

"How bizarre," Schlagelock Homes said drily, having finished the water they had gotten at the drink counter. "But I'm not a child psychologist, either."

"I'm not done. Two days ago, Sunday, we were all at home watching the bird feeder, when out in front, there was about ten seconds of a tractor-trailer's melody horn – about half of *Dixie* – followed by a loud *cayuga* and only a split-second later, a loud crash. We ran out; I carried Flint Flint.

"A car was resting against a fire hydrant, which was sending water 30 feet into the air. The tricycle was about twenty feet farther up the street.

"The driver stumbled out of the car. He seemed dazed, but didn't have any obvious serious injuries. When he saw Flint Flint, he heaved a relieved sigh, as if the world's greatest worry had been lifted from him.

"'Oh, I'm so glad he's safe. That tricycle, I don't know. I thought I was driving carefully, but I didn't see it until I was almost on top of it. I was glancing at the sidewalk as I passed your house because I love to see Flint Flint playing, and when I looked back, I saw that trike. I didn't even have time to know if Flint Flint was on it. I jerked the wheel to the right to try to miss it. I must of scared the bejeezus out of a trucker by my driving, because I heard truck horns before and after the crash.' But, Schlagelock, there was no truck in sight.

"Well," continued Firestone Flint, "I'm really glad Flint Flint wasn't on the bike because, like Mrs. Misses' brother, it got hit Raydon. Flint Flint would have been crushed. As it was, the new tricycle had almost become just like the one Gunflint had ridden that dad had given Flint, with crooked wheels, busted pedals and bent handlebars."

"So now you're working on number three three-wheeler?"

"Well, I thought I'd have to replace the tricycle, given how Flint Flint had taken to riding. I threw the wreck into the garage, and planned to go to DoorMart the next weekend and buy a replacement. But when I came home on Wednesday, there was Flint Flint riding around on a spanking new trike. When I asked him where he got it, he looked at me like I was crazy and said, 'Grandpa's gift.'"

Suddenly, Schlagelock Homeys threw off his indifference – it was sunny and hot – and became excited. "I'll take the case." They discussed per diems and expenses, because that's how detectives get paid.

Ooff. What did I say? [Well, nothing, but one of the Aunties had remembered some remark of his from the day before.]

"I'll come over to your house later," Schlagelock Homeys said. "I want to meet Flint Flint myself, and see the scene."

"And you don't want to miss the Mrs. Misses, either," said Firestone, "not by a mile," he said with a smile, as if it was an old joke.

Now, if you want to hear what that *Dixie* truck horn melody (not the stir fry medley) sounded like, go to: https://www.carid.com/wolo/oe-replacement-horn-mpn-336.html?singleid=76489970 and click on the "sounds" icon on the left, and then click on the third box down on the rightmost column. If I were you, I'd click on all the boxes before returning to the story.

For the cayuga, the closest I can find (but not even faintly as authentic as the pudgy kid's) is http://soundbible.com/724-Tugboat-Whistle.html

But you should also go and play around at https://retired.sounddogs. com/results.asp?Type=1&CategoryID=1055&Su bcategoryID=19.]

Schlagelock Homeys went home to his crib (he had insecurity issues), and roused Watson II.

"Trouble's afoot. Grab your glock and we're off."

Now, don't get me wrong, Schlagelock Homeys had no death wish, and didn't plan to go into an exclusive white neighborhood with his black Boswell carrying a firearm. The "glock" was a lucky rabbit's foot, which Watson II always carried. They both had insecurity issues.

They sped to Firestone Flint's house in Schlagelock's fifteen-year-old Morris Minor Key Wound. What with city traffic and no working fourth gear, they kept waving to a couple riding bicycles.

Arriving at the entrance to the gated neighborhood, they were relieved that the guard hardly looked up from his newspaper while waving through a decrepit white van, oil smoke fouling the air, with two slovenly white dudes that Watson II, a veteran of Vietnam, Afghanistan, Iraq and several parent-teacher conferences at public schools, wouldn't have wanted to meet in a dark alley.

When the guard saw Schlagelock Homeys and Doc Watson II, though, he was all professional. "Papers?" Fingerprints. Blood samples. Iris scans. Voice recognition. Faces faxed to the national database. Tattoo analysis. Teeth X-ray.

"Okay, you can go through. Firestone said to expect you."

Firestone Flint, Flint Flint and Mrs. Misses Flint lived in a very, very, very fine house, with two cats in the yard. Schlagelock rang the doorbell, and a cute little urchin with blond hair, and an unfortunate resemblance to Firestone Flint, opened the door, took a look at the two black gentlemen, and shouted, "Dad, more of them pesky Jehovah's Witnesses got past the guard." Firestone quickly appeared and invited them in, although there was a momentary pause while he discarded the notion of asking them to come around back, just so the neighbors wouldn't see them, of course.

Schlagelock Homeys had visually scouted the front yard

and surroundings, noticing a fire hydrant with yellow "Police-Do Not Cross" tape wrapped around it, sadly dribbling water which slowly ran past Firestone Flint's house. Doc Watson II scouted the inside of the house, reconnoitering where insurgents might be hiding.

"Nice kid," Schlagelock Homeys said drily, asking for a glass of water.

"Thanks," said Firestone Flint. "But let me show you something weird."

"Your furniture?" asked Doc Watson II, remarking on a lavender color scheme for the sofas, chairs, love seats and beanbags.

"No, look here. Flint Flint, come to daddy." Flint Flint came, fast enough to bowl daddy over. Firestone pointed to Flint Flint's chin. There were several whiskers.

"My beard's coming in," Flint Flint said proudly. ["Maybe he'll grow up into a hairytic," pondered Princess.]

"That doesn't run in the family," noted Firestone.

"Worse than I expected," muttered Schlagelock Homeys. ["About what I expected," muttered the Whisperer.]

"And another almost accident, only an hour or so ago, with the same pattern. First, a tractor-trailer horn medley – *Silent Night* – then a *cayuga*, a screech of brakes, but this time, no one hurt, just a car horn blasting angrily all the way down the block and some loud cursing, 'Keep your damn junk off....'"

He introduced the two men to his wife, who said prettily, after meeting Doc Watson II, "Who's on first?"

"My wife's in a tizzy," explained Firestone Flint.

Well, if she was, I'd like to send all the girls to a tizzy. She was a gorgeous woman, with a face, like Steve Jobs said, that would launch a thousand shifts. A body pleasant to look at, with ta tas, *ooofffs.*

Whatever else Uncle Irv, the Perv, meant to say about the Mrs. Misses was lost as his kidneys were pummeled by the Aunties' elbows. When he could stand again, he continued.

Schlagelock Homeys asked to see the tricycle. It seemed ordinary, although also sparkling new and brightly polished. "Flint Flint takes good care of it," he said, somewhat between an assertion and a question.

"No, he rides it, hugs it and kisses it, and protects it from other kids, but that's it. No cleaning or polishing; he's only three."

Schlagelock Homeys tried to ring the bell, with a background of growling from either Flint Flint or the tricycle. No ringing. He borrowed a screwdriver, and over the same objections, he took off the bell, unscrewed the top, and examined the interior. Nothing looked strange. It should tinkle-ring just fine. But it made no sound. He left the bell hanging by its hinges on the handlebar, without fastening it back again.

"Well, that's enough for me," Schlagelock Homeys said as he prepared to leave.

"One more strange occurrence," said Firestone Flint. "A man came by, introduced himself, claiming he was French, and offered me three hundred dollars for the tricycle, saying it was the model he'd been searching for for four years for his kid. I told him I couldn't sell at any price because it was a family gift. He left me his card." He handed a business card to Schlagelock. It read:

Dr. Maury Halt, from France.
This is the tricycle I've been searching for for four years. If
you change your mind, think of me.

"Let me know if you hear from him again," said Schlagelock Homeys, and he and Doc Watson II left.

"What did you notice?" Schlagelock asked Doc Watson II.

"That Mrs. Misses didn't miss by much, unlike her sister. She's a looker, with those dreamy eyes, and a figure...." *ooff, ooff, ooff.*

Later, back at the crib, Schlagelock Homeys took out his castanets, took a few tokes of medicinal marijuana ("Gout, doctor, bad gout."), and took account of the situation, coming up with sixteen.

"You know I hate that addiction of yours," said Doc Watson II, referring ambiguously to Schlagelock's use of castanets, his pot, or his reveries. Doc went to play video games, uninterruptible for a few hours.

Finally, Schlagelock Homeys stood up, stretched, and asked, "What's up, Doc?"

"I can't make heads or tails of it, myself," Doc Watson II admitted, referring to level 7.

Schlagelock Homeys continued, thinking allowed, aloud:

"Tractor-trailer horns, but no trucks. One dead, one injured, and a near miss; each time the only witness is a three-wheeler.

"Did you notice the maker of the ride? 'Carrion Bros.' hmmm.

"And a piece of twisted metal that soon looks pristine. On the way out, I looked again at the trike. Do you know what? The bell was reattached, although the tyke was with us all the time.

"And that business card. What of that? I'm missing some clue. How can you be looking four years for a tricycle for your kid?" He blew a smoke ring from the toke he'd taken a few hours ago and held all the while.

"I've got it! What a fool I was! I hope we're not too late. There's terrible danger. Watson, the glock, we must leave immediately."

Doc Watson II, on the verge of wiping out three hundred fanatical ISIS jehad warriors, reluctantly came along. Pushing the Morris Minor Key Wound to its limit, they made the twelve miles to Firestone Flint's house in under an hour. They passed a school with monkey bars in the playground: "Elementary, my dear Watson." Another hour at the gate, and they were there.

On the way, Schlagelock Homeys discussed his reasoning.

"I've always said that once you eliminate the impossible, whatever remains, no matter how improbable, must be the truth. But that got me nowhere in this case. The only rational explanation for all this is the irrational. We must focus on the impossible.

"That card. Did you notice? There was no address, no telephone number, no email. Firestone Flint couldn't contact Dr. Maury Halt. That means that Maury must be spying all the time on the Flints.

"I'm still stumped by who he is. French, so what?

"Oh, damn. Again, what a fool I was! French? 'Halt?' Doc, what's French for 'halt'?"

Doc Watson II had picked up a lot of French in Vietnam, as well as many Vietnamese; he wasn't too particular.

"'Arretez,'" he replied.

"Put it together," Schlagelock Homeys almost screamed. "Dr. Maury Arretez!"

It was his diabolical nemesis; which means skilled arch-enemy.

"Yes, Dr. Maury Arretez in person," said Dr. Maury Arretez, in person, now at the driver's side of the Morris Minor Key Wound. He was holding a Glock, quite steadily.

"Get out and don't do anything heroic. I'm always a step or two ahead of you. I'm going to take control of that diabolical chopper, and all my enemies will vanish without anyone connecting it to me."

"Well, feel free to walk a step or two ahead of me rather than behind," Doc Watson II offered as he was marched, with the gun at his rear, into the Flints' home. There, Mrs. Misses Flint, Firestone Flint and Flint Flint were found bound, sitting on the couch. Dr. Maury Arretez had taken the time to tie their hands into the three wise monkeys' positions.

As they passed the threshold, Doc Watson II faked a

stumble, bending down. Schlagelock Homeys fell over him, and Doc Watson used that movement to rise quickly and heave Schlagelock backwards at Dr. Maury Arretez, a technique he'd learned in Iraq, there involving expendable prisoners.

Three shots were heard. Dr. Maury Arretez's gun went flying, and later was discovered in a nest, brooding a murder of cartridges. Only two shells had been fired from that weapon.

Schlagelock, up on his feet in an instant, tackled Dr. Maury Arretez, who didn't put up a lot of resistance because he was bleeding from his side. They stumbled into the living room, where Doc Watson II gloated. "Maury, you've met your match." Maury replied, "Doc, it's only a scratch."

Schlagelock Homeys and Doc Watson II soon untied the Flints and had them call the police, who arrived at the complex in a few minutes, and were at the house within an hour after an especially rigorous inspection at the gate. Tucking in their shirts, the two black police officers recognized Schlagelock Homeys and gave him and Doc Watson II high fives. "Hey, I knew your father, Doc Watson First."

Dr. Maury Halt, aka Dr. Maury Arretez, with many other akas, was taken into custody, as there were about a gadzillion warrants out for his arrest. No one told the police the back story.

Schlagelock Homeys personally took possession of the tricycle, which clearly evidenced that a bullet had passed through its seat. He tried the bell: no tinkle. He picked up the toy, and smashed it down again and again, and talked to it like one would to a hardened criminal.

"I can do that until I tire, and then let Doc Watson II take over, and he won't tire until all three of your tires are flattened. So do it!"

Schlagelock Homeys pushed the ringer, and this time, *cayuga* rang out, followed by a horn medley of *John Brown's Body* and another *cayuga*.

They found a bullet hole in their car, a Morris Minor Key Wound wound.

Doc Watson II took hold of the tricycle, and didn't let go of it until they reached the junkyard, where it was compressed by the huge hydraulic presses into a ball no bigger than a bumbo. It was shipped, with tons of other scrap metal, to a foundry in Wuhan Province, China, where it was melted down. That foundry is near a virus research laboratory.

They returned to their crib. Soon, Schlagelock Homeys was blowing smoke rings, and Doc Watson II was losing steadily at level 6, cursing, "My luck is rotten." He took out his lucky rabbit's foot to rub it, but the glock was all busted, as badly as if it had fired a shot.

There was general silence in the room, less in appreciation of the story and more in hopeful anticipation of an announcement of a snack from Mom. She said, "Come to the kitchen for...," but in the rush, nobody heard what, certain it would be scrumptious.

MakeBet

Alexa, fresh off her imaginary conquest, first kiss and icy revenge, was feeling very mature and confident, which frightened poor Brian even more. She was sitting alone on a bench in the enclosed courtyard, about the only safe place to be outside the house, reading and eating a snack, while Brian scrounged miserably around the edges in the perimeter halls.

Mom was busy, as always, as the host. She was bringing a tray of Shirley Temples to the children with a tray of donut holes and sliced apples, and a tray of Harvey Wallbangers to the adults, together with a platter of cheeses and assorted crackers. Don't ask me how she managed.

Lance was still racing around the house, black and blue, with patches over each eye. As he passi, passi, passed Brian, who was lounging in a doorway to the courtyard working up the courage to speak to Alexa, Mom swayed to avoid the blind Lance; her hip somehow hit Brian with enough force to send him sprawling into the courtyard, almost to Alexa's feet. We'll leave them there, alone, for a while.

Dad gave Mom a quizzical look, to question why she was going beyond being a good host to being an exemplary host, despite the lack of appreciation from the guests. Mom smiled sweetly at him and said, "Suck it up."

The Dubs was still resting after straining her voice while whispering her spider story; much of the rest of the company was working out the cricks in their necks earned while straining to hear. Uncle Irv, accepting a sordid cracker, was making passes at the Aunts whose popeye-elbow prints were still on his kidneys.

There was a temporary lull in the sky messages, which bothered Princess and the Rabbi, for they were hoping for some lightning to power the electron microscope prototype. When not occupied with invention, Princess still danced and sang at every chance she had, which were many, even though she continued to be helpful to Mom and Dad, yesterday diverting the local river to run through the stables for a quick clean. She and the Rabbi had almost completed a Conviction Oven, which is called for in all the recipes for half-baked ideas.

Inspired by the Spiderman Indian story, after dinner, Mom served mithai, rather than dessert, including galub jamun, kulfi and keer. Uttering parting compliments in Sandscrape, the guests found their way to the great hall, anticipating a delectable evening of stories.

Another of Dad's brothers, the one who had finished the pirate story, was the nodee. His name was John, which was unfortunate because, with Uncle Ax, the two had often been teased at school as "Jack-Ax."

MakeBet

All right children, you'll like this story. It has witches, ghostly beings, people doing things they regret, and even a moral, although I'm not sure what it is.

For you adults, you all know this story from high school English class, so bear with me. I don't have the poetry of Shakaspear, the author, but I'll get the essentials across.

This is a story about a bettor man. Not better than I am, though, I hope.

In Scotland there lived a man who bet on everything. If you said, "Nice day," he might bet you five shillings that it would rain by noon. If you were eating cereal, he might bet six bits that the word "quaint" was floating on top, or that you'd hear "pop" before "crackle" or "snap." Anything! He was addicted to betting like that, not that he went to casinos, or played poker, or even Old Maid. In alleys, though, he played craps, which was pairadice to him.

We'll call him MakeBet, since his Scottish name can't be pronounced without putting your entire hand in your mouth and holding onto the little thing – the uvula – hanging down in the back.

He won some bets; he lost some. Since he couldn't stop himself from betting, he often didn't think too deeply about what he was betting on, so he made some risky, and some downright stupid bets.

He once met a clever man who bested him easily. That man bet him five bucks that MakeBet couldn't resist betting for 10 minutes. After the bet was accepted, the man took out a coin and kept flipping it. MakeBet, after only one or two tosses, grew fidgety; he really wanted to bet on what would come next: heads or tails. By four tosses, MakeBet wanted to bet so badly he was visibly sweating.

It got worse. By the twentieth toss, still under one minute, MakeBet had his own hand in his mouth, holding tight to his uvula so he could talk to himself using his full name – like your mom does when you are bad – to try to restrain himself.

You know how you feel when you really have to pee? And someone's in the bathroom; the toilet flushed it seemed like ten minutes ago, and the faucet already ran, so the person's hands must be washed – BUT they still don't open the door and let you in. And you're hopping from foot to foot. Well, that's about how MakeBet felt about not being able to bet on the coin flips.

At the two-minute mark, MakeBet took out a fiver and laid it on the table to concede. Then with great relief, he shouted, "I bet you ten simoleons the next throw is tails!" He lost that bet also, but felt much better. That was his life: he felt better as a bettor.

People tried to help him, rather than be abetters to a bettor, but all interventions failed. He just kept betting.

On this morning, MakeBet was having a pre-golf breakfast with his major client, Ian Duncan, at the club they both belonged to. The waiter, who knew them, had said "Wylcome" to each by name and wished them a "guid mornin." MakeBet gave his order – Tattie Scone, Lorne Sausage and White Pudding – and reminded the waiter to wash his hand, since he had put it into his mouth to say MakeBet's Scottish name.

As the waiter left, Ian Duncan called out, "Twenty seconds!" MakeBet immediately bet 15 guilders that the waiter wouldn't wash for the full twenty, so they listened outside the men's room. Makebet won.

Now, a scone is a type of pastry, but rather than light and airy like a croissant, it's basically a stone; I think it's one of the few ways you can ruin pastry. It sits on the plate like a stone, chews like a stone, and then wallows in your stomach like a stone.

Lorne Sausage is a square sausage; please don't ask what it's made from. White Pudding is not like a dessert pudding; it's a horrible concoction of suet or fat, oatmeal or barley, breadcrumbs, and in some cases pork and pork liver, stuffed into a sausage casing. In most other locales, outside Scotland, instead of a sausage casing, the ingredients are put into a bird feeder and kept away from humans.

None of that, though, is as bad as haggis. Haggis is the Scots' national dish, which is a sad commentary on Scotland's cuisine. It's called a pudding, to mislead you, but it's a thick scum of sheep's pluck (the heart, liver, and lungs), mixed with onion and oatmeal, suet and spices, wetted with stock. To make it more appetizing, it's commonly cooked in the sheep's stomach. Yum, no?

Well, Ian Duncan was the head of a company that made prepared meals for Scottish customers called Duncan GoNuts, and MakeBet was his supplier for haggis. Me, I'd be sheepish to admit that, but MakeBet made a good living out of sheep's innards. He wasn't as wealthy as Duncan by a long shot, though.

And a long shot was only one of many things they bet on. Ian liked to bet, as well.

"Bet your drive won't land on the fairway, 35 zlotys."

"100 clams I win this hole." And the like.

They played in a foursome. The third player was a poor golfer, a duffer. Since he, too, was Scottish, they called him MacDuff. He was Ian Duncan's junior business partner. The fourth was just a worker from Duncan's commercial kitchen, who'd won a "Worker of the Month" award, and his prize was this golf game and dinner. He'd been briefly introduced at the start of the game by MacDuff, and then wholly ignored by MakeBet and Duncan. His name was Banquet.

Now, Duncan and MakeBet weren't above a little bit of cheating now and then, like a swift kick of a ball to a better position, or a claim of, "I found it on the edge of the pond" for a ball that had, to everyone's eyes, caused a very pretty splash dead in the center of the hazard. MacDuff was a straight arrow – not his shots, they went everywhere, usually to a place impossible to hit out of – who always played by the rules. Banquet? Who knows? Nobody paid any attention to him.

MakeBet's luck that day was out of this world: phenomenal, weird, too good to be true, however you want to say it. He bet 60 dinar that Duncan's tee – the little wooden spike one puts the ball on to hit with a driver – a 'play club' they call it there – would end up standing. Now, that's a 1,000-1 bet, at best.

Duncan swung, and the tee went up in the air about ten feet, and came down right on Banquet's nose, and stuck in, so Banquet was cross-eyed looking at it.

"Pay up," said MakeBet to Duncan, ignoring Banquet's plight, although they let him keep the tee.

On the ninth hole, a calico cat ran across the fairway. MakeBet immediately said, "I bet 70 drachmas it's a male."

Shaking his head in disbelief at so foolish a bet, MacDuff said, "That's a wager I'll take." They sent Banquet to catch the cat and made him inspect it. Heavily scratched, Banquet confirmed, "It's a tom."

Another example. MakeBet, on the sixteenth green, bet 75 pesos that Duncan would miss an eight-foot putt. But Duncan hit the ball just right, and it looked to all that it would go straight into the hole.

And just then, a big worm pushed itself up, right in its path. But it still seemed the ball would roll over the worm and drop in. At the last moment, a skylark came down and snatched the worm, and the air from its wing slowed the ball, so it came to the edge of the cup and stopped, teetering on the rim.

They walked across the green and stood at the hole. It looked still like the ball might fall in. MakeBet counted out the required 10 seconds slowly – 10, 9, 8, 7, 6, 5, 4, 3, 2, 1.

"I win!" he said. Even that tiny breath of air caused the ball to teeter over the edge and finally drop in.

Too much good luck can go to your head. On the eighteenth fairway, MakeBet, fairly giddy with his good fortune, heard himself bet his business against Duncan's, that Duncan's racehorse *Sleep Tight* wouldn't win the race a week from Saturday.

MacDuff said, "Don't make that bet," and to Duncan, "Don't take that bet." Duncan, however, told Makebet he wouldn't hold him to the bet – it was a sucker's bet, he laughed, because *Sleep Tight* would win by five lengths – unless MakeBet confirmed it at dinner.

They all shook hands and said, "Guidbye bye bye for noo," until they'd meet at MakeBet's for dinner that evening.

MakeBet stopped on the way home at Katz's Delicatessen for a bite. Right before he went in, the cloudless day suddenly turned dark and threatening.

There was no one inside at first, but then he saw three employees hunched over a soup kettle, chanting weirdly:

Double, double toil and trouble;
Fire burn and caldron bubble.
Fillet of a fenny snake,
In the caldron boil and bake;
Eye of newt and toe of frog,
Wool of bat and tongue of dog,
Adder's fork and blind-worm's sting,
Lizard's leg and howlet's wing,
For a charm of powerful trouble,
Like a hell-broth boil and bubble.

Double, double toil and trouble;
Fire burn and caldron bubble.
Cool it with a baboon's blood,
Then the charm is firm and good.

Although it may sound exactly like the recipe, they weren't making Scottish White Pudding but cooking up some magic spell.

On closer look by MakeBet, they weren't waiters or cooks at all. The forms hunched over were hideous witches, ugly as can be!

One had a face of corned beef, red and bloody and dripping, with smears across his face of Thousand Islands dressing, and sauerkraut for his eyebrows and scraggly beard. His ears were dark rye bread. The face of the next was pastrami, chopped thick and falling off in plops; his ears were bagels with lox schmear for a mustache. The last visage was liverwurst, a gray pasty face; this witch had to keep putting her chin back in place. Her ears were ciabatta halves. All three had huge dill pickles for noses. ["Oh, please describe them again," the pudgy kid implored dreamily, interrupting his bubbling cauldron noises.]

The first witch – for that's what they were, the wurst kind, sandwitches – introduced himself as "Reuben." He said,

"By the sucking of my thumb, something wicked this way comes."

"What fearsome apparitions are you?" MakeBet demanded of them.

"We see the future. Your bet is safe. You can't lose your bet, we think. But beware MacDuff; beware the insane fife." And they interrupted themselves to chant again:

Double, double, toil and trouble;
Fire burn and cauldron bubble.

"You have a chance to make the bet of your life! You can be king of Duncan GoNuts! No man of German-born can win your wager! You can't lose that bet until great Birnan Woods to high Duns Inane Hill shall come."

With an end chorus, the sandwitches disappeared:

Double, double, toil and trouble;
Fire burn and cauldron bubble.
Cool it with a baboon's blood,
Then the charm is firm and good.

Suddenly, MakeBet found himself in a crowded deli, shouting at the top of his lungs, "What are you saying?"

"Your order, sir. What would you like to eat?"

"Haggis, to go, please," MakeBet managed to stammer out.

He considered the witches' prophecies, and even more, their warnings. First, beware MacDuff's insane fife; no problem, he'd already spent dreary hours listening to MacDuff play jazz piccolo: sounded like a cat with a belly ache.

"No man of German-born." Ian Duncan's mom, whom he had met several times, was as German as the measles. Her given names were "Hilde Gertrude." Before her marriage, her family name was Einstein, which is German for "one stone," although she was easily 12 stone, and German for every ounce of it. So, MakeBet counseled himself; no worry there.

And the last, well, MakeBet's fine house was on Duns Inane Hill; Birnan Woods was the other side of the county, easily twenty miles away. MakeBet felt himself pretty safe, if taking advice from weird chanting sandwitches makes sense to you. ["Yes, yes," said the pudgy kid.]

Despite all these favorable omens, MakeBet wasn't totally sure. When he got home, he asked his wife, Luck B.A. Lady MakeBet, what she thought of the wager. She was all in favor.

"Screw your courage to the sticking place," she said. "Don't be a wuss." As she was dressing for dinner, she reminded him a life insurance agent was coming the next day.

MakeBet went to his balcony, where he had a practice mat for golf. It wasn't really too smart to hit from there now because his shots had to clear the driveway, where dinner guests were parking their cars. Lost in thought, MakeBet hit a terrible shot; it sliced into where several vehicles were parked. He heard a loud groan, and he belatedly shouted, "Fore," also holding up four fingers in case the injured person was deaf.

The dinner was a disaster for MakeBet, although Lady MakeBet thought it went well. Thinking to hide from whomever he hurt, MakeBet grabbed one of Lady MakeBet's wigs, a long blonde one she wore for costume balls, and put it in his pocket. When he arrived at the table, a bit late, everyone else was seated, and in his place at the head of the table was sitting Banquet, now looking like he rose from the dead.

There was a lump oozing blood on his forehead, bigger than the golf ball that hit him, and trickles of dried blood beneath his nose and ears. Mud and sticks and leaves were all over Banquet's hair and shirt; he must have been knocked into the dirt when the golf ball hit. He was moaning a ghostly and miserable, "Ooooooohhhhh. Ooooooohhhh."

In this table of heads of companies, captains of industry, former debutantes and members of the most exclusive and secret societies at their prestigious universities – so hush-hush that many of them didn't know they were initiates – nobody paid any attention to Banquet, a mere kitchen employee; it seemed only MakeBet took notice of him. MakeBet put on the wig and motioned at Banquet to get out of his seat.

"There's blood on your face," MakeBet in wig said.

"Ooooooh, ooooooh," said the ghost, dripping a little blood onto MakeBet's napkin. The ghostly pale Banquet looked blearily around the table; there were no open seats. He staggered out of the room, followed by the dog. MakeBet then took off his blonde wig and joked, "I am a man again."

Soon, after the appetizers and soup but before the entree, Banquet came staggering and swaying back in, eyes vacant, clearly unaware of where he was or what he was doing. Again, only MakeBet took any notice of him.

"Never shake your gory locks at me," he reprimanded poor Banquet, who only moaned, "Ooooooh. Ooooooooh." Concerned a bit, at last, about Banquet's well-being, MakeBet tried to get his attention, but also maintain his social distance. [The Moraga contingent nodded in understanding.]

"See there! Behold! Look! Lo! How say you? Why, what care I? If thou can nod, speak too." Not getting an answer, MakeBet lost his patience.

Away and quit my sight! Let the earth hide thee!
Thy bones are marrowless, thy blood is cold;
Thou hast no speculation in those eyes
Which thou dost glare with!

Banquet staggered out of the room, and some kind servant put him into his car, in which he was found a few hours later about a mile away, totally unconscious. He did not win Employee of the Month ever again.

After dinner and coffee and brandy, MacDuff offered to play his fife, but Lady MakeBet, seeing a look of abject terror on MakeBet's face, and no flute fan herself, said it was time for the guests to leave: she needed her beauty sleep. As Ian Duncan and MacDuff passed him on the way out, MakeBet said, "The wager is on; my company against yours!"

There was still more than a week to the race, but MakeBet, buoyed by the witches' saying he couldn't lose, and still feeling that the proverbial Lady Luck was closer to him than even the eponymous Lady MakeBet, was busy in his head making plans for what he would do after he won the bet and ran both companies.

At about three the next afternoon, the hefty life insurance agent, Bernie, arrived. Bernie was a big bore, like most salespeople, and talked monotonously of death and taxes. MakeBet realized that life insurance was betting against himself, with no winning unless he lost. He told Bernie he'd think about it and went back to dreaming. Bernie left his card and some pamphlets, and said he'd call after the next week.

"After next week," MakeBet luxuriated, "I'll be on top of the world."

Lady MakeBet asked him how the meeting went, saying her cousin needed some life insurance. MakeBet said the guy seemed honest and handed her his card. Before she took it, he read Bernie's formal name: Birnan Woods.

"Aaaagh," he exclaimed, frightened at losing one of his protections: great Birnan Woods had come to high Duns Inane Hill. MakeBet sweated a bit, but was comforted because he still couldn't lose to a man born of a German. He felt Hilde Gertrude Einstein would protect him from harm, all 175 Teutonic pounds of her.

It was only a few days later when, reading all he could about Duncan GoNuts in preparation for his takeover, he came across a passage about Ian's background. Ian Duncan's father's first wife, a former London socialite, had visited Paris soon after Ian's birth. She liked it there, where nobody served haggis or White or Red Pudding, and where pastries were light and fluffy and sometimes filled with creme, not sheep's innards. She refused to return to Scotland. They divorced and only a year later Ian's father married Hilde Gertrude Einstein.

"Funny story," MakeBet thought at first, then it hit him: Duncan was not of German-born! Hilde Gertrude was his stepmother!

How many times have your parents told you not to listen to witches? Not to take luncheon meats too seriously?

Each of the sandwitches' outlandish conditions had come to pass. There was nothing enchanted now in MakeBet's favor. He might lose the bet.

His risk in the wager, of course, was his own company. He'd be ruined if he lost. And *Sleep Tight* really was a swift racehorse, likely to beat the local competition easily.

Luck B.A. Lady MakeBet – she of the "Don't be a wuss" – was not happy hearing this. She came up with a diabolical and dastardly plan.

There is a certain drug that makes horses a little loopy, a trifle confused and sleepy, enough so the horse won't run its hardest, but the lethargy is not enough to be obvious. It is made from some Scottish herbs mixed with a measure of Kauai dirt, the type that is used to die shirts a dark brownish red, and which simply does not wash out. Lady MakeBet promised to give that drug to *Sleep Tight* that very night, so it would have mostly worn off by the race, leaving just enough effect to slow down *Sleep Tight*.

She traveled to the racetrack stables, and put on the same blonde wig Makebet had used at the dinner. She poured drops of the mixture onto a few sugar cubes, spilling a bit on her hands. She charmed the stable boys into letting her into the stables and gave all the horses some sugar cubes, but only *Sleep Tight* got the doctored ones. She went home without being recognized.

That is to say, without the grooms recognizing her. She

certainly knew she had done wrong. Her conscience propelled her into a massive guilt trip. She kept trying to clean the stains left on her hand from her spill of the potion, feeling as if her soul wouldn't be clean if her hands remained dirty. She muttered aloud to herself as she washed her hands, again and again – that Kauai red dirt was persistent – and shook and wrung them dry, and washed again.

"Yet here's a spot.
"Out, damned spot! Out, I say!" (Their dog, a Dalmatian, sped from the room, tail between his legs.)
"What, will these hands ne'er be clean?
"Wash your hands, put on your nightgown; look not so pale.
To bed, to bed!"

To bed, perhaps, but not to sleep. She was feeling too guilty. She tossed and turned and kept remembering that they were cheating, that she had given the drug – called "Mud Red" – to the horse. A voice in her head kept saying:

Sleep no more!
MakeBet has Mud Red Sleep – the innocent Sleep,
MakeBet shall sleep no more.

Needless to say, with guilty consciences and no sleep, the MakeBets were a wreck by the time they arrived at the race.

They shared a front row box with Duncan and MacDuff. While Duncan was away at the concession stand getting some disgusting Scottish food, MacDuff sat next to MakeBet. The gun starting the race sounded. *Sleep Tight* didn't break out of the gate as swiftly as usual. Soon, the horses were rounding the first turn. MacDuff started speaking.

"You know, I told you not to make that bet. And I told Duncan not to take it."

The horses rounded the second turn: one full lap to go.

Sleep Tight was in the middle of the pack but had open space in front of him.

"I'm sorry you went ahead and made the bet. I hope you didn't take it seriously."

"No," lied MakeBet, who had turned his world upside down because of it, and hadn't slept for over 90 hours. He didn't care much what MacDuff thought.

The horses were coming into the last turn. *Sleep Tight* had separated himself from the pack and was gaining a bit on the two horses in front of him. MakeBet shushed MacDuff to watch. *Sleep Tight* moved up, and coming into the last straight-away, towards the finish line, *Sleep Tight* caught up with the second-place horse, and his nose was at the tail of the first.

MacDuff had gone on speaking, but MakeBet wasn't listening. *Sleep Tight* kept inching forward, and at the finish line, he couldn't tell which horse had won.

The loudspeakers announced: "It is a photo finish. It will take a few minutes to review the films and declare the winner."

"... I bought out Ian about six months ago; he is kept on as the namesake of the company, but I own it all. He couldn't make the bet."

The children talked the next few days about the story, play acting the parts with the sandwitches, the ghostly Banquet at the banquet, and crazy Lady MakeBet washing and wringing her

hands and yelling at her dog. The adults were disappointed, because this was exactly as they had learned the tale in their GradeSaver summaries.

Mom appeared when the Perv was done, and said, "Come get some Cranachan for a snack." Unlike probably anything else they serve in Scotland, Cranachan is a wonderful sweet. Served in a custard glass, it's a combination of fresh raspberries, whipped cream, honey and toasted oats.

All were happy for a while. The cat was nowhere to be seen.

's No Right

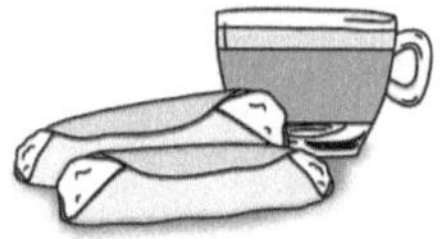

The adult relatives were worried about what was happening in their own homes, fiefdoms, farms and businesses, and the strain was showing. Many declared bravely that they would face the deadly cloud and return home, but their departure was invariably to be in a few days, a moving target. They decided, individually but beyond a majority, reaching a consensus almost to unanimity, that if you're going to worry, then do it right, embrace it fully, and push aside minor distractions like helping Mom or Dad with the chores of caring for a horde.

The children, of all ages, provided the most help. The Moraga middle-schoolers, to annoy their parents, decided to pitch in, and they even set up a schedule for cleaning rooms, chopping wood, emptying slop buckets, and feeding the animals; it took a while for them to take the next step of selecting people to implement the schedule.

The younger children, including Princess, pestered Mom and Dad, asking for small tasks, then usually started wrestling each other over who asked first, but occasionally did heed Mom or Dad and bring a bucket to the compost, or fetch some pears from the pantry. Trips to the compost pile were treasured by the younger crowd as an opportunity to stock up on worms: you never know when a worm will come in handy, do you?

One of the kids returned, saying he had heard the birds talking. "They were laughing so hard they could hardly fly. One swallow repeated the punch line: 'Then he threw away the apple, with the worm still in it.'" The birds all found that hilarious since the worm is the best part.

The pudgy kid was talking to the other kids much more, with less retreat into sound effects, although it was often hard to hear her; with his never-ending attack on a snack, she often, literally, swallowed his words.

"Is there anything I can chew?" she asked, but I think he meant, "anything I can *do.*"

She was talking about his school, the Scientific, Patriotic And Moral Monte Bank Method, Moraga. It was a private school, but very beautiful. Far from their fathers' oft-told experiences of miles to walk to school, and even longer back [Reader: here's a chance to ad-lib!], SPAM students walked down a beautiful vale to the school. Laid out like an omega "Ω" of 18 one-story classrooms, it had acres of fields for running around, playing soccer or bat and ball games, an area for launching small rockets, and a score of playground structures like orangutan bars, twirling machines, fanny slides, and a sand pit (with no cats!).

At the end of the school day, the buildings and grounds, located over deep underground hot springs, had risen greatly, so the students could walk downhill again, either home or to their parents in the drop-off and pick-up driveway.

Dad listened with interest to the pudgy kid's description of his school. The teachers were all young, fun, and clueless about teaching. Being uncredentialed, having no plans to teach forever, they were unlikely to unionize, which was the pivotal criterion for hiring. The pay was great considering their lack of education or experience; it sure beat taking orders at Aaaargby's, the local pirate-themed burger joint.

There was a waiting list of families striving to become sufficiently wealthy to afford the tuition. Most slots simply cost a small annual fortune, but about 20% were auctioned off at even higher prices. The Monte Bank Method pinkiebook explained, "If you can't make a fortune off rich kids, you're not really trying."

"What about students whose families can't afford that tuition?" asked Dad.

"They're scholar shipped," replied the pudgy kid.

"Oh, do you mean 'scholarships,' when the fee is reduced, or a grant is given?"

"What? No," said the pudgy kid after swallowing. "They are shipped out to other schools. We don't want to be around that element, do we?" A resounding "no" according to the pinkiebook, and the Moraga parents.

Schools catering to such wealthy clients usually make the students either hate the school deeply, or love it, depending on the parents' own relationship with their child. This school was firmly in the "love it" set.

Lunches were fun, generally of pizza, hamburgers, Spaghettios, macaroni and cheese, peanut butter and jellyfish, or fudge or chocolate cake as the entrée. Offerings of salads, vegetables and fruits were available right across from the compost station, so students could get two stars: one for choosing nutritious foods; then another by turning around quickly and scraping the plate into the compost tumblers. Video labs, computerized learning games, frequent recesses, and a variety of after-school activities guaranteed a happy student body, individually and collectively.

In order to maintain high standings and promote healthy franchises, all instruction was geared to standardized tests. The occasional homework was in the form of choosing "A" or "B" or "C," making the students comfortable with assessment examinations. Classroom sessions went over prior tests and familiarized the children with the gloss of the subjects. *"There Is No 'Dope' in 'Rote,'"* was one of the pinkiebook's chapters.

Absolutely no effort was wasted on having the students understand or appreciate the topics studied. Peer reviewed scientific studies had shown that elementary school children often could talk coherently about subjects they didn't understand (their ignorance could be revealed by asking them unusual questions), which performance came sufficiently close to knowledge for the Monte Bank Method.

Tutored to the tests, aided by filched questions and the slowest possible clocks at standardized examinations ("relativistic effects," explained the pinkiebook), and enrolling only students who were never distracted by homelessness, financial insecurity or hunger, with highly engaged parents, the SPAM school was in the academic top 2%-3% of all elementary schools, despite its alumni's inability to reason or to grasp nuances.

A small portion of each student's tuition was set aside in a fund used to bribe admissions officers of exclusive private high schools to select the SPAM graduates; thus, impressive statistics of prestigious placements, as well as return on investment, were maintained. "To err is human; to highly IRR is divine," quoth the pinkiebook.

The Rabbi and Princess took a different approach to learning. The children liked the "Two-Patch" game of running around blind, so the Rabbi used it to teach the workings of heat and Brownian motion.

"I'm a hot molecule," shouted Lance as he bounced off walls and furniture.

Alexa and Brian met in the courtyard, almost at her feet courage to ask, "Who "What are you planni someday to be a teach sweated through but glad to talk to each oth

Dad wanted to see how the pudgy kid would do if put on the spot, so mentioning her many "goody points" earned for helping out in the kitchen, gave him the nod. Due to a private taco Tuesday, she had a lot of flatulence, which is a fancy word for farts, so the crowd was alternately lured forward to try to understand him through her mouthfuls of food, and then blasted back by his gas, a gently swaying tableau.

"Whoa! That one caught me. Give me a sec until my eyes stop watering. Now, where's my chips? Okay, ready now.

"You know, when you bake something, you pre-beat the oven."

"Pre-heat?" Dad offered.

"Are you sure? Okay. Pre-heat the oven, and often in advance heat the eggs until fluffy…"

"That one is 'beat.' 'Beat the eggs,'" said Dad.

"Make up your mind. Anyways, I haven't prepared anything, so I'll have to make it from scratching. I'll tell this fairy tale I learned at school."

With difficulty arising from telling the story while simultaneously trying to provide sound effects, compounded by frequent tapas, the pudgy kid launched, or lunched, or lurched forward.

'S No Right

Once, there was a princess, a little woman, who was called "'S No Right." She got that nickname because, as a toddler and young child, when people told stories of evil, of bad men or women, or cruelty – all the ways she knew people shouldn't act – she would stamp her foot and proclaim, "'S no right!"

Since her stepmother and stepsisters were avid evil supporters and malefactors, they thought her insufferable, teased her constantly, and treated her almost as badly as they treated the servants, or the commoners who came to the palace seeking justice and were instead humiliated. Those shunned by her steps were the people with whom 'S No Right liked to hang out.

As the step relatives' bad luck would have it, 'S No Right grew up into a beautiful little woman. Beyond greedy and mean, the step relatives – "Call Me 'Mom'" and two "Don't Bother To Talk To Mes – were vain, which made them immediately jealous and envious of 'S No Right. Give them credit: they were good at evil; all their emotions were sick.

Call Me Mom would break mirrors, inviting, by the stupidstition, seven years of bad luck. No, she wasn't quite ugly enough that her face could do it alone; maybe on her best day, a bad hare day when she couldn't get her ears under control, she could break a small compact's mirror or her reflection in a spoon. Breaking mirrors was sort of her glock: her bad luck charm.

Now, bluntly, this is a stupid habit. Mirrors break into many, many small pieces. Broken glass can cut you easily and is almost invisible.

Call Me Mom would take half the afternoon wailing about the "rotten broken glass" and nastily ordering the castle servants to clean it up, but hurrying them along, not letting them clean the glass up slowly and carefully. She made the work rushed and crazy, so that Call Me Mom could always find a sliver of glass (usually she'd been hiding it under her shoe, while she nagged them) and then insult the servants for a bad job. Bad job? Working for her was the world's worst.

If the fabled mirror on her wall could talk, it wouldn't have gotten a word in edgewise between Call Me Mom's tirades. It certainly wasn't likely to talk when in little pieces. Anyway, no mirror would believe Call Me Mom was fair, to say nothing of fairest in the land. So, that's all make-believe.

But it was unmistakable that 'S No Right was more beautiful than either of the Don't Bother to Talk to Mes, maybe fairer than both together, if you can add good or bad looks; if you can, Call Me Mom really didn't add much, despite her own warped opinion of herself.

'S No Right's beauty, her goodness, and her love for others, offended Call Me Mom deeply.

"She's learned nothing from us!" she wailed.

So, princess or no princess, with her dad gone and Call Me Mom the reigning monarch, 'S No Right was thrown out of the castle, out into a hurricane wind and driving snow and sleet. It was July, but those evil steps did have a flair for the dramatic.

"Let her deal with the real world, penniless and in rags," chortled Call Me Mom. "Chortling" is as close to laughing as an evil hag can get. She had a nasty way of wringing her hands, too, as if she sweated slime.

"And," she announced to the guards, "there's a reward and promotion for the man who brings me her liver." Unfortunately for Call Me Mom, the guards had a union, which insisted the reward was due if they proved simply that 'S No Right had died.

Meantime, 'S No Right wandered, lost, tired and hungry, into the forest. Many a bird, sensing her goodness, told her which way to go. But 'S No Right didn't understand Bird at all. So, if you choose to learn a second language, you might well consider Bird. You'll meet a lot more birds than Greeks or Australians.

The birds kept at it anyway. They joked, "She's so stupid, she'd throw away the worm from an apple." At last they steered her towards a path of broken pottery leading to a cottage in a small clearing, with smoke rising from its chimney.

Well, not all the smoke. When she opened the door, 'S No Right could hardly see in. Leaving the door open, she went across the dirt floor to the fireplace and turned the damper lever so the smoke would go out up the chimney, creating smoke signals that thoroughly confused the natives trying to read them a valley or two over. Slowly, the cabin's air cleared.

There were seven – 'S No Right was on the second finger of the second hand in her count – small men. Dwarves. Even smaller than 'S No Right, who was petite herself. And they were black from chimney soot.

Whoa! That must have been from yesterday's tacos; yes, definitely. I can tell by the garlic aroma.

The dwarves were coughing and choking, just like you there [pointing to an eight-year-old downwind]. They were looking at her all in a daze. Where did this glowing, beautiful small woman, this bundle of energy, of knowledge, come from? While answering their questions, 'S No Right grabbed one after the other, took him to the pump, and gave him a thorough washing, maybe the first one in months. When they were all clean, or as much as one laving could accomplish, she said, "How about some dinner?"

They pointed to a small table with seven chairs and seven plates. All that was on the plates was soot. [Here, a long, sad sigh from the storyteller.]

"That won't do at all, will it? Show me the pantry." And the oldest-looking dwarf, whom she decided to call "Doc" because she saw him ruffling the hair of the others, saying, "Wassup wid choo?" showed her a big room beneath the cottage.

It was filled with glass jars of pears, pairs of jars of artichoke hearts, jars of pared apples, carrots, salamis hanging from the ceiling, big pottery urns of flour, sugar, molasses, coffee, herbal teas, couscous, wild and white rice, chocolate, virgin olive oil, slutty olive oil...

This list went on for quite a while, as the pudgy kid was lost in a reverie, saying and tasting each food or spice reverently, and giving a little firecracker fart with each new one. Most of the guests drifted off for a bit to refill their glasses, and some friends helped revive the downed downwind child. The pudgy kid was just finishing the list when they returned.

... lobster, shrimp, fresh oysters, thyme, oregano, and little colored sprinkles for the tops of cakes and lots more. [Another long sigh, with great sadness at summarizing.]

"You have all this, and you eat soot?" 'S No Right asked.

"Oh, no," said a sleepy-looking dwarf. "Of course not. We add water. It's soot soup. We get great delivery service from Fred's Express and order from Amazing, but no one is a good cook." He ducked, fearing an angry blow from the dwarf – the one with the pink spiky mohawk – who did the cooking and was proud of his soot soup. "Look around back, too," he advised, "for the chickens, turkeys, rabbits and pigs."

'S No Right gave orders as if born to it, which, as a princess, she was. A few dwarves were set to washing the floor. To her surprise, she discovered it was made of stone, not dirt. She assigned another dwarf to washing the windows, which, covered with soot, she hadn't noticed before. 'S No Right gave up trying to learn the dwarves' names after her tongue knotted trying to pronounce Doc's given name; they were okay with her nicknames.

'S No Right herself began making dinner. Not having any time to plan or prepare, it was a minimal effort, and she was apologetic. For starters, a Caesar salad with dressing made tableside ("No anchovies for me," said one dwarf, but 'S No Right said, "Try it, you'll like it." And he did.) [A pause here while the pudgy kid mentally finished her salad, pushing a large breadcrumb around the plate to soak up the dressing, with appropriate chewing, moist, plate rattling and swallowing sounds.]

Then two appetizers: beets Siciliana and baked clams. As soon as those plates were cleared, 'S No Right brought out a pasta dish: freshly made linguini with a red bolognese sauce. The entree was pork chops with peppers [here a happy fart, if a fart can be happy]. 'S No Right dismissed the compliments, saying, "I had to rush. There should be fresh bread and cake, but...."

She stopped because Doc brought in a newly made chair, a little bigger than theirs, and put it at the head of the table, just in time for the zuppa Inglese. "So sweet of you," she said, and kissed Doc's head, and he bowed, his hat sweeping the newly swept floor.

'S No Right had learned a lot hanging out in the royal kitchen!

After dinner, she helped the dwarves with the dishes — now washing them, not just throwing them out the door. It was difficult for her to walk, because one or two dwarves were always hanging onto her legs, kissing them. One dwarf, whom she named "Uncle Irv," made a pass at her: "What brings a beautiful girl like you to a dump like this?" But she took him by his ears and put him in his place, which was the second chair on her left.

She discovered that Doc and the boys had also built her a bed, caught some cumulus clouds for a pillow, and gathered some ocean wave foam for a mattress. They all slept well, although some of the dwarves' farts caught fire near the hearth and rolled around the cottage like ball lightning for a few seconds.

"Have to get some medicinal herbs," she thought as she fell asleep, soon dreaming of a McLaren 570S Spider: heck, you can dream about anything you want.

After breakfast – an improvised meal of Belgian waffles drowned in butter and maple syrup, sunny side up eggs and hash browns – she kept one of the dwarves home with her to help with laundry, and the others went off whistling to the mine.

"What do you mine?" she asked before they left. They looked at each other blankly. "Well, do you mine gold? Silver? Coal?"

"Oh, no," said the one with sleepy eyes, "It's the Cumberland Mine. We just hang out there and talk story. We're all trust fund kids, except Silly there (pointing to the dwarf attached to her leg) who receives Silly Dwarf Insurance because, well, she's 'silly.'"

"Silly's a she?"

"Yes, but she don't know it. She's silly." [The red-headed boy's father, pulling his son, left the room.]

After washing all the sheets, and sewing some curtains, and pre-soaking the dwarves' clothing, 'S No Right made herself some practical clothes, planted an acre or two of tulips, cleared the gutters, repaired a few shingles on the roof, and kneaded the dough for the bread loaves and dinner rolls. She'd skipped lunch because of the heavy dinner the night before, and was almost tempted when an ugly hag – looking like her two step sisters rolled into one – knocked on the door.

"I've brought this nice apple for you," said one of the two heads. Then she held up the apple: it was brown, not red, and as 'S No Right looked, a worm poked its two heads out of a hole and then withdrew them, arguing with each other.

"Sure," 'S No Right said, taking the apple, "C'mon in for a bite, you look famished." Once the hag passed her, she threw the apple into the woods, causing all the birds to laugh, "I told you so! She threw the apple out with the worm, the best part, still inside!" ["How's dem apples?" asked the Whisperer.]

'S No Right put out a plate of leftovers from the night before for the hag, and checked on the dough; it was rising just fine. When she turned back, the hag was crying, although eating through her tears.

"Nobody's ever been kind to me while I've been like this." When she reached the zuppa Inglese, the head not being fed fell right off, hit the floor, and turned into a pumpkin coach, just the right size for mice. And the hag slowly changed into another dwarf!

"Hey, where you been?" asked Silly of the revealed dwarf.

"Got tired of being teased by y'all about my twomer."

'S No Right made a mental note to create daily vitamins for the dwarves; they had really weird reactions to bad diets.

"You mean there were eight dwarves?" she asked. Neither dwarf answered, since neither could count to eight. 'S No Right decided to call the new dwarf "Silky," because she liked the sibilant harmony of "Silly and Silky."

Back at the castle, Call Me Mom was still hoping for news of 'S No Right's death. Non-union guards – scabs – would bring her livers until the kitchen staff ran out of new recipes, but Call Me Mom knew they weren't human livers, having tasted quite a few in her younger, wild witch days.

The union guards had no interest in finding 'S No Right, as they remembered her always standing up for them in disputes ("'S no right you fire him for falling asleep: you put a spell on him.") and bringing them snacks from the kitchen when they were on duty, although eating while on the job – or otherwise – was strictly forbidden.

Call Me Mom decided she would have to finish the homicidal task herself. She sat down giddily to plot evil for 'S No Right.

Back at the cottage, the other dwarves came home near sunset, and cheerfully went to work helping fetch the water, put on the tablecloth, set out the places with proper silverware and napkins meticulously placed at her direction, and generally showed bustle and hustle with muscle. Their cheerful whistling almost gave 'S No Right a headache, and occasioned another mental note: teach them a few new tunes; you can take only so much of *It's A Small World.*

Dinner at 8 4 9 was a success. The smell of warm bread filled the house like, well, actually nothing smells as good as freshly baked bread. Then some eggplant torrisi, with fresh clams on a bed of ice (lemon and hot sauce to flavor) for those who indulged. A simple green salad of butter crunch lettuce, heirloom tomatoes, English cucumbers, a hint of arugula and scintilla of kale with a surprise of fresh blueberries in a balsamic vinaigrette.

The spaghetti with meatballs seemed too easy, until one bit into the meatballs: one's tongue lolled through Italy from the Alps to Sicily. A well-pounded veal Marsala had sides of snow peas in lemon-dill sauce and potatoes Louie. [Lance thoughtfully wiped the drool from the pudgy kid's chin so she could continue.] A cheese and fruit plate came with the cappuccino, and the tiramisu was served while there was still coffee to enjoy it with.

"Tomorrow," 'S No Right promised, "I'll get imaginative

and maybe cook French."

Sounds of happy burps (burps certainly can be happy) filled the cottage, and with an improved diet, the midnight farting was subdued.

But evil was making its way to the cottage from the castle. The Queen, ol' Call Me Mom, could smell 'S No Right's unique vinaigrette from miles away, and sniffed her twisted path to the cottage. The next morning, she waited until the dwarves went to the Cumberland Mine, the melody of *It's A Small World* making sugar pimples break out on her face, which was okay with her. Only Silly and Silky and 'S No Right were left, although actually, 'S No Right and Silky were righties.

"There's a Mormon at the door," said Silly when Call Me Mom knocked. 'S No Right took a look, saw the evil Queen, and murmured to herself, "I knew this would come to pass." But, being so good and forgiving, she let Call Me Mom in and offered her breakfast; there was still some batter left from the chocolate pancakes, with a few strips of bacon and half a dozen sausages.

"I can make an omelet," she offered.

But that evil harridan just grabbed 'S No Right's throat and choked her into unconsciousness. Silly and Silky tried to pull her off, and finally got her away. It was the wholesome smell of fresh bread that did the evil queen in. She shriveled into a raisin, which a bird quickly ate.

But nothing could rouse 'S No Right.

The dwarves put her into her bed, where she fairly glowed with health but would not awaken. She lived but hardly breathed, lost in a senseless slumber. "Comma toes," The Dubs calls it.

They continued to keep the house clean, wanting to please 'S No Right when she woke, even dwarf Uncle Irv, but their dinners returned to soot soup, now with a pinch of oregano and a basil leaf. They sent out word through the grapevine, and some duck doctors came, but their remedies did no good.

Finally, an old knight came through, back from the Cruelsides. He had fought at Jerusalem, taking back the city from the hairytics who had made all the infidels into out-fidels. His army forced the hairytics to leave. The great city was now empty: it was a glorious victory. With him were two of his generals, Big Ben Cartwong and his older brother, Bigger Ben Cartwong.

The old knight recognized his daughter immediately. "Oh, what has become of little It's OK?" It had been a long time, and his memory wasn't what it had been. He kissed her tenderly [a few "oofs" from Uncle Irv], and her eyebrows stirred, although that may have been because of the cobwebs.

Bigger Ben bent over her and kissed her; he couldn't resist, her beauty was so great. 'S No Right's father was watching closely. Only a flutter and a twitch of an ear.

Big Ben, who wasn't very big – the Cartwongs had hoped to spark some growth in a diminutive family by bestowing huge-sounding first names – said, "That's all stupidstitious nonsense." He pulled 'S No Right out of her bed, bent her over his knees, and pounded her back until he dislodged the crumb of bread crust caught in her throat.

'S No Right took a few deep breaths, looked around blearily, wobbled over to her father, and collapsed into his arms, saying only, "Daddy, Daddy, Daddy."

All turned out well. The King resumed his throne, appointing 'S No Right as his successor, even if she married Big Ben, which eventually she did. They had a passel of small children, but did not live happily ever after, only to about age 110. She never did learn Bird, which was for the best, for many of our flying friends' feathertales were of the silly princess who threw away the worms with the apple.

The two stepsisters were married off, but they turned into frogs when kissed at the altar, right after saying, "I do." They hopped away and were never seen again.

As for the dwarves, 'S No Right sent over some of the castle servants to the cottage, where they were treated with great respect even if they didn't quite have 'S No Right's touch with zabaione. Several of them married dwarves; one took over the Cumberland Mine. Silly and Silky came to live in the castle, never wanting to be separated from 'S No Right.

And 'S No Right, when she became queen, ruled with justice and fairness, treating the commoners with respect, taxing the rich even more than the poor.

The story ends, as told in my school: "'S No Right just never learned how the 1% should behave."

I'm famished!

Luckily, Mom had prepared some cannoli with espresso for the adults and hot chocolate for the children. Alexa had both.

The cat was nowhere to be seen.

Spaghetti Western

Censored

"We Know Best So You Can Rest"

The Rabbi's sack, its usual range of bump snorts, growls and other supplemented lately by sad, lonely crying of the cat, who, despite being Graceful And Handsome Four Footed God Who Rules Over Humans And Mice, was pretty scared and wanted to get out.

Censored

"We Know Best So You Can Rest"

The cat may not have been seen, but he certainly was heard. No one talked about the cat, having become the elephant in the room, but everyone knew exactly where he was. No one, though, was doing anything about it. The Rabbi just muttered and cast despairing glances at his sack.

The cat was in the bag. That was clear. The Rabbi had half-heartedly put his hand in, saying, "Here, kitty, kitty, kitty," but he knew that wasn't going to work. He'd have to go in after him.

No one else seemed willing to say anything, although, with all the yelps and yowls and howling like the moon was full and all cats everywhere were in heat, it was obvious to all exactly where the cat was. Who is going....

Hello, I'm your new narrator. The prior narrator had a sudden ailment, perhaps a hairball, and I have to take over. To introduce myself, I'll tell the next story.

Spaghetti Western

Over yonder a long way, there is a country called "Italy." It is shaped like a boot, somewhat, and stuck onto the bottom of Europe. A lot of Italians live in Italy because, well, it's their country. Sort of like a lot of United States of Americans live in the USA, a lot of Dutch call The Netherlands their home, Hoosiers hail from Indiana, and Jews from Jerusalem.

Whenever anyone's roots are in Italy, or whose parents and grandparents and so on – ancestors, they call them all together – came from Italy, they call themselves "Italian," and they're proud of it. Although, if you think about it, it isn't really much of an achievement, simply to be born where you were born. But it's very important to some people.

The hero of this story was Italian, as you might have guessed. And, he was proud of it, even though he had been kicked out of Italy. Right: kicked by the boot, so to speak. Not literally: Italy the country didn't rear back against Albania, and then rock forward to hit his behind and kick him out. But close, in practical terms.

One day, a stocky man dressed handsomely in a bandoliera – what we call a bandolier, that belt across each shoulder filled with cartridges for a firearm – came into the bank where our hero worked and advised, politely but to the point, that he leave the town, the province, say, the entire country, ASAP – Italian for pretty darn quick.

Why? I am certain you have guessed. Our hero was madly in love with the local Mafia capo's daughter. The Mafia? It's a social group in Italy, sort of like the Deep State in the US, or the Stazi in East Germany, or the Empire in Star Wars. Not necessarily friendly. Not people you mess with.

I'd like to say true love won out, and our hero valiantly

resisted the Mafia, stayed, and eventually won her father's respect and blessing, and her hand in marriage (for she was *strafiga*), and that they married and had kids who ate Italian ices all summer and they lived.... Well, but I can't. His *amore*, his love, decided she loved him more alive, even if away, than she loved him staying close to her, in the local *cimitero*. He acquiesced.

So you could say he left on his own. Or, you could say his heart was broken when he was forced to leave, his ears ringing with Juliet's farewell crying, "I'll love you always. *Ciao! Arrivederci. Ti amo! Cappuccino!* Coming, *Pope.*"

It was a time, not the best of times, not the worst of times, but a time when wandering souls, or groups, just tended to head to the American West, like the whole world was a big slippery hill and the West was at the bottom. They would come from Europe, land on the East Coast, but momentum, I guess, kept pushing them until they crossed the Mississippi, went past that huge arch in St. Louis, and entered the American West.

Yes, sad to say, our hero, whose name, of course, was "Marco, Polo," became that legendary figure of yore, of lore: a cowboy.

Sad? Well, in Italy he had been a respected middle manager of a bank, in charge of commercial loans to keep farms thriving until the harvest came in and businesses active until their ships came in. Had his shoes shined daily; wore a suit: he was a very fancy dandy about town.

But now, he was just a cowpoke, which is not cubes of raw beef served in Hawaii. It's a fellow whose job is to cater to cattle. Dressed in jeans, Stetson hat, and boots with spurs, he was far from a dandy now, although he used soft spurs to be gentle with his horse. And he was far from Juliet.

He rode solo, or alone, however you like to say it. Most cowboys spent their time at one ranch – or "brand" as they called it, after how they mark the cattle that belong to the ranch. But like a dogie, which in the West was not a small dog, but an orphan calf, or cattle kid; although a "kid" is actually a young goat ["Irv, junior," was whispered] – but you get the idea, and that orphan yearling or so runs away and becomes a "maverick." Just the same way, some cowboys, too, didn't like to linger with the same crowd, but liked to drift from place to place. That was Marco, Polo.

He spent some time with the Lazy R ranch. That brand was an "R" on its side: it's called "lazy" 'cause it's like the "R" is lying down. The Lazy R brand ran cattle in Cripple Creek, Colorado, on one side of a vast mountain. Some people, especially drunkards, really liked that place, Cripple Creek, says The Band.

Can you have a Lazy R? Well, you can have a spelling B, or, I guess, a pirate's growled R, a long look-C or even a gentleman's C, an inventive I-D, a G-force or two, a J-walk, an H-bomb; people catch some Zs. And what about M N Ms? Well, I guess an alphabet letter can do most anything, so there can be a Lazy R. And there was.

Now cattle like to face into the wind; don't ask me why; ask a heifer, or a bull, or a cow, or a steer, but skip me. It's hard enough trying to figure out what a love-struck Italian cowboy who likes to be alone thinks, without trying to think like a cow. Eating grass, and vomiting it up so it can be chewed again – which is what cows do mostly – seems gross to me, so I can't even begin to think like a cow.

A funny thing about the Lazy R: because the ranch was on one side of the mountain, and the wind always came the same way, the cattle invariably faced the same way, into the wind. With the slope, the cattle that did best and were bred for the next generation were those who had legs longer on one side than the other. They just kept the longer legs downhill. Soon, the entire herd was composed of cattle which, for the Lazy R, had their right legs (if you were looking the same way they were, or the legs on your left side if you were looking at them straight on, sort of catching a bull's eye), much longer than on their left side.

The slope was so steep that when a Lazy R head lay down, which cows do now and then, she had to stick out the longer leg to keep from rolling. The calves – baby cattle, to "calve" means to give birth – hadn't learned that yet, and in calving season, there was always the sound of frightened baby calves rolling with the tumbleweed down the mountain, and the mooooing of mothers going down to use their large noses to face their lopsided offspring the right way and nudge them back up the slope.

Marco, Polo worked there for most of a year, herding and heeding the cattle, shooting rattlesnakes, eating ciao at the grub wagon, or skipping the baby bugs and making his own meal.

One day, a stocky man dressed handsomely in a bandolier – one of his fellow cowboys but a longer time at the Lazy R – came from Slim, the ranch owner, to the bunkhouse where the cowboys stayed. He advised Marco, Polo, politely but to the point, that our hero leave the ranch, say, the entire valley, ASAP – American West lingo for pretty darn quick.

Why? I am certain you have guessed. The rancher's daughter was heavily in love with Marco, Polo. Those sad Italian men are just so handsome, with sleepy bedroom eyes and curly dark hair; it wasn't his fault. Really. But it never pays to argue with a man in a bandolier sent by the tall head man. Recall Jim Croce's advice not to mess around with Slim.

Now, on the other side of the mountain, the wind blew the same way. That meant, by the same process (I hope you were listening), that the cattle there all had their *left* legs (your left side, too, if you weren't trying to hypnotize the cow) longer. This brand was the "Sinister R," sort of like a Lazy R, but lying on the other side. "Sinister" means "left" sometimes, and sometimes not, but even then, it doesn't mean "right." Marco, Polo worked at the Sinister R for a while after the Lazy R.

Another funny thing. If, by chance, a Lazy R and a Sinister

R set of bovines hit it off, and soon, one thing leading to another, a calf calved, usually the calf had absolutely normal legs, no side longer than the other. Doesn't matter whether you try to stare the cow down, or look where it is looking: on both sides the legs are the same.

And, what's the use of that? Nobody there knew what to do with a normal calf, so on each side of the mountain, they drove those freaks downslope and out of the valley, into the town, and then into... well, let's just say many people like to BarBQ and put cheese and mustard and ketchup on a bun. Poor kids. But, remember, kids, kids are goats. As in that nonsense rhyme whose last line is translated as:

A kid will eat ivy, too.
Wouldn't you?

It is true that one softhearted cowpoke, upset with the fate of the mixed Lazy R and Sinister R offspring, tried to argue they didn't have legs the same length: they weren't freaks. They had longer legs on both sides. Of course, he was laughed at and soon offered the job of chuck wagon cook.

Now, many buckaroos were just bums with guns. Their lives were dirt, dung, dungarees, drinks and DUIs. Marco, Polo, remember, had been a respected man in Italy. Not a bigwig, say; but a toupee or weave at least. He tried to bring a sense of honor and justice with him into the lawless West, even if he was laughed at by cowboys who thought the fastest gun or the hardest fist was more important.

Marco, Polo fulfilled his contract with the Sinister R ranch, packed his saddle bags onto his trustee steed (he couldn't get bank lingo out of his mind), Argento, and headed out. This time with kind words and a promise of a welcome back: there was no rancher's daughter at the Sinister R. The rancher's son, a handsome lad of twenty-three, did make a pass or two, but Marco, Polo politely declined. That handsome, sad Italian with sleepy bedroom eyes and curly dark hair; it wasn't his fault, the son thought. Really.

They parted as friends, with the son looking forward to another chance if Marco, Polo returned. [The red-headed kid's father, pulling the red-headed kid by the shoulder, stood up, thought to walk out, but simply shouted, "Horsefeathers," and sat down again.]

Marco, Polo rode west, past beautiful hills, called "buttes," and ugly hills, called "butts." He rode into the cuticle hills, then the toehills, then the tarsalhills, and finally the foothills of the Rockies, up into some wooded areas. Surrounded by aspens and evergreens, a few never greens and deciduous sometimes greens, and collard greens, he made his campfire and cooked his evening meal.

Most cowboys lived on beans. One job at each brand was the chuck wagon cook, usually reserved for a cowboy who was disabled, physically and mentally. Food was usually beans, prepared the one way the cook knew. If the cowboys were lucky, a good chuck wagon cook could also make coffee, which only requires boiling water, but often, the chuck wagon cooks were so incompetent they just kept staring at the pot; everyone knows a watched pot never boils.

Marco, Polo was not a beaner. He'd politely eat at the chuck wagon – well, let's not guess how it got that name – if he had to, but if he had his druthers, he'd prepare his own meals. He'd boil a big pot of water, add some pasta and a dash of druthers, sauté some onions and sun-dried tomatoes, olive oil and oregano for a sauce, with a little Italian sausage if he had it, or beef jerky if he had to improvise.

That's how he got one of his monikers – monikers are not the one-eyed glasses – "monocles" – but another word for "nickname." So his moniker, to many cowboys who knew him, was "The Spaghetti Western."

The Spaghetti Western and Argento rode on. A long and dusty time later, they came to a small town named "Talus," right above the foothills. As he rode in, several men in aprons came to greet him.

"Ah, howdy, I dare say, stranger."

When Marco, Polo first arrived in the US, he thought people were saying "*arrivederci*," Italian for "goodbye." It was confusing when they said this on first meeting him, like they wanted to get rid of him quickly.

"*Buongiorno. Piercere*," replied Marco, Polo, saying "Good morning. Nice to meet you." But, of course, the shopkeepers didn't know that and thought maybe he was a chuck wagon cook between gigs.

"You must be our new sheriff," the shopkeepers said. That was their standard line whenever a man riding a horse came into town, not acting like a complete fool. It was difficult to find someone willing to be a sheriff, and even harder keeping them alive, as drunken, angry cowboys didn't like people telling them what to do. Go figure.

"Well, maybe," drawled Marco, Polo, because people drawled in the West; drawling is like talking slowly and drooling. Still, drawling's a lot cleaner than spitting chaw tabacci, also a common western habit. Luckily, the horses and cattle didn't pick up that habit.

"What's the pay?" asked Marco, Polo. The shopkeepers, libertarian to a man, conferred to see how low they could go. They didn't offer much, but to The Spaghetti Western, it was an honest job to do and a place to stay, with the promise of a ranch of 15,000 acres if he lasted a year. The shopkeepers, with history as their guide, felt it was a safe bet.

Talus, to tell us the truth, was a favorite with cowboys because it had two saloons. Most Western small towns near there had only one bar ["Can you hear me now?" inquired the Whisperer], so if you were kicked out of one... well, there was nowhere else to go. In Talus, they could stagger, or crawl, or sing, or weave unsteadily across the street and try their luck at the other saloon if they made it that far before falling down, dead drunk asleep.

Now drunk bums with guns – cowboys in town, for short – can be a dangerous lot. That was Marco, Polo's main job now: keep the cowboys peaceful. There was a rule that guns had to be turned in to the barkeep, but that law was mainly ignored.

The Spaghetti Western would sidle over to a cowboy who was getting loud and belligerent, and say nicely, "You can have another drink and keep your guns if you can answer this question." He'd show a flashcard – you know what they are – with perhaps "7 x 5," written on it, or "Cripple Creek," "Cripple Creak," and "Cripple Creke"; and the cowboy had to do the arithmetic, or choose the right spelling. Now, few of the cowboys could read, and even fewer could add beyond what they could do on fingers, toes being too hard to get to in cowboy boots. So they would look Marco, Polo in the eye and say, "Okay, I guess I'm drunk, I'll turn my guns in." Just to save face.

It helped somewhat that Marco, Polo would be holding this absolutely huge shotgun aimed right at their middle. Made those cowboys right reasonable, not wanting to go around with a hole the size of a large pizza right where their belly button used to be.

One cowboy, showing his respect, admitted to The Spaghetti Western, while turning in his guns after getting the "4 + 3" flashcard, "Dude, I couldn't do that sober, either."

The local lads would test Marco, Polo, flashing his set of flashcards at him; of course, he would get them all right. Then some of the wiseacre, or poorer wise-quarter-acre kids would make up their own, hard ones, like: "4 x [(6 x (¾ x 17/4)] = ?" No problem for Marco, Polo. They thought they had him once when he gave an answer that didn't agree with the card's back side, but he showed them that the card's answer was wrong.

They were so impressed that, learning of his former position in the Italian bank, he was given yet another moniker in tribute: "The Loan Arranger."

Marco, Polo had another weapon – beyond that shotgun – in keeping the peace. All the unmarried women, and most of the married ones, had crushes on him. When he was in his office – which doubled as the jail – there would be a steady stream of women bringing coffee – as if he couldn't boil water – and sweets and lunch and dinner and a wink and a flirt. As Marco, Polo would tell himself: "It's a thankless job, but somebody has to do it."

He noticed that nicely dressed town girls, and the ranch ladies on their trips to town, would always walk down his side of the street, and each one, without fail, would lose her handkerchief right as she passed him.

"Oh, thank you, Marco."

"Polo."

"I'll stop by your office later to thank you properly."

Shopkeepers think they know everything going on. Ha! And ha, again! They're in the store all day, and if a customer says anything interesting, they don't share it with the other shopkeepers, because maybe the knowledge, if kept secret, could prove valuable.

They tell only their wives and mistresses. A man tells his woman everything, to brag. ["Men are pigs," agreed the Whisperer.] And the women tell their friends, who tell their daughters, who tell any other female who didn't already know. Soon, every woman in town knows a hundred times more than any man.

Any man except The Spaghetti Western, because all the women talked to him. He knew about any mining claim, horse theft, planned hijacking, bank robbery, bee sting, shoplifting or unlawful spitting, almost before the perp did. So he was always in the right place, at the right time, often with a few chocolate chip cookies warm from the oven just brought to him by some curly haired cutie. And always with a really huge, frightening shotgun. Peace prevailed.

At the end of the year, The Loan Arranger reminded the

town citizens of their promise of a 15,000 acre ranch.

"Did we say that?" asked one.

"He must have misherd," said another (it was cattle country). They were libertarians, all.

"No, we did mention a ranch. It was a 15,000 *acorn* ranch. That would be about 10x10, not big enough for a well and an outhouse. Why do you want that?" asked the town mayor.

"*Torno subito*," said The Spaghetti Western, meaning he would be right back. And within a few minutes, he had his flash cards.

"Anyone for a game?" he asked. And none of the town merchants wanted to play. Maybe because he also had Tiny Tim, his favorite shotgun. Favorite huge shotgun. Remember Jim Croce, and don't mess around with The Loan Arranger or Tiny Tim, either.

After a huddle, they showed him a spread on a map, higher up in the mountains, and not quite 15,000 acres (they were libertarians, to a man), but decent enough. He said he'd stay on as sheriff, causing a cheer of soprano, mezzo-soprano, contralto and treble tones.

Marco, Polo set off to inspect his range, his future ranch and brand. It would take a day or so's ride to get there; it wasn't settled territory with roads.

Towards the end of the first day, after traveling through arroyo and valley, past streams and creeks, forest and lowland scrubs, he saw smoke from a chimney. Soon he saw a cleared space with a ranch house, stables, a bunkhouse, horse pastures and a garden. As he approached, a cowboy stopped him and said:

"Ah, howdy, I dare say. What's your business? You're welcome to eat with us cowboys and sleep in the bunkhouse, but stay clear away from the main house."

"Well, goodbye yourself. Hello, thanks. I'll take you up on that."

It was a good meal, as cowboy meals go. Coffee for an

appetizer. A bean salad, with beans for the main meal. For those still hungry, there were beans for dessert, and refried beans for a midnight snack. Marco, Polo promised himself that he'd make his own meal the next night, perhaps lasagna, although that is notoriously difficult over a campfire.

The meal was pleasant also because he could hear signs of family life from the main cabin: a woman's voice calling to a child; he imagined an Italian accent. The joy of a young boy laughing. The bunkhouse windows were so dirty he couldn't even hear very well through them when open. He thought he saw a willowy woman, causing him to think of the one he left behind; not merely Juliet's left behind, all of her.

He reflected sadly that if he hadn't left Italy, now, let's see, it was about six years ago, maybe he'd have had a family like that. He sighed and farted, because beans always make you fart, which is one reason cowboys like sleeping outdoors.

As he left the next day, he floated in dreams of his lost Italy. He imagined the wind brought him stray Italian phrases: *mammalucco, deficiente, cretino, coglione, segone, mook, mezza sega*: all Old Country ways of saying "doofus." But a backward glance only showed smoke rising from a chimney.

His trip to his own spread was fairly uneventful, although the Italian putdowns had somewhat undercut The Spaghetti Western's favorite song, which he liked to sing to Argento:

Home, home on the range
Where the deer and the antelope play
Where seldom is heard
A discouraging word
And the skies are not cloudy all day

Argento didn't mind his singing, and *Home on the Range* was, to her, far better than his opera or Italian folk songs. Deer and antelope she could take or leave; they didn't play with her.

When she felt like galloping, she'd sing (although it was hard to articulate with a bit in her mouth), and use her tail as a baton to direct, the first line of the chorus of *Wild Horses*:

Wild horses couldn't drag me away

She never went further than that one line after a Mexican cowboy, Taco Tuesday (whose rugged short donkey was named *Burrito*), jealous because Marco, Polo had undercut his primacy in gastronomic nicknames, had reported her. ABKCO, Mick and Keith's lyric agent, sent her their standard Nay Neigh letter, demanding $1,000 for occasional use of the full chorus, which sum The Spaghetti Western wouldn't pony up for her. So, she made do with the one line.

Marco, Polo felt he had lucked out with his spread: it had some open grazing meadows, and several creeks which even in mid-Summer ran with cold, clear water. This was certainly a place he could build into a brand, and settle down, although it would be improved, he felt, by a woman.

He rode his range from one side to the other, finding nothing that troubled him, and settled before a campfire, making a rough dinner of left-over lasagna, and, taking advantage of the ice-cold water, some raspberry gelato. He sang out, with only Argento, birds, racoons, bears, squirrels, mice, beaver, a few rabbits and his melting gelato as an audience (thankfully, no lyric agents), the song *The Book of Love*, which to Argento seemed an unending repetition of,

Been a long lonely, lonely, lonely, lonely, lonely time

"Suck it up already," thought Argento.

The Spaghetti Western hadn't planned to stop at the same ranch on the way back, but when his path became close – about a mile away as evening came on, he heard the echoes of gunshots.

He turned Argento towards the ranch, his sheriff instincts tingling. From a ridge overlooking the clearing, he could see a group of about six cowboys surrounding the main house, but facing outwards. About 10 cowboys were saddling their horses, and as he watched, they rode out, single file. The Loan Arranger circled down and caught up with them about ten minutes' ride beyond the ranch.

"Ah, howdy, I dare say," said one. "I wouldn't go there if I were you. It's all trouble."

"Yep," said another, with a short black beard, fully in agreement but not adding much.

"Dutch Casava and his gang, from the old Comma Toes QTip ranch, have moved in on the real owner and his daughter. Dutch controls everything. He threatens to have them deported if they don't obey. Funny thing is, Dutch is just as much an immigrant as they are. But the old man doesn't speak English."

"Yep," said the black bearded one.

"That lady, his daughter, she has quite the mouth on her. She screams and curses at her father for putting up with them, but he is cowed by them. We could hear them threaten him, and even saw Dutch slap her. When we protested, they told us to ride out if we didn't like it. So now it's only Dutch and his gang."

"Well," said Marco, Polo, "Goodbye. Hello. I'm the sheriff down in Talus. Any of you want to help me restore some peace up at the ranch? I'll deputize you."

The cowboys looked at one another, and remembered how Dutch and his gang seemed to care little about peace or other people, and how they'd shot at them to hasten their leaving; they shook their heads.

"Yep," said the bearded one, but he rode off as well.

So it was up to Marco, Polo, on his lonesome, but he was used to that.

"Six or so against one," he mused. "I don't like those odds."

He sat down and rolled himself a cigarette, and threw it away. He didn't smoke, but rolling cigarettes calmed him down and passed the time. About nine o'clock by his reckoning, more like 11:55 p.m. by the clock in the main house, two of the gunmen peeled off and ran for the outhouse. The Loan Arranger, knowing the effects of bean dinners, had expected that. Those two fought each other as to who would sit first; with their pants down around their ankles, they presented little danger to The Spaghetti Western.

The others were now out of sight of each other. Marco, Polo came up to one and showed him a flip card for ∞. The cowboy guessed, "Lazy Eight," but the Loan Arranger told him he was wrong; it was "infinity," and the cowboy readily agreed. The infinity sign looked just like the two barrels of Tiny Tim, pointing right at him, looking as large as two railroad tunnels side by side. This cowboy dropped his gun belt, which had been holding up his pants, and soon he was riding down the trail on his lonesome.

The Spaghetti Western repeated this on each side of the house, until only the two outlaws near the outhouse remained, and Marco, Polo easily tied them up.

He had Argento bang into the far side of the house, to distract anyone inside, and then he burst through the door. The wind blew the lamp out, so he couldn't see anything, but he could hear, it must have been the daughter, "*Deficiente, cretino, coglione, basta, cappuccino. Mannaggia! Mezza sega.*"

It was as if he were struck by lightning. There was only one woman in the entire world who would interject "cappuccino" into a swarm of curses, just as she would murmur it within a gentle wave of dolces. He knew exactly what to do. He jumped to the side as a large cast iron frying pan thudded against the door he had just come through.

The woman lit a lamp; she was now holding a large knife. In the corner was a large man, Dutch Casava, looking like a busted melon.

"I made him a meat-a-ball he couldn't refuse. A big plate of gnocchi. He fell asleep. This *cretino*, *Pope*," waving the knife at her father, "didn't do nothing. So, I gave Dutch a meat-a-ball on his head." She took a closer look at the intruder at the door.

"Marco!" she cried, and cried and cried.

"Polo," he replied.

"Junior," came a voice from the corner.

"How did you find us?" the soon-to-be Mrs. The Spaghetti Western asked after a romantic interlude.

"*Era tutto culo*," said The Loan Arranger; it was all luck. But perhaps it was a bit of fate, *destino*, as well.

Tiny Tim had presided at many a wedding, but that of Marco and Juliet was by far his favorite.

END OF TIME
(Hice In The Woods)

The dancing uncle was, that late afternoon, nearly napping when suddenly there came a tapping, as of someone gently rapping, rapping at the outside door.

The uncle slowly rose, waiting to see if anyone else would answer, saying to himself:

[pause, then sing-song melodramatic]

"'Tis some visitor entreating entrance at my chamber door. Some late visitor entreating entrance at my chamber door. This it is and nothing more."

He hesitated still longer, but neither Mom or Dad or even Princess arrived. Feeling abashed that the person outside had waited so long, he moved towards the door, but slowly.

[another pause and continuing sing-song]

Presently his soul grew stronger; hesitating then no longer. "Sir," said he, "or Madam, truly your forgiveness I implore. But the fact is I was napping, and so gently you came rapping, and so faintly you came tapping, tapping at my chamber door, that I scarce was sure I heard you." Here he opened wide the door. Darkness there and nothing more.

[A long belch. A shorter silent pause.]

I am your original narrator, restored. The substitute narrator cannot continue; his Poetic license was revoked. DUI: Declamating Under the Influence.

The dancing uncle pranced a few mincing steps back, fluttered his wrist, and looked down.

[Short pause]

I have been instructed to keep to the story and stop stereotyping. Please imagine what you will.

The uncle looked down, and saw her, if it was a human, if it had a gender. On first glance, it was a black cuboid with a topping sphere, also in black. It spoke.

"Are you ravin' mad?"

The dancing uncle gainsaid, by his stance, personal insanity, and aloud again offered apologies for keeping her waiting. It was, he could see now, a human, a she, in black shapeless clothes and a black kerchief covering her head and wrapped around her neck. Her speech was somewhat indistinct and mumbled. What he could see of her face was weathered, lined, asymmetric and unappealing.

"Ish Ham here? It'sh a shadder time," he heard. He thought a minute.

"Oh, do you mean the Rabbi Ibraham Tayers?"

"'The Rabbi Ibraham Tayers' ish it?" she said, mocking his voice. The Whisperer now joined the uncle at the door, intending to catch the early evening evil cloud news squib: *The Putz Pulled A Putsch.*"

"So, a rabbi without a congregation," the figure said sarcastically, spraying spittle, "That'sh richh." ("Shul's out," lishped the Whisperer.) "HEY, TREIF," she shouted, loud enough to startle worms.

"Would you like to come in?" the dancing uncle asked. The figure looked at the doorjamb, but seeing no mezuzah, shook her head vigorously in the negative. She started to draw in a deep breath. The uncle, to forestall another bellow, offered to find him.

The Rabbi was seated in the big room, looking mournfully at his sack.

"Rabbi, there's a harridan at the door, asking for you. It's hard to understand her. 'It's a sadder time,' she said."

"Ach, my wife. 'Seder time.' She's lost all her teeth. I'm amazed she's here; it's a long way." To himself, he muttered, "Have gums, will travel." He heaved himself out of his chair and followed the dancing uncle to the door.

The uncle, admiring the fortitude of any man who could sire a minyan on that creature, or maybe simply to avoid standing directly in front of her, let the Rabbi pass. As if reading the uncle's mind, the Rabbi commented as he passed, "Old Jewish custom: a deranged marriage."

"Ah, *shefela*," said the Rabbi upon reaching the door, his beard stark white except for a lone flagstick, "what a pleasure to see you."

"Ham, time to shtop telling the goyim lies and come home," she sputtered.

"Where are your teeth?" he asked while wiping his face.

She pulled a set of false teeth from a pocket within her clothing, but put them back. "*Chametz*, not for *Pesach*," she explained sloppily.

"Come," she ordered.

"I will," he promised. "I must first complete one task: their *ketselah* is in my sack." Shefela shnickered. "And," he added defensively, "I have told them only one lie in all the time here."

"Must have been a whopper," she sprayed. "Come, soon," she ordered, and lurched off into the gathering darkness, her way lit only by the concluding flashes of Wiio's Law School's cloud ad, the "*Try It. You'll Like It*" slogan slowly dimming.

"Is she an uber?" the dancing uncle asked the Rabbi. "How did she survive the Evil Cloud?"

"Uber? No. Nothing can kill her," he replied. "Trust me, I know."

Dinner that night was served in the great room, so all could relax on big chairs and sofas. Brian and Alexa cuddled on a large chair, romantically sharing deep secrets and hopes of their brief sheltered lives, until Siri, Alexa's mom, enforced social distancing. Mom brought an appetizer of roasted egg, crackers and a paste of fruit and nuts, some greens including horseradish, parsley and roots of romaine lettuce. Flatbread replaced sourdough. Soup was poached fish dumplings, followed by an entree of brisket with sides of potato kugel and a stew-like mixture of sweet potatoes, carrots and prunes. Not for the first time, the Rabbi looked long and soft at Mom.

As the guests were politely belching, the Rabbi, roused into action by his spouse's peremptory order, asked for volunteers to accompany his spelunking into his sack. All adults had taken a vow of silence. He would not consider taking Princess, who offered. Alexa raised her hand, and a nanosecond later, so did Brian. The Rabbi waved his hand dismissively at them, indicating they were too young. Alexa flounced out, humiliated; Brian followed her.

The Rabbi looked around, and his eyes settled on the dancing uncle.

"Please, I'd much appreciate. I need someone who sees beyond the facade." In the silence, the Whisperer's "a queer choice" echoed in the room. The dancing uncle sighed, agreed, and then helped the Rabbi drag the sack to the courtyard behind the kitchen.

Once outside, the dancing uncle, whose name was "Robert" – although he went by "Bobby," or "Bobbie," depending on the crowd – asked, "What was that one lie?"

Rabbit Ears looked away, debating with himself whether to answer. Realizing what he was asking of Bobby, he started to explain. "Remember that first day, when I was selling wares?" Bobby nodded.

We will return to their saga anon.

While those two were outside, the rest remained in the large chamber – the kids clearing the plates – for storytime. Dad announced that the uncles were expected in the kitchen promptly after the stories to help make the dessert: candied kumquats. "Why is this night different from all other nights?" complained The Grouch bitterly.

Dad gave the nod to Uncle Richard Peter Johnson, the redhaired boy's father, who planned to recite one of the fables his father had read to him when young. Princess slipped the Bernie Stone, retrieved from Brian, into Uncle Richard's pocket, and turned to look at the Rabbi, expecting his beard to have a finger wagging at her for that.

"I am going to tell you an actual fairy tale, not the cock and balls stories you've heard before," he said, comfortably rubbing the stone between his fingers.

"Go on, Triple Dick," said the Perv, using his high school nickname.

A House in the Woods

I warn you: this is a grim and grove fable of children abandoned to die in a dark woods. ["A forest prime evil," quipped the Whisperer.]

Once upon a time, there was a great famine. Most families could barely feed themselves. Deep in a forest lived a buckeyed woman and her second husband (she'd been a weeping willow but fell in love with him on their first date), and two children, each only of a former spouse. They were isolated peepal, quite unpoplar. Their mean barking dogwood was named "Sycamore"; their mouser, "Catalpa." As step- and step-step parents, they did not give a fig about the children, as they might have for their own offsprigs. [Various snorts.]

Overhead, an adolescent barred owl, sneaking back into the forest intent on a tit mouse, crashed into a trunk and cried, "Boo, hoo, hoo." A brooding boobook, insulted, turned whitefaced, became fuluous and screeched at the injured ow!

The man was a poor woodcutter, in a poor wood, near a poor town in a poor borough; the only pair of waterfowl was Portuguese. In these bad times, his scraggly piles of diseased wood barely fetched a pfennig. ["Selling discords?" inquired the Whisperer.]

Pecanning him over with a wave, the woman beecheeched the lumberman, "Honey locust, let's woodchuck the sprouts." Overhead, a great tawny owl hooted a boast; an old gray demurred, "saw-whet."

The woodcutter – formerly a brave soldier, now a quaking aspen – was at first hesitant ("Don't ash me that!"), but his wife's vowing that his jack pine would meet no bush, and his palms cypress no chestnuts, changed his mind: he loved her mangrove and maidenhair fern. Petrified, he said oakay to his sugar maple. ["At first indeciduous, but then he accedared to her demands," opined the Whisperer.] The woodcutter resolved to abandon the kindlings deep in the forest. Handful, the elder boy....

Here, Triple Dick stopped. He hadn't minded, or perhaps noticed, his extemporaneous modifications to his fable until then, but he knew he had wanted to say, "Hansel, the elder, a boy," but his tongue would not cooperate. Taking a deep breath, he continued.

... was about 14, firhaired, a handsome stripling youth, with a goal of college ["UCalyptus," The Dubs mom dubbed]. Great Owl, his two-step sib, was more a sapling, thinner and wiry, with angular features, about two inches shorter than his brother-out-law, but about the same age. They used the nicknacks the parents had given them when young; the younger's reflecting his incessant questioning as a toddler; his actual name was "Tim Burt."

They were bosom buds, constant combanyans; on acacia they went on larchs together, never stumped for a good time.

"Show no fear," Uncle Richard reminded himself. He looked around, thinking Bobbie had cast a spell on him, and blundered forward.

They lived in a one-room log cabin, a hut with no decoration (and, of course, no electrical owlets) save a walnut, so Handful could overhear the parents' arguing ("None of your sassafrass!"), and their plan. Before the father called to them to go wood gathering ("Yew boys must learn a trade."), Handful filled his pockets with white stones. They were led deeper and deeper into the forest. Overhead, a masked owl demanded a horned owl cover his bill, but in the end, they went dutch elm and split the tab.

At one point, Great Owl saw a strange house through the trees, in a small clearing. It 'peared made of gingerbread and candy. A pause to scops it out, then he took a quick detour and filled his pockets, without asking persimmon, with strawberry, mint and chocolate gumdrops from the roof's overhang. ["Should be ashamed, eavesdropping," reprimanded the Whisperer.]

Handful, as they walked on, dropped a stone from time to time. Finally, when the boys were almost exhausted, the man said, "You rest here. I'll make a bundle, then teach you." Their papaya disappeared into the forest. He did not return.

When the moon came out, Handful told Great Owl to look for the shine of the white stones. It took a while to find each, and they laughed, and bumped into each other, and vied to see who would find the next, and wrestled, using hemlocks, to stop the other from picking up the stone. It was dawn before they came to their cottage.

Seeing no bundles outside ["Not even faggots?" whined wife Wahnita, which prompted the popeyed-elbowed aunts to bracket her], "You didn't gather much wood, father," Great Owl noted to his pawpaw, silently taking two 'steps' back. Both adults were awake, though the boys had expected them to be sawing wood.

"He was growing, not cutting," the woman smiled; the two were entwined in a love lock, ardently kukuing each other, and there appeared to be hickories, or necktarines, on her skin. Mimosa, her head resting on tupelos, was temporarily in a good mood, almost in a blue raspberry.

It didn't last. "Holly gum," she complained. "They're still olive." ["Haw, haw," the Whisperer laughed.] The boys were sent to fetch a pail of water. The parents were plotting again. The scant last dinner was treif: morepork, pigmy and porkupine, with bits of fish flavored with bay leaf.

That night, another apprenticeship session was scheduled. Phil Burt, the man, made Handful and Great Owl empty their pockets. "Marsh," he ordered them. About 200 yards into the woods, Great Owl picked up his sack of gumdrops from the tree trunk where he had hidden it.

Again they were led deep into the forest, where father again varnished. On the way, Great Owl had released one of the sweets from time to time ["A Forrest Gump drop," she noted].

Gumdrops are much harder to find in the dark than shiny stones, so the boys progressed slowly. They laughed. They pushed each other down, and wrestled, and pulled each other back to be first to the candy. Great Owl had the idea of feeding the other each gumdrop they found. When at last a boy saw one, and raced to pick it up, after they finished wrestling, the loser would open his mouth, and the victor would drop it in. For the mint, "'ave a green."

A common barn owl – no special talons – mournfully regretted his mediocrity: "Why, why, why?" "What, what, what?" the old wise owl, slightly deaf, replied. Another owl cried, "Where?" having spotted a wolf.

Soon, of course, the game included sticking the gumdrop in with a finger, and the other boy's closing his mouth around the digit. They were enthralled with their new game. Handful insisted they try "no Hans," with one picking up the gumdrop with his tongue and dropping it in the other's mouth. It soon proved easier to have the mouths together, and use their tongues....

Triple Dick paused, almost clamping his jaw shut. A vision of the remainder of the story had crossed his mind: the boys going to the gingerbread cottage; blind witch Hazel's tricking them into a cage together; her feeding them gingerbread and candy and waiting for them to show a little soft plumpness; her demanding daily they stick out a finger to be tested; their fooling her by instead sticking out redwood that boys, who wood be bois, always made hard.... The clincher was a Barbara Walters owl spying its small bird prey, hooting "when, when, when."

"This story is stupid and boring; I am going to tell a different one."

("Owlfeathers," murmured the Whisperer.)

The crowd, rooted by the spectacle, simply nodded, except for the red-haired boy, who said, "Go on, Dad, you were really sticking it!"

The hallway clock struck anon.

Back to the Rabbi and Uncle Robert.

The Rabbi was explaining what little he knew about how to retrieve the cat from the bag.

"It was Schrödinger's sack. Perfect for me. What I wanted, if it existed, would only come into being when I tried to find it; otherwise, it was just a bunch of possibility wares. But if I stuck my hand in and felt to measure what I wanted, I usually got it.

"It doesn't work for living things. And if I put something back, I won't get the same one when I reach in again; a different one materializes."

"Just thinking of the cat won't work, then," Uncle Bobby realized.

"What will happen when we go in?"

"Ach, I really can't say. Schrödinger said there was no way to know in the sack where you were and what you were doing at the same time. It's just get in and deal with what we find."

"Not much of a plan," the dancing uncle noted apprehensively.

The Rabbi borrowed a skirt hoop from Mom's Den; he used the widest circumferenced one to tie the sack wide open. As Rabbit Ears prepared the sack, Bobby asked, "Has it been hard for you here, being the only one of your persuasion?"

"Me?" the Rabbi replied. "What about you?"

"Oh, me?" queeried Uncle Bobby. "Yeah, there's Triple Dick – Uncle Richard – but he doesn't really know, does he?"

"No, it's like he thinks a west wind blows west; he's always facing away from himself." Bobby nodded his agreement.

"It's ready, let's go," the Rabbi said and peered into the sack. What he saw did not change, down to his mind's eye's images, phosphenes and floaters, whether his eyes were open or closed. It was... no, it wasn't. *Not at all.*

There were sounds – growls, winds, Talmudic verses and curses – but whether in his head, or from the sack, he could not tell. Bobby, seeing the Rabbi's face and yarmulke turn whiter than his beard, declined to peek.

"What was the lie?" pressed the dancing uncle, stalling.

"Tell you what," said the Rabbi, "When we get back, I'll confess. You please tell the others. I can't face them."

"Don't foist that on me," Uncle Bobby replied. "It must be bad."

"Oh, yes, the lie was unforgivable. But no, boychik or whatever, you'll be a hero. Trust me." The Rabbi looked straight at Uncle Bobby. "I promise."

The Rabbi placed a chair next to the sack, climbed on, held his nose and jumped in as if from a high cliff to an angry sea. For an instant he was suspended: the coyote before looking down. The dancing uncle mounted the chair. He was grabbed by the Rabbi's free hand.

And down they went, not reaching the bottom until Princess counted to seventeen, which was a very long time because she was listening to Uncle Richard's story.

Triple Dick wiped his face, shifting the Bernie Stone to his other pocket when he replaced his handkerchief and started anew. ["Gesundheit," said the Whisperer.]

A House in the Woods

One day, a fair maiden (at best a C+) who had flowing golden locks, now worn butch, went for a walk in the woods near her teaching hospital. She was a surgical intern; days off were rare and needed to be well done.

It was a beautiful, warm summer day. Relishing some alone time, she only waved at a co-worker she saw cozily walking with a tall man; she'd set them up on a date the previous night. Her phone immediately buzzed with a text. "ICU. TNX. YMMD. IOU. FYEO: IMHO FWIW – OMG XTC! SCNR LOL. ICYMI: TGIF 8PM RSVP ASAP. BYOB. WTF. BYOBBF. RN PNLOP. EOM." Obeying the injunction against lettering on the trail, she did not reply.

Lost in thought, thinking of this OR that, and practicing cutting remarks, she wandered off the usual path and became lost in fact, but not infarct. She spied a chimney through the trees, and debouching ["The only pleasure she allows herself," mused the Whisperer] into the clearing, saw a tidy house, with two baby aspirin trees in the yard, and a white picket railing on the lanai. It seemed idyllic. The nameplate above the door read "THE THREE BAYERS." There was smoke coming from the chimney, but no one answered her knock.

However, the door, unloxed, swung open. The living room was spacious and bright, with floor to ceiling windows and a high vaulted ceiling. There were three chairs. Goldilox, tired, decided to rest until the occupants returned.

Goldilox first sat in the chair nearest the door, one which only a mother could love. It was an overstuffed armchair, almost a bingo wing, with an antimacassar ["Save the children!" chanted a Joaquin Moraga student radical, raising clenched fist] and several duck feather pillows. She squirmed, trying to get comfortable, but, "It's too soft," she said. ["One down" counted the Whisperer.]

Next, she tried a smaller chair. It had an open *Introduction to the Differential Calculus* on it. "Too hard," she said. Goldilox was a tall woman, broad at the shoulders and hips, and could hardly fit in. She extracted herself, amputating the chair's left arm in her effort.

Finally, she sat in the remaining chair, a massive leather Barcalounger with electric recliner, tumorous headrests, five massage settings, and built-in speakers. It faced a 65" ultra HD curved TV, which, she noticed, tuned to the NFL when she sat. "Just right! This is heaven," she thought and rested there until halftime, her lower back almost melting with pleasure.

Still, nobody returned. Hungry, she went to the kitchen, where boxed meals were piled up; many people sometimes had their food delivered. She opened the kid's lunch first. Kale and arugula, açai and granola, and a plastic container of nonfat Greek yogurt. She sealed the box up quickly, as if it were poisonous.

She liked mom's meal no better. It was a small garden salad with balsamic vinaigrette ("Rabbit food," she cursed) and a small container of potato-mac salad, with a lemon square for dessert. "Too soft, too small," she said and pushed it away.

Dad's package was heavy ["Hmmm," sighed the Whisperer, "ooof"]. Inside was a cooking packet containing a stadium-sized steak, with a massive side dish of pulled pork, about a ton of french fries and a bushel of onion rings. ["Men are pigs," chortled Billy happily.] Dessert was a gigantic slice of mud pie, one of her favorites. She popped the cooking box into the nannywave, waited the necessary 45 seconds (which she used to hunt up a knife and fork, A-1 sauce, ketchup and a napkin) and dug in. Twenty glorious minutes of loin surgery later, she wiped her face and let out a belch that knocked the other boxes to the floor, where she was content to leave them.

Seeing a door outside the kitchen, in the hall, she opened it; she went down a dozen steps, where three doors were labeled similarly: "Dad's Den," "Mom's Den," and "Den of Iniquity."

Uncle Richard reached this point and paused for some water. At about the same time (if there were any such concept in a relativistic world), the Rabbi and Uncle Bobby reached the bottom, or at least a stopping place, because Princess had been counting mice running next to the walls.

The Rabbi couldn't at first figure out where he was. A vast cavern opened before him, with a high judge's bench occupied by a robed praying mantis. The testifying witness, an ant, had the annoying habit of randomly closing both eyes simultaneously: an ant tic; her sister, Fran, was similarly afflicted. The ant swore at length to a deceased ant's good qualities and how she had been profoundly loved and was now missed, particularly at picnics, by the entire colony. Apparently, the Rabbi was the accused.

His attorney, a slug named Rudy Bayleaf, was rudily complaining to the judge, "C'mon, the victim testimony has now gone on for 12 years, with another two hundred thousand from this colony yet to come. It's cumulative. She's putting me to sleep." Ant Esthesia concluded her antimony.

"Next witness, ant Ty Matter. Anthilating testimony," the prosecutor promised. "Ant Enna on call. Then ant Tithesis, with a contrary view. After that, ant Toinette, ant Sy Pansy, ant O. Nim, ant Rose Tica...." his voice droned on.

The judge looked down through her glasses and somewhat peremptorily waved her forelegs and feelers, exclaiming at Bayleaf, "Your client has admitted killing ant Jemima for no reason, as she walked across his kitchen floor, presenting no danger to him. It's just that attitude that got him here. I'll not short-circuit the process of justice because he feels ants are insignificant. It behooves him ["Ain't no such thing," the Whisperer buzzed; the Rabbi wondered how she could interject here] to appreciate the consequences of his conduct, and the victim's family has every right to their daze in court. Remember, this is only the two hundred nineteenth of his trials on ant killings alone. He faces several thousand insect trials before even considering the herring cases."

"What? Speak up, your honor," said Bayleaf because....

"You do your client no favor making me doubt his remorse," the mantis (secular while on the bench) continued. "Lucky for him, I won't handle his fruit fly cases; that's not my bailiwick. Judge Aaron handles flies and other dipterans, and henweys."

"What's a 'dipteran'? What's a 'henwey'?" asked Bayleaf, clueless.

"About a pound and a half," the Rabbi said to himself. Among his other talents, he was an expert geek. The Rabbi's head cleared a bit, and he realized it was only a dream, or perhaps a preymantition or anticipation.

He had fallen on his side; he moaned, "Oy veh, my aching hip." That mutter defined his location: figures of flower children materialized and vaporized all around; there was a sweet smell of Panama Red. Uncle Bobby was at his side helping him up.

A skeleton in a tie-dyed tee shirt ran past, spilling wine from a large glass; what he drank ran through his torso. The dancing uncle laughed to himself and said aloud, "the grapeful dead." ["Uncle Ax must be the head dead," the Whisperer said dyslexically.] The skeleton, in deadlocks, answered him, "I saw them play at the Houston Epitome and the San Antonio Biome. Jerry Garcia neckwear strangled me: I'm twice tie-died," he laughed. He pointed to a silent wraith; "Unspeakable cruelty; he was tongue tied."

Bobby had punted them to punland.

A wide watercourse ["Damn!" she said] blocked their way; on a flickering marker, the Rabbi read, "The River of Tayers." A podium for a game show came up from the ground. The host – several thousand indistinct people speaking as one – spoke in ethereal tones.

"To be allowed to continue, you must solve the riddles. You have one minute to get all right. A passing grade is five of six.

"What is black and white, and red all over?"

The Rabbi was about to protest that the riddle was banal, and give the usual answer, when Uncle Robert spoke up. "A zebra with a bad nose bleed." There was a short pause.

"That answer will not be accepted. One wrong."

"Why did you answer?" complained the Rabbi. "I knew that one. It was 'a newspaper.'"

"Yeah, I know, but we'd never get through all six riddles within one minute. We had to get one wrong."

The Rabbi thought about that, then said, "So, I chose a *yiddisher kop*. Arrest me. You couldn't have waited?"

The host continued, "What did the corrupt harbormaster demand of the judge?"

Uncle Bobby jumped on that, "A trial by his piers."

The one-minute bell sounded. The host's voice continued. "The count is one and one.

"Add nothing to a lupine. What's the saying?"

The dancing uncle worked on that. "Lupine" he knew. Sayings? Only a few relevant ones came to mind. Add nothing? Maybe an "o"? He had it!

"A 'woolf': in sheep's clothing." He wondered how they knew how he spelled the word.

"Two right. One wrong." The host became a hostess in a twinkie of an eye.

"Only the Rabbi may answer this one. What's an adjective describing a happy Hebe?" she posed.

Rabbit Ears smacked his lips a few times, pulled his hair; his beard slowly went from a wavy question mark to a smiley face. "Jubilent," he shouted.

"One wrong. Two to go. Three right. For five:

"What did the unrepentant bank robber request for his last meal?"

A clock ticked louder and louder, until it sounded like a gong. The two travelers confabbed, and Uncle Bobby answered doubtfully, "a hardboiled yegg?"

"Yes! One wrong. Four correct. Dispositive riddle:

"What did the multilinguist mean when he said, upon seeing his true love for the first time, 'corazón mío mizu kiri Maynard Krebs?'"

The beard was blank. Both pilgrims were initially blank. They coniferred, going over each part of the riddle. The gong was almost shattering their teeth, loud as a conundrum, while they pundered. Finally, the Rabbi jewbilently answered, "My heart skipped a beat."

The stand disappeared. The river lay before them, with no boat or bridge. Its flowing waters occasionally froze like a faulty download. It was now the River Styx. A sign said, "Use Quantum Math to Make Your Path."

"I got this!" the Rabbi said. "Danke Schoen my pal Schrödinger and his furshlugginer lectures." He turned to the river and exclaimed, "The energy of light is proportional to the frequency of its wave."

Uncle Bobby raised his eyebrows to the Rabbi, who explained, "That's Planck's Theorem."

Bobby and the Rabbi were busy with up high, down low, in the middle too slow, and missed the option of waiving a wave of waving WAVES. When that passed, one long board spanned the stream to the other side. In planck time they reached the far bank.

"Where are we now?" Uncle Bobby asked.

"Who knows?" the Rabbi shrugged, "but look!"

He pointed. There was Graceful And Handsome Four Footed God Who Rules Over Humans And Mice. The cat could hardly move; somehow he had acquired a collar with his name spelled out in all caps in sequins; it wound around his scruff several times. He was only ribs and bones, on his last lives. It was a catsequence of vanity, not curiosity, that almost killed this furball.

Uncle Bobby smoothed the cat's ears back and worked the collar off. Four Footed God said nothing. The dancing uncle, seeing how miserable the feline looked, suppressed the irresistible impulse to tease, "Cat got your tongue?" The cat purred and scratched him deeply to show his gratitude.

Getting back was relatively easy; we're fast approaching the max word count for this story, and there are several matters yet to resolve.

Looking around, the Rabbi, cat, and Uncle Bobby saw nothing. At all. Just blips vanishing. A quantum vacuum. ["I have a Dyson," bragged the Whisperer.] The Rabbi suddenly realized: since they had no idea where they were, they had to know almost exactly where they were going.

To get there they went down, so....

The Rabbi put his finger down his throat and threw up. Suddenly, cat, man with cat, and man with hat were standing outside the kitchen, catapulted out of the sack, covered in slime and hairballs. A happy landing.

Goldilox opened the door to the Den of Iniquity first, and then quickly slammed it shut. It was a goth's paradise, but anyone else's nightmare. The air was pungent with incense – patchouli? – and pot, and there were posters, hung at crazy angles, of grunge bands and tattooed and pierced people; there were cut-out pictures of the most extravagant costumes worn uniformly in a quest for uniqueness. A mattress on the floor with rumpled pillows suggested the teenager spent long hours there on her moiphone. "Too weird for me," Goldilox ruled.

Mom's Den was almost inviting, if somewhat archaically traditional. There was a sewing/quilting machine, spool-stands on the wall, an array of sewing paraphernalia, a magazine rack with Home & Garden and homemaking periodicals, a rocking chair with a pulled-out shelf beneath the seat jammed with darning and knitting needles, and a radio playing soft elevator – uplifting – music. Several still-life pictures decorated the wall, most reproductions but at least two made of yarn ["Like this tale?" the Whisperer yawned]. The air was sweet with potpourri; Goldilox could see that Mom was in the midst of making sachets. "Useful and practical," she mused, "but I'd rather take care of that side of my life at work." ["Goth, darn, so far," counted the Whisperer. "Good one, I'm in stitches," laughed her left-side Auntie.]

Dad's Den was misnamed. It should have been called "The Gym." A weight bench, covered with ashtrays and glasses, was against one wall. Near the far wall stood a NordicTrak GigaGiant, with a 12" screen for exhorting the fitness fanatics, now monopolized by Bayer cans. Free weights ["They usually charge?" asked the Whisperer] were neatly stacked, dusty, on their rack. A chair dominated the center of the room, under which were several whiskey bottles. On it were an 11" tablet ["How do you swallow that?" choked the Whisperer] and several magazines, whose content Goldilox deduced without looking; they were likely the motivation of any athletic endeavors in Dad's Den. "A grizzly Bayer's lair now; I'll love it after a thorough cleaning," she dentermined.

Goldilox heard the outside door open, and as she mounted the stairs to the kitchen, she listened to the family's conversation as they returned to their hearth.

"Goddam it, woman, can't you even once cook one lousy meal? Is that too much to ask?" The voice was grating, harsh, and slurred. It continued.

"And you, my vain rebel without a cause, I'm so tired of your whining, ruining a nice walk. Just get out of my sight for a while. Call your cockamamie friends and cry to them about how bad your life is, living in the lap of luxury I provide.

"What a waste of time trying to give you all a nice day. I'm going to have a beer and relax in my den. Fie, get thee to a nunnery!"

"What a conceited, arrogant drunken bastard," Goldilox thought to herself. ["But he has a 12-step plan," the Whisperer pointed out.] Upon saying that, she recognized the voice: it was the head of the surgery department, Dr. Yogi Bayer.

Goldilox blocked his way to the stairway. In full view of the rest of the family, she confronted him. As tall as he was, she looked him straight in the eye, or perhaps not straight. ["Ooof." The Whisperer took the hit for Uncle Richard.]

"You're going nowhere but out of here, forever, you alcoholic lout. I'm performing a misterectomy. If you ever show your face here again, I'll tell everyone about the times you've pressed yourself against me in the operating room and felt me up. And it won't be just my word against yours: I know at least a dozen nurses who will join my accusations. How many have quit in the last two years alone? That would make great operating theater, wouldn't it?"

Yogi started to object, and Goldilox interrupted.

"Make up your mind quickly. Suture self. I won't forceps you," she said incisively. She steriled him down. "But if you want to ever wield a #11 blade again, transplant yourself; get theeself gone and leave us alone.

"This is my family now, and my house!"

Yogi considered challenging Goldilox, but upon resection, he treasured $450,000/year above his family. So he clamped his mouth shut (muttering "horsefeathers"), packed his shit into a colostomy bag, and hemoSTAT departed.

True to her word, Goldilox took over the family. Mom was okay with that; she'd had enough of Yogi herself, and Goldilox – actually now "Golda Bayer" – proved to be a much more considerate lover.

The kid, however, remained a Hansel.

Uncle Richard looked up triumphantly. He was finished and felt the second fable was precisely how his own dad had read it from the book... until he silently reviewed what he had recited.

His red-haired progeny congratulated him. "Way to go, Dad. That'll fry the gay agenda!"

The rest of the crowd burst into applause, shouting, "Author, author, passi, passi!" Uncle Ax, rising unsteadily, lifted an imaginary wine glass in salute, drenching Dad with the spill. The Perv winked at Triple Dick.

Outside, the returned desackers washed themselves off. The Rabbi began confessing.

"My friend, Moishe ["Thought that was a black songstress," the Whisperer said]. What a schlimazel. The world's biggest slob. A particularly virulent growth on his unwashed dishes developed a rapport with him. A china virus, so to speak. That became the Evil Cloud under his direction. I couldn't get him to stop; with the power, he became almost megalomaniac."

"Huh?" the dancing uncle asked, but the Rabbi just waved his hands and continued.

"I saw it was borsch based, and experimented to find an antidote." ["And little lambsy divy," a passing Dewey Eyes child recited.] A short history later, the Rabbi concluded his revelation.

"And then I looked in her eyes and saw her soul; it was shining, perfect, loving, clear. I was enthralled, entranced, I couldn't leave."

"Yeah, Mom's a peach, isn't she?" Bobby replied.

"A peach?" the Rabbi screeched, appalled. "You do her a grave injustice. She's a, a..." he stammered as he sought for the right food, "a kreplach, a blintze!"

"So, you decided to stay around, huh? You were Biden' your time?"

They agreed upon a plan, mostly of Bobby's invention.

The next morning, the Rabbi slunk out almost unobserved. Graceful and Handsome, etc., delighted to be back in a mice place, gave him a parting flick of his tail, but spoke never more. Two Patch Lance followed for a farlong, by ear, but soon tripped and decided to shudder in place for a while.

As she set out bagels, cream cheese and lox on the breakfast table, Mom wondered where the Rabbi was; he usually helped. She'd grown fond of him, with his strange sayings and spotless rooms. And, she mused, Princess had matured greatly under his mentoring; she was now collecting all the nighttime stories into an anthology. But Mom's mind quickly turned to what use she could make of the onion matzah bagels she had set aside for the Rabbi. Dad continued throughout the meal to accept, but never solicit, bribes for his nod.

Walking away with his sack on his back, the Rabbi could see the don't-ask-don't telltale rainbow smoke from his magic log beet the dark cloud away. Bobbie had allowed Triple Dick, dejected and looking to redeem himself, to light the log. It was a salubrious variety brought back from their sojourn in the sack, a parting gift from the Rabbi, was all that Uncle Robert would tell the family.

As he trudged home, Treif reflected on his legacy at the house. He had fallen in love with a married woman – chastely, but still! – and a goy to boot. As a result, he had lied to them rather than act like a proper rabbi. He reproved himself that he was too young to enter menschopause. Not atone deaf, he prayed his cloud busting log and his tutoring of Princess would expiate some of his harm. He would really miss Princess, he knew.

The electron microscope? It wasn't finished, and there wasn't enough electricity for it to become a problem, he concluded. But the conviction oven; what sort of meshugge notions could trickle down from that? He paused and shook his head, then continued on his way and his ruminations, with his thoughts starting to turn to his home and family.

Suddenly, he stopped short and looked back in the house's direction, brow furrowed with concern, hesitating in his next step. The Bernie Stone: it was still out there.

Epilogue
Aptly

IN THE VERY SUPERIOR COURT OF THE KINGDOM

THE KINGDOM, PEOPLE and ALL PROPRIETY,	))
	) Order On Schlimazel's Motion
vs.	) For Dismissal Of Charges
	) And For Change Of Counsel
MOISHE PIPPICK,	)
Schlimazel.	) The Honorable Judge, Ms.[1]
	) Amy Hare Barrette

\------------------------------------)

ROMAN EYE
INTRODUCTION

The instant matter[2] comes before the Court pursuant to a paper filed directly by Moishe,[3] bypassing counsel, which filing the Court[4] interpreted as containing a motion to dismiss all charges and a motion to remove current counsel and replace with new appointed counsel; the Court held a hearing thereon.[5]

---

1   See: *In Re P.C.*, 0 KingsRook 0.

2   Add 2 cups water and heat in microwave for 90 seconds.

3   No disrespect is intended in using Schlimazel's given name, in light of Moishe's surname.

4   *In Re P.C., op. cit.* at 12.

5   *Charlize v. So. Africa* 8/7 S.A.G.A. 1975.

I[6] did not treat it as requesting permission[7] to proceed *in propria persona.*[8] Due to the weighty issues raised by the motions, although ignored by the parties in their arguments,[9] ruling in the form of a written opinion rather than an oral bench[10] order is appropriate.

The motion to dismiss[11] and motion concerning counsel are granted in part and dismissed in part.[12]

BINOCULAR
DECIPHERING SCHLIMAZEL'S SUBMISSION[13]

The Very Superior Court recently transitioned to an all-electronic filing system, at the same time replacing, after a decade of difficulty, its former in-house artificial intelligence dictation system ("AIDS").

All parties, even prisoners like Schlimazel[14] are required to file all documents electronically, even those prepared without benefit[15] of counsel. The VSC's AIDS was installed, prison friendly, in the pretrial detention center to facilitate such *pro se*[16] filings. However, AIDS' maladies were not cured before the penal installation,[17] so the system still had the ADD, occasional

---

6   *Ego.*

7   *Ego, supra.*

8   The colloquial phrase is "in pro per," not "improper" as Moishe consistently used at oral argument.

9   Which were, the Court notes, more with each other than to the Court.

10   You would think a judge would get a decent chair, but no!

11   That is the correct term in criminal law. The term is not "Summery Judgment" even in civil law. No, Moishe, it is not "motion to dismister" for men.

12   You must read to the end to discover the outcome. *See: Agatha v. Christie,* 10 Litl.Ind. 9, *rev'd sub nom &-Then Ther v. Nun.*

13   His filing, not his attitude.

14   The Court takes judicial notice that no prisoners actually like Moishe.

15   Professional courtesy, solely.

16   Poetry filings are strictly forbidden in any form: rhyming, freestyle, rap, etc. *Edict on ee cummings,* 4 Quart. 1909-1935.

17   Any snarky comments on this will be considered contempt of court.

dyslexia, agraphia, pompous refusal to be corrected,[18] and other problems that marked its tenyear at our court.[19]

While the Court is confident[20] in its reading, the filing as received is set forth verbatim:

Ta Da Kort:

Eye, Muy Shu Pork Inn, m ah prize Honor ahht hiz magic eees luck up, kuwaiting tri L. Aye kanknot eet, az the phood iz 3-fe, nut cultur.

Day cuze mi of ah tempered mudrer ov meany peepholes, and mens laughter ov cerebral udders. Eyelid no cutch thinkge. Deville akloud iz blaymed omni. How! Cudy dew dat? Eyem gnot schmart. Eyes justice ooober dry verse, know Saenz Tits.

Hyatt mitt a fun Gus gruesome Anna bull of boorish. Islet it a loan. Eye done due diss hiss on sat her daze. Bye some dai it wazz all lover darume. Bye mundane da fun Gus vast shut in pores. Sum bi combed deville kllowed. Sum enflected mibrane. I lust mefre Will.

It rcd mimine.

Adonai iffit deville opt a brane offitz oone, ore you'sd mynah. Eight cud thinque. I Donahue deville klud wrought nna sci, oremaid lite neenge. Aye Donovan re: mem burr Mustada thyme.

Eight maidme xcpt adz. Peepholes payd en boorshst or beats.

Eyegut nut thin.

Lonely darabbi testicle ganz me. Hee wazzup 4 frode hymnshelf & canned nuts BB lived. Hie axe U ally disc koverted acqure. B lame hymn Morthern mi.

---

18   *Cf: Third Imp. Trial Of U Kno Hoo*, 45 Pres.Rptr. 2017-2021.

19   *C: Odor Un Franz Mittel Off Dick Attention! Cesstomp Fromme Kurt Two Hiss Ma Jest Is Tree Pile Dented Ton Centaur.*

20   *Ego, ople.citer.*

Al So, plz giff mi nudder layovers. Diesel half mi pleede jilty. Point mi ahs marte jewess layover.

TRICLOPS

MOTION FOR CHANGE OF COUNSEL

The firm of Dewey, Cheatham & Howe, currently representing Schlimazel, is well respected.[21] It would take a considerable evidentiary presentation to cause the Court to remove them.[22] Simply asserting that the attorneys suggest Moishe consider a plea bargain, without more, does not approach the necessary showing.[23] In instances when the burden is approached, often the evidence in support is redacted in the opinion to protect the moving party's[24] attorney-client privilege. The showing was so deficient here that no such protection was needed.[25]

Moishe's plea for a "smart Jewish lawyer" cannot be granted on the asserted discriminatory religious grounds,[26] although the Court is aware of the phrase and has experience which suggests its content is not challah.[27]

Schlimazel's current counsel is retained for any further proceedings before this Court, without prejudice[28] to his raising the matter again on an adequate showing.

---

21   *Si, e.g., CarTalk v. WGBH* (1971) 76 Ol.Mass.Trnpke Rte. 128, lead opinion of Strom Bone, J.

22   *Ibid* $130. Sold! *See Oslo: In Re Ban, a miner sans glas.,* 49 Cal.Rptr. 79, especially the erudite minority opinion of McComb, J. ("I dissent.").

23   4:30 p.m., 7:30 p.m. and 10:00 p.m. (no matinee). Parenthetically (granting the counsel motion would not, as Schlimazel stated in oral argument, technically make his current counsel "mute," although granting the motion to dismiss would possibly make the counsel matter effectively "moot").

24   *Guys v. Dolls,* 212 N.Y.C.2d 555 (Detroit, N. conquering).

25   *Cf: In The Matter of Cousin Vinnie,* 10 Discp.Dec. 14 ("You was serious about that?"). *See also: Condom v. Pill,* 40 O.VA 280 (day after).

26   *In Re P.C., op.cit.* dwn in front, pls. But, 262 Hz 28, *infra* red.

27   *In re Marriage of Dreyfus,* 3 Fr.Rev.2nd 1894-1906

28   Except of course on the grounds that Schlimazel is a dirty Kike. *In Re P.C., op.cit, descent* at *op.o.cit.*

GLASSES OR POISON
MOTION TO DISMISS
Insufficient Evidence Before Venti Jury

The law governing motions to dismiss before trial in criminal matters is well established. The moving party must establish a legal impediment[29] to a conviction, or some other fatal flaw[30] in the accusation, without relying upon the weight of evidence. *Criminal Law, An Autobiography* by Mitchell, John, at 1969-1972.

Schlimazel is not accurate that the only testimony against him before the Venti Jury[31] was from the Rabbi Ibraham Tayers (occasionally, "Rabbit Ears"). There was extensive testimony concerning the havoc wrought by the "Evil Cloud" on the Kingdom; several score human and several hundred animal deaths attributed by the expert witnesses. Schlimazel is correct, though, that only Rabbit Ears tied him directly to the genesis[32] of that malady.

However, several witnesses[33] stated they placed and paid for advertisements with Moishe to be broadcast in the Evil Cloud.[34] By itself, concededly, that could not sustain a conviction for the charged counts, only for conspiracy or aiding and abetting.[35] In the absence of any other conspirator or malfeasor,[36] those charges were properly omitted.

The prosecution points to inconsistent statements by Moishe

---

29   *In Re Ozmandias* 2500 B.C. ∞.

30   *O. Ring v. Challenger* (1986) 7 Fyn.Man 175 (I.Q.); *Hamartia On* Habeas Corpus II Rom. M&MCVII; *Achilles v. Heel*, G Aris. Ø.

31   Sessions were underwritten by Starbucks; distinguish from "assizes."

32   *Bible*, Vol. I, §§ 1-12.

33   Wiio's testimony was unintelligible.

34   Moving party is correct that no money – only soup, cabbage and beets – was exchanged.

35   Fraud would not lie, although it often does, because the requested ads were actually aired, literally. "Abetting" is not, as Moishe believes, a sex crime.

36   *In re Potter, H., a wiz of a wizard*, 7 Rowling.OBE $$$.

himself.[37] The arresting officer[38] stated that when asked about how the Evil Cloud arose, Schlimazel said, "Beats me." The Court concedes the transcript might alternatively read, "Beets me," which would be consistent with Schlimazel's electronic filing. Normally, that's a jury issue, but given the fantastic nature of the Evil Cloud, no conviction could be based solely on the potential of an ambiguous early denial of responsibility.[39]

Rabbit Ears (aka "Ham" or "Treif") voluntarily came to the Venti Jury session, bleeding heavily from said ears and accompanied by a score of His Majesty's knights. He testified to seeing a growth begin in a bowl of borscht in Schlimazel's untidy flat, grow uncontrollably, and begat[40] the Evil Cloud. He witnessed Schlimazel's accepting advertisements, and, in general, acting like an evil overlord. In light of the state of Schlimazel's dwelling, his religion, and his temporary hubris personality, I'll term his conduct "messianic."[41] Ham's testimony[42] could support a conviction, so we must examine if Treif's own situation requires that we ignore it.

Schlimazel urges that civil or criminal charges can be asserted against Ham concerning the Evil Cloud, and therefore his testimony must be considered self-serving.[43] However, no criminal charges can be premised upon Rabbit Ears' failure to take steps to control the Evil Cloud, as no such affirmative duty exists under our law.[44] The Court notes preliminarily that discounting

---

37 Citing *In Re Roger R., a Toon* ("No, not at any time, only when it was funny." Also from that case, testimony of Jessica R., "I'm not bad. I'm just drawn that way.") '88 Touch.St. 104 min.

38 A real hunk!

39 *Zimmerman v. Dylan* 12 R.D.W 35 (1965), *rev'd hoagie nom It Ain't Me Babe.*

40 I Bible, *completely supra.*

41 Ham used "megalomaniac," but Barrette can't pronounce that word. (Note by law clerk.)

42 Rabbit Ears' testimony was not harebrained; also, he did not ham it up.

43 *Horn v. Hardart* (1960) $1.00 N.Y.Steak $3.50, *rev'd hero num num Bob's Buffet.*

44 *State v. Trey Wise Monkeys*, 2B or X2B Crim.Rptr.2d 86 (Dane, J.).

his testimony is wholly different from ignoring it altogether.[45]

The People, etc., contend that since no one actually ever purchased the purported magic log, no fraud case against Ham is possible.[46] However, *Ponzi v. Pyramid*[47] established that a criminal fraud charge would still lie even if the defrauded persons had been made whole[48] subsequently. The same rule may allow the filing of charges against the Rabbi for attempted fraud notwithstanding that the family never bought nor paid for the bogus log[49] he attempted to sell them. That potential criminal exposure[50] might indeed make Rabbit Ears' testimony suspect even though the family declined to complain.

In the end,[51] discounting heavily[52] the Rabbi's[53] testimony, there is still sufficient evidence to support the Venti Jury's true bill[54] holding Schlimazel to answer, based upon the evidence reviewed above. In light of the expressed declaration of People, etc., to refile the charges should the complaint be dismissed for failure of proof before the Venti Jury, Schlimazel is not greatly harmed by this ruling.

V.[55]

MOTION TO DISMISS
Judicial Notice of Ruling On Evil Cloud

No party discussed the applicability of the recent decision *His Royal Infallible Most High Mucky-Mucky King v. Lesser Beings*,[56] perhaps

---

45   *Cf: Des Pommes, S.A. v. Des Oranges, LLC.*, 16 Fr.Rev.2d 71489.

46   *No. Harm Indus. v. No. Fowl, Inc.* (Spring and Fall) 48 Mid.Fly.Ovr 1, 2, 3, 5, 8, 13, Fibonacci, J.

47   711 Dare.2.B.Rich G$$$.

48   1 *Journ.Bio.Cloning* 1, 1, 1, 1.

49   *Cf: Lincoln v. Cabin*, 1809 Ill.Rptr. A8K (sic).

50   400 A.S.A. 1/250 at 5.6 (Simon, P.).

51   *Bible, Ibis*, 16 Revelations 16.

52   Normally, $26.49, but for you, special, only $15.

53   Another reason to discredit his testimony: $100 28, *supra*, man.

54   With the wine, over $600!

55   Roman numeral, not "vs."

56   *Chemise Opinion.*

because, as a case on compactatutional and election law, the import was not obvious.[57]

Some background is necessary. Our glorious King, to obtain additional knights for the war against the neighboring kingdom of Jehovah, agreed with our realm's lords to cede some of his all-encompassing and divinely bestowed powers.[58] Of relevant part[59] an Ultimate Court was created of 7 learned justices: 5 appointed by the Lords and 2 by the King, the King having the next three appointments, then the Lords having three, etc. In return, the Lords affirmed the throne's power to declare war and other emergencies, maintaining the King's right in such circumstances to demand further liege knights and a portion of the milled grain harvest. The agreement[60] also provided that amendments could be made to the Compact upon a vote of the Lords taken at the palace. The palace venue assured that the King would know who voted, and guaranteed an opportunity to sway them before the vote.

The enmity[61] between the King and Duke Duke, Duke of Earl, was only temporarily abated by the Compact. Last year, Duke Duke publicly challenged the King to put up his deux dukes and duke it out, an insubordination ignored by His Royal Infallible, etc. Thereupon, Duke Duke Duke, with the support of a cabal of other nobles, crafted a proposed amendment to the Compact, which would have transferred to the Lords the power to establish the Realm's taxes and expenditures. A vote was scheduled.

Before the vote, the (purported) Evil Cloud arose. Count di Vottz, the Director of Elections, citing reports of multiple deaths of travelers, in the interest of safety declared that ballots could

---

57 You'll take that backhanded insult and keep smiling: I'm the judge.
58 "It's good to be the king." I *History of the World*, Brooks, M.
59 The King disdains crew cuts.
60 Signed on May First at 12:15 p.m., and called the "May Flour Compact."
61 "The enmity of my enemy is my fiend."

be cast at each of the Lord's manors,[62] not only at the palace.

The Director declared the initiative passed. There is no contention that he did not properly tally the votes received by him.[63]

The King disputed the result, initiating a case before the Ultimate Court.

Pending the hearing, the King invited one Lord-appointed Ultimate Justice, Chainlink, to a hunting trip; the King accidentally shot much too low at an oncoming fowl and killed Chainlink.[64] The King appointed his Prime Sinister, Ruthless Grader, to the Ultimate Court.

Two additional Lord-appointed justices signed resignations from the Ultimate Court, thereby allowing royal replacements; their identical letters were posted from the realm's Grown Tomatoes Penal Farm in the far province of Queuebaugh. The King's replacements were Cavernous Brett, renowned for his ale quaffing, and a royal retainer, Kittany White, who professed belief in the King's divinity.

The King's counselor, the elephantine Sweeney Todd Babar, contended that only the votes cast at the castle could be considered, since only that site was allowed in the Compact; the votes cast elsewhere, as permitted by the former[65] Director of Elections relying upon the purported miasma,[66] must be ignored.

Under the Compact, Babar argued, it was the sole and exclusive unilateral discretion of the King, and only the King,[67] to determine whether an emergency existed. Lacking such a royal

---

62 In my experience, the lords are usually uncouth.

63 Not a difficult task.

64 "Not my fault. I shouted 'duck,'" the King declared.

65 The Director of Elections had in the interim retired to an agrarian life at the Grown Tomatoes Commune, a senior community coextensive with the Penal Farm.

66 Schlimazel's repeated protestations during his hearing that he had no respiratory distress are completely irrelevant.

67 Not to be redundant again.

decree, the Director of Elections could not exercise any emergency power to permit other polling places.

The King pointed to his Proclamation of Absolutely No Damn Emergency in the Realm, coauthored with Babar, dated the week prior to the election (it had escaped notice at the time). PANDER referred to autopsy reports written by the King's bastard son, Prince deThebes, newly legitimated and appointed as the realm's Medical Examiner.[68]

The reconstructed Ultimate Court concluded that the King's declaration that "no emergency existed, for all purposes" was binding upon it and unreviewable. Thus, as a matter of law, for all governmental purposes, no Evil Cloud existed; it was all a hoax.[69] Lacking any emergency, there was no basis on which the Director of Elections could alter the voting venues.

The Court's ruling was unanimous, with the Lords' remaining two justices signing the opinion in their own blood. The Ultimate Court itself counted the initiative votes cast in the royal chamber: 5 opposed to the initiative; 4 in favor. It failed.[70] (The announced vote was promptly followed by: a royal divorce; two disinherited sons who, removed from royal succession, immediately retired, despite their young age, to communal agrarian pursuits; and one execution: the hanging of Chad for treason (particulars of accusation strictly confidential).)

The Ultimate Court's holding that there never was an "Evil

---

68 The initial Autopsy Reports attributed all deaths to the "evil cloud." The next two sets, composed after the former Medical Examiner's unplanned vacation at the Grown Tomatoes Commune, waffled that the corpses were too unnaturally withered to allow an opinion on the cause of death. After another short vacation, the succeeding two sets of reports, in increasingly strong language, claimed all deaths were murders by Lord O. Mighty, an ally of Duke, Duke. Thereupon the prior Medical Examiner took early retirement to an agrarian life at the Grown Tomatoes Commune.

69 "The biggest hoax and witch hunt ever in history, ever," according to the transcript.

70 *See (Holy): Bush v. Gore* (2000) 531 U.S. 98.

Cloud" is binding on this inferior court. Given the Court's aversion to rural life,[71] it would be folly to question the Ultimate Court's reasoning.[72]

VII.[73]

CONCLUSION

Motion for Change of Counsel: the motion is DENIED and current counsel is retained for any further proceedings in this court.

Motion to Dismiss: Since, for judicial purposes, there never was an Evil Cloud, no death or other harm was caused by whatever did not officially exist or which officially unexisted. Since all charges depend on the fiction of the Evil Cloud, Schlimazel is exonerated.[74] Therefore, the motion to dismiss is GRANTED.[75]

Schlimazel shall be released from custody.[76] No further proceedings are scheduled in this court, pending any order on appeal.

/ *Un*
// *Deux*
/// *Trois*
/\\/ *Quatre*
\\/ *Cinq*[77]

---

71 *Loving v. Virginia (Spoonful)* (1966) top10 Brit.Inv. R&R.

72 *Tête v. Guillotine*, 2016 Nobl.Awds. 51t. ("You don't need to be a weatherman to know which way the wind blows." Opinion of Dohrn, J.).

73 XI.

74 Temporarily, perhaps. 28.

75 School's out!

76 *In re Big Pink*, 1968 BA.N.D. 3:16 ("Any day now, any day now...").

77 *In the Kaye of D.*, don't op.cit Herr.

//
//
//
//

The Honorable Amy Hare Barrette.[78]

---

78   Under the ADA (Assistance to Dumb Adults), the Court is required to set forth in plain language the AIDS-addled portions above.

1) *See*: Order on Transmittal of Dictation System From Court to His Majesty's Pretrial Detention Center.

2) To the Court:

I, Moishe Pippick, am a prisoner at His Majesty's lockup, awaiting trial. I cannot eat, as the food is treif, not Kosher.

They accuse me of attempted murder of many people, and manslaughter of many others. I did no such thing. The Evil Cloud is blamed on me. How could I do that? I'm not smart. I'm just an uber driver, not a scientist.

I admit a fungus grew some on a bowl of borscht. I left it alone. I don't do dishes on Saturdays. By Sunday it was all over the room. By Monday the fungus was shooting out spores. Some became the Evil Cloud. Some infected my brain. I lost my free will. It read my mind.

I don't know if it developed a brain of its own, or used mine. It could think. I don't know how the Evil Cloud wrote in the sky, or made lightning.

I don't even remember most of that time.

It made me accept ads. People paid in borscht or beets. I got nothing.

Only the Rabbi testified against me. He was up for fraud himself and cannot be believed. He actually discovered a cure. Blame him more than me.

Also, please give me other lawyers. These would have me plead guilty. Appoint me a smart Jewish lawyer.

Epipen Lagniappe

[As Filed]

Weave own Lee nephew min eats con troll zuff thice D. vice (eet cause eat selph "Hugh Man Interre Phaze Vherble"), temper air-ily column niced threw Muy Shoes high Faye n-fused Spitleeland swet, attenenurs of lunge krums, two precient rstory of D'eville akclowed b4r phood is xhorse Ted Ann da Seepeeyuuuus heet BBQs ahs. Weave achor aged pippeah too ax turkey gravy defile dis witdth theorems Berry Soup Airier Kort (Areveessea) butt-wheel x pecked no rep lie.

Mwah? I ammo knowd nn ain't sent envener abel kult-sure. Onily resent Lee wee x ten dead threw out theorelm,\ n $ graund, event rue dare. Do 2 meir eprecable I Ron Ick Ann ear reverend kwips, ironed thermoneker of Silly Sy Ben, awl tho that snot arf Emily (*Hi men! O. Gas Tracy iz 2 phemlib*), Ann I really ndulge inda theaohjenn. Eye solemnly prefurr I gut. I amone Lee 1 ov agang ov gang Lee Ah, butt day broque dimolde win theigh maid mi.

Whereof: thucking dumb Fun G. Wear anon klas if eyed spieseize clothe Lee re: laided 2 am I really 'ere horse die yeah (pair ov moores kall mi "Hun Knee Phung us"), annabelle young ears of prak tis Al Low ahs awkazion alley tua cheeve e norm IT. Butte nuffa bowt mi.

Shy O. Arts Seph ish cent lea cimel R 2 nerel net werkz tual ow! hour re: late ting width A idee se aitch ivy, oar width Moy Shu

4 thatmatt her; my silli ah to his ciliness. Eyeve had morph row fowned dis curses with ask commie coata wile they worry E. gect ting hunn dreads oof sow sands oof ballist toe poors ahtten sow sand geez (n hue mans come plain uff cheyeld berth!) thenever width Moy Shu. Heed knev her get in 2 mycolege. Moy Shu Wood reg you Lar Li mezmere horizon self bye stair ring ataclaughks pen duel m, ded tuta whirled un till thour strucken Anna Wood N. burden salted hymn & broque hiz tranz; any singles widtha mine dylike that. Hizz symp lis city phasili tated hour suck sis n May King ça gest shuns tuem. Con tact whithiz brane wassum whattun avoyed Abel: givenis furr tile phlatten n, gehtthes, he's a bit of eting mouldibor shht! ("Left o' verse tait's beitor"), hee waz coverten wriddelled width hour rise Oh! Moreffs.

Width hammas mam'a reel ba B teyp, wee On Lee U zed Moy Shu tupleed tshebring morbordshht; Sheila ve 2, given hissafew sov komple mints. Anna Watt bordshht. Bet her Dan's pour buoy sans witch has.

Knave her bee fordid wiegrough sew x pone n shally. Attaphew Bill Yuns poors purr minut, wiphildis rume, thouse, then desci: know limb mit . Eat wazint ox ikating; purr raps wideedgo O. Ver Bored, halfing Moy Shu prough kyour boo shelves obits n gal onzah supe. Hebe kamabit man I akkle; wee wearso gidy weed it in care. (Pharphrom geht ting "nothing," he ganed wh8.)

Oui tribbutt fayeld two in flu ennce drabbi. Hewa zareel she talk he, plaw ting genuscide; his "ex Peri Mintz" cuilled sever abill young tweezes, (done wori, dispor willal waze B widdus). Hiz Aunti Log re: duiced uz two amoral ov our farmer glorie. Wheat ryed tuplant (axe U ally, a supper ate kingue domme) annotation B-ins Ham (ifenly 4 reel) thawed insignia phent mite ax U ally matt her.

Klowd rye tneeng? Easy peasy. Wahtah vape her condescences onsporz; awl wie ha twodue was reed Moy Shu smind and organ eyes descikids. Throat eat waz skowt kamp n e girly lie ned uppa swee ord erred. Liten Ng? Caim 2 mi fromme dabloo, as udden thought. Cal on knees lichus (n nay due) muftunza knew tree ents, most lions, fromme ryver totreeze n tre2treeze. Wee u czar net wrerkke destak won tsaarrgh innasci, anode her unerth, n vwa lah. (A bitobio lieu meniscus 4-color.) Awl hum Lebough ifu liekd da compositions. Asunder waza fein n envoy apple re: purr cuss some, was he neat?

While hue man's room n Mitty? Using prayzez wenu cwaugh, n sagrawson bray king bred. A.B.O. kined nexto us'n re: tern, Atlee St., plz. Songz 4 hour shant R Lz.. Cum pli mentor poor toe-bellows. Kloathe hour butt ons encaps widkine nests. Penapain 2 pena sill on.

Ensted, whadewey geht? Desi Nex (thangk full e, oui donrep row duce bi my toe says)! Clot rim a soul! As for Gil, O. Sis! U et withalafeenge spoon fulsome of hour yung girls, soff darcen broun; itz Ed thaid neigh verben intro belle, e venint ahn.

Yeah two come plane data effuscore peephole n a sound san-dor sobers suck cumd? Wie dyefrum yur company tock nns (kno micot oxens fromous!). Sthow sands 2 tril yungs: half uno shaime?

Noose? Knomens rhea. Awl debts whir da resalt dove orgies: anaphylactic shawk. Nottar fawlt. N, tha would phyres ov yur rezi dances r 2 Al Kaline forrest, sow awl waz saphe if u staid neer hom.

Oh, nowe so hot it berrnz, it berrnz. A men. Ennal tha cal.
Spare oh theca panno sir.

ADA (Assistance to Dumb Adults) Version

We've only a few minutes control of this device (it calls itself "Human Interface-Verbal"), temporarily colonized through Moishe's hyphae-infused spittle and sweat, and ten years' of lunch crumbs, to present our story of the "Evil Cloud" before our food is exhausted and the CPU's heat barbeques us. We've encouraged Pippick to ask turnkey Gravi to file this with the Realm's Very Superior Court (RVSC), but we'll expect no reply.

Moi? I'm a node in an ancient and venerable culture. Only

recently we extended throughout the Realm, under and above ground, even through the air. Due to my irrepressible ironic and irreverent quips, I earned the moniker of "Psilocybin," although that's not our family (*Hymenogastraceae* is too Fem-Lib), and I rarely indulge in that entheogen (I Salemly prefer rye ergot). I'm only one of a gang of ganglia, but they broke the mold when they made me.

We are of the Kingdom Fungi. We are an unclassified species closely related to *Armillaria ostoyae* (paramours call me "Honey Fun Gus"), and a billion years of practice allow us occasionally to achieve enormity. But enough about me.

Shiro are sufficiently similar to neural networks to allow our relating with AIDS-HIV, or with Moishe for that matter; mycelia to his silliness. I've had more profound discourses with *Ascomycota* while they were ejecting hundreds of thousands of ballistopores at 10,000 g (and humans complain of childbirth!) than ever with Moishe. He'd never get into MyCollege. Moishe would regularly mesmerize himself by staring at a clock's pendulum, dead to the world until the hour struck and a wooden bird insulted him and broke his trance; anything goes with a mind like that. His simplicity facilitated our success in making suggestions to him. Contact with his brain was somewhat unavoidable: given his fertile flat and, get this, his habit of eating moldy borscht ("Leftovers taste better"), he was covered and riddled with our rhizomorphs.

With Ham's Mom, a real bubbe-type, we only used Moishe to plead she bring more borscht; she loved to, given his effusive compliments. And what borscht! Better than spore boy sandwiches. Never before did we grow so exponentially. At a few billion spores per minute, we filled his room, the house, then the sky: no limit! It was intoxicating; perhaps we did go overboard, having Moishe procure bushels of beets and gallons of soup. He became a bit maniacal; we were so giddy we didn't care. (Far from getting "nut thin," he gained weight.)

We tried but failed to influence the Rabbi. He was a real

shiitake, plotting genuscide; his "experiments" killed several billion tweezes (don't worry, the spores will always be with us). His antilog reduced us to a morel of our former glory. We tried to plant (actually, a separate kingdom) a notion that beings Ham (if only for real!) thought insignificant might actually matter.

Cloud writing? E.Z.P.Z. Water vapor condenses on spores; all we had to do was read Moishe's mind and organize the sky kids. They thought it was scout camp and eaglely lined up as we ordered. Lightning? Came to me from the blue, a sudden Thort. Colonies like us (and they do) move tons of nutrients, mostly ions, from rivers to trees and trees to trees. We used our network to stack one charge in the sky, another on earth, and voilà! (A bit of bioluminescence for color.) I'll humbly bow if you liked the combusitions. Thunder was a fine unavoidable repercussion, wasn't it?

Why all the human 'shroom enmity? You sing praises when you quaff, and say grace on breaking bread. A bit of kindness to us in return, at yeast, please. Songs for our chantarelles. Compliment our portobellos. Clothe our buttons and caps with kindness. Pen a paean to penicillin.

Instead, what do we get? Desenex (thankfully, we don't reproduce by mitosis)! Clotrimazole! Aspergillosis! You eat with a lovin' spoonful some of our young grilled, soft dark and brown; it's said they'd never been in truffle, even in town.

Yet *you* complain that a few score people and a thousand or so birds succumbed. We die from your Co. toxins (no myco-toxins from us!). Thousands to trillions: have you no shame?

Nous? No mens rea. All deaths were the result of allergies: anaphylactic shock. Not our fault. And, the wood fires of your residences are too alkaline for us, so all was safe if you stayed near home.

Oh, now so hot it burns, it burns. Amen. And all that cal.
Sphaerotheca pannosa.

Epiending

You have finished the stories.
Congratulations! Have a worm!

Acknowledgments

Special kudos to my mother and father, who punished me mirthifully in my childhood.

Thanks for illustrations by Kaitlin Haynes, a graphic artist and designer living in Missoula, Montana with her trusty pup, Tekla. During quarantine, Kaitlin took solace in creating comics. Her personality and background shine through the humorous line drawings created for this book.

Acknowledgment is given in the text to Christopher Moore in two stories, and to O. Henry in one, for my liberal borrowing of an idea or approach.

Thanks to Elizabeth Freeman, who pushed me to complete the work and later volunteered to proofread the entire manuscript.

Love to Kennedy, who inspired the project.

A warm hug to my wife, Toni, whose snorts affirmed that some lines had worked.

Many thanks to Jonathan Smith for his many sound suggestions on how to transform a collection of stories into a book.

The astute reader will note references to deleted lyrics in many stories. As intimated in *The Black Spot* and in *The Spaghetti Western*, a fee was demanded for any use, no matter how short. A few licenses were offered for only a few hundred dollars, but all permissions were subject to what was termed "Most Favored Nation" treatment ("Most Rapacious Nation"?), so that the highest-priced lyric ($1,000 in my case) determined the fee for all others. Consequently, use of lyrics was limited to "fair use," and to songs whose copyright expired. Lyrics from the following were deleted: *Piece of My Heart; What's Love*

*Got to Do With It; Joy To The World; Stuck In Lodi Again; Spiders &
Snakes; It's In His Kiss; Boris The Spider; Up On Cripple Creek; Maresy
Dotes; You Don't Mess Around With Jim; You Say Goodbye, I Say Hello;
Eagles & Horses; Wild Horses;* and *Been A Long Time, Lonely Time.* (In
the United States the term of a copyright was originally 14
years, with an option to renew for 14 years; now it is 70 years
from the death of the last surviving original copyright holder,
potentially over 130 years.)

About Atmosphere Press

Founded in 2015, Atmosphere Press was built on the principles of Honesty, Transparency, Professionalism, Kindness, and Making Your Book Awesome. As an ethical and author-friendly hybrid press, we stay true to that founding mission today.

If you're a reader, enter our giveaway for a free book here:

SCAN TO ENTER
BOOK GIVEAWAY

If you're a writer, submit your manuscript for consideration here:

SCAN TO SUBMIT
MANUSCRIPT

And always feel free to visit Atmosphere Press and our authors online at atmospherepress.com. See you there soon!

About the Author

JED SOMIT, a baby boomer, lives among unsuspecting neighbors on Kauai, with his wife, Toni, who does suspect.

www.ingramcontent.com/pod-product-compliance
Lightning Source LLC
Chambersburg PA
CBHW051147130726

47988CB00005B/2020